From the Start

An American Valor Novel

CHERYL ETCHISON

AVONIMPULSE
An Imprint of HarperCollinsPublishers

FROM THE START. Copyright © 2017 by Cheryl Etchison Smith. All rights reserved. Printed in the United States of America. No part of this book may be used or reproduced in any manner whatsoever without written permission except in the case of brief quotations embodied in critical articles and reviews. For information, address HarperCollins Publishers, 195 Broadway, New York, NY 10007.

Digital Edition MAY 2017 ISBN: 978-0-06-247109-3
Print Edition ISBN: 978-0-06-247108-6

Avon Impulse and the Avon Impulse logo are registered trademarks of HarperCollins Publishers in the United States of America.

Avon and HarperCollins are registered trademarks of HarperCollins Publishers in the United States of America and other countries.

FIRST EDITION

17 18 19 20 21   HDC   10 9 8 7 6 5 4 3 2 1

For my dear friend, Gloria Jones.
Her love for Myrtle Beach and Duke University
are just two of the fingerprints she left on this book.
Sometimes I think Michael MacGregor
was as much her creation as mine
since her stories helped shape the character he became.

Rest in peace, my friend.
You will forever be in my heart.

Chapter One

May 2013

KACIE MORGAN RAISED the cloudy glass tumbler to her lips and licked the course salt from its rim, all the while surveying the bar, knowing she was officially in hell. Despite it being a fairly new establishment—and a nice place as far as bars went—it just wasn't her scene. The cowboy hats and cowboy boots. The painted-on jeans that both the men and women wore. The line dancing and mechanical bull.

Then there was the fact she couldn't stand country music. She might have been born and raised in the South, but the appreciation for songs about racing pickups down red dirt roads, getting drunk on Jack, and skinny-dipping in farm ponds must have skipped a generation.

She sighed and turned back around, catching a glimpse of herself in the mirror behind the bar.

Dear God in the heavens. She shouldn't have looked.

She squeezed her eyes shut and tossed back the remnants of her margarita on the rocks. A tang and tart shiver raced the length of her spine, her body squirming involuntarily to shake it off.

Her empty glass met the cow-print bar top a little heavier than intended, the upside being it garnered the bartender's attention. "Another?" He shouted to be heard over the music.

"Sure," she said. "Why the hell not?"

He came over to clear away the empty glass and his eyes roamed her chest as he took his damn sweet time to read the front of her shirt. She didn't have to glance at the mirror again to know the club lights ignited the rhinestones across her shirt, the word BRIDESMAID glimmering in the relative dark like a '70s disco ball.

"Eight weeks," she chanted to herself. "Eight. More. Weeks."

Just eight weeks until the bachelorette weekend, the holiday weekend, the rehearsal dinner, the wedding, all of it would be over. Her baby sister would be happily married and, more importantly, her maid of honor duties would be complete. No longer would she have to be overly friendly to women who were not her friends. No longer would she be guilted into wearing questionable attire or spending money she didn't have on all of the cutesy little things they wanted her to "chip in" on.

Kacie handed the bartender a few bills as he returned with her drink, then resumed leaning against the bar, watching as the country music gave way to hip-hop and the puritans bolted for the bars and seated areas. In the span of a few minutes, the dance floor became an instant bump and grind session for anyone under the age of twenty-five or with more than a few drinks in them.

In a sea of cowboy hats and baseball caps, her baby sister was easy to spot. The rhinestone tiara with attached veil on her head glittered in the pulsing lights as she bopped around the dance floor. And all the other bridesmaids were right there with her.

If she were a better maid of honor, a better big sister, she'd suck it up and join them. But she just couldn't find it in herself to move. Ever since her well-planned future with a man she loved—or at the very least thought she loved—had taken a deep dive into the toilet nine months earlier, she found having fun an almost impossible feat. How sad. How pathetic.

With a pang, Kacie realized at the age of thirty-one she'd become what she always feared most—a total buzzkill.

MICHAEL MACGREGOR STARED at the wooden double doors leading into the historic brick warehouse and tried to will himself inside. Far older than most of the revelers partying along Savannah's River Street, he was suddenly feeling every bit of his thirty-five years; the last place he wanted to spend his Saturday evening was in a country bar with a bunch of twenty-somethings. But this was where his sister-in-law wanted to celebrate her birthday:

enjoying live music, doing a little line dancing, and maybe even taking a ride on the mechanical bull.

So he was here. For her.

"There are worse places in the world than a country bar," his brother, Danny, had said when he called with the invite.

That was definitely true. He'd spent his fair share in them during his five years serving as the 1st/75th Ranger Regiment's battalion surgeon. In that time he'd been deployed, along with his younger brother, to Afghanistan and Iraq, to Western Africa, and to a few other places neither could speak of.

His phone chimed in his pocket and suddenly he found himself wishing there was some kind of minor emergency that would save him from going inside.

You better be coming to my party. Don't you flake on me.

He laughed and shoved his phone back in his pocket. There were very few people in the world willing to call him on his shit, but his sister-in-law, Bree, like a sister for most of his life, was certainly one of them.

Hip-hop music assaulted his senses as Michael paid the cover charge and made his way into the crowded bar, stopping at the edge of the dance floor to survey his surroundings. Almost immediately he was spotted by Jeff "Gibby" Gibson, who waved his arms so wildly Michael would've thought he was in dire need of medical attention. But really, that was just Gibby. The man didn't know the meaning of the word *subtle*.

Michael must have taken too long to acknowledge him, because the next thing he knew, Gibby was making his way across the dance floor. He paused momentarily, turned to a crowd of women in matching shirts surrounding one woman in a tiara and white veil, and waved for them to follow.

Shit. A bachelorette party. He was too sober to deal with this at the moment. Not so Gibby, judging by the glassy look in his eyes.

"Doc!" Gibby shouted once he was within a dozen feet. "Just the man I was looking for!"

Within a matter of seconds Michael found himself surrounded by a crowd of very young, very beautiful, very inebriated women. And if he didn't feel old before he walked in here, he sure as hell did now.

"I got someone I want you to meet," Gibby shouted over the music. Then he turned and took the hand of the cute brunette wearing the veil.

"Oh, hell, no," he said, almost immediately backing away.

"Get your head out of the gutter, man. It's not like that." He turned and smiled at the bride-to-be. "This is the guy I was telling you about," he said, slapping Michael's chest.

"Oh, hey!" The veiled one stumbled toward him with her hand held out in greeting. "It's nice to meet you."

Reluctantly, he took her offered hand. "Likewise."

She was a pretty girl, especially when she smiled, but something in his gut told him things weren't quite right.

"I need a favor."

He immediately dropped her hand. "I don't think so, sweetheart. I'm not really interested in helping you celebrate your last night as a single woman."

Her eyes widened, and then she began to laugh . . . and laugh, and laugh, finally placing a hand on Gibby's shoulder just so she wouldn't fall over as she bent over at the waist and laughed some more.

"Well, that's quite the ego boost," Michael muttered to himself.

Finally, her laughter subsided and she wiped the tears from her cheeks as she looked at him. "I didn't want you to do *me*! I want you to do my sister!"

He shook his head, unable to believe his ears. "I'm sorry. What did you say?"

She waved her hand. "I didn't mean it like that. Well, I do, but—" She waved her hand again as if that was going to magically erase all she'd said. "What I mean is that my sister is here, she's not having any fun, and I'd like it very much if someone would show her a good time."

At a loss, Michael looked at Gibby for help, but his fellow Ranger was currently occupied with not one but two bridesmaids.

"We're going to try out the mechanical bull," one of the ladies said.

"Okay," the bride-to-be answered. "I'll be right there." Then she turned back to him. "Seriously, you seem like a nice guy. I'd really appreciate it if you'd go say hello to my sister. She's over at the bar and will be easy to spot." She pointed to the far side of the venue. "I'm gonna go ride a bull." And then with another laugh she disappeared into the crowd.

Michael shook his head in disbelief. He'd had plenty of women throw themselves at him during his lifetime, and in his younger years he'd obliged his fair share. But to be offered up the wallflower, the outsider, the loner of the group? Uh, no. Taking on a pity date was the job of a wingman. And he *never* played the wingman.

With a sigh, Michael weaved his way through the crowd, finally locating Bree and Danny seated at a large round table along with fellow Ranger Ben Wojciechowski and his wife, Marie. Immediately, Bree rose to her feet and threw her arms around his neck.

"It's about time you showed up!" she yelled.

He wrapped his arms around her waist and gave her a squeeze, lifting her a few inches off the ground, just as he'd always done since they were kids. As he set her down, a waitress came over with a tray full of shots, lime wedges, and a saltshaker.

Bree clapped her hands and grabbed two glasses from the table. "You're just in time."

"I don't think so," he said, trying to avoid the shot she was holding out to him.

Bree raised an eyebrow. "You have to. It's my birthday."

Michael laughed at that. After all, she wasn't *his* wife. "I don't have to—"

"I'd do as she wants or she just might cut off your cookie supply," his brother interrupted smoothly.

Michael's gaze drifted from his brother, to Bree, to his secondary cookie supplier, Marie, who was shaking her head. And then he saw Ben, who was fighting to hold the laughter in.

"Fine," he said, taking the glass. "Then allow me to make the toast." He raised his glass and waited for the others to join him. "To the best sister any man could ever ask for. May the coming year be even better than the last. Happy birthday!"

Bree's smile lit up the room as the others chimed in with birthday wishes of their own and clinked their glasses together. Then after a quick tap to the tabletop, Michael tossed back his shot, choosing to forgo the salt and lime. He placed the empty on the table and glanced around for the waitress.

"If you're wanting something else to drink, it'd probably be quicker to go to the bar," Danny said as if reading his mind.

Michael asked the group if they needed anything, and when he was met with nos, he headed for the counter. As he was searching for an open space, sparks of light caught his attention. After a moment, he realized he'd found the lone bridesmaid.

The bright club lights glinted off the rhinestones on her shirt as she leaned back against the bar with one foot resting on the low brass railing that circled the bottom. His gaze traveled the length of shapely legs in short shorts upward to the now-familiar tank top. Her wavy blond hair was piled high on top of her head, exposing the length of her neck and the curve of her shoulder. While she looked to be older than the rest of the bridesmaids, she was by no means old. And she was, in a word, gorgeous.

Clearly, he shouldn't have been so quick to dismiss the bride-to-be's request. And really, what kind of man would he be if he let such a beautiful woman spend her evening standing all alone?

"CAN I BUY you a drink?"

Kacie looked at the full drink in her hand to the glassy-eyed cowboy standing in front of her. Actually, *swaying* in front of her would be more accurate.

Disheveled and more than a little dirty looking, she guessed he was a good twenty years older than her. In other words, much too old for most of the single women in the club. He leered at her chest while drinking from his longneck and she fought the urge to crisscross her arms over her breasts. Damn rhinestones. Never in her life had her B-cups garnered so much attention.

"I'm fine, thanks," she replied, waving her nearly full glass in his obvious line of sight. Hopefully, that would be enough to get him moving along to somewhere far away from her.

No such luck.

He stumbled a few steps closer.

"You're a pretty little thing, ain't ya?" His breath was a mixture of stale smoke and cheap beer.

She didn't want to cause a scene. Really, she didn't. Although she'd run this gauntlet during her college years with drunken frat boys, she was a bit out of practice now. And back then, there'd been safety in numbers, a friend or two nearby to help you out of a jam.

"Thank you, but I really need to—" She tried to squeeze past him, but found herself effectively trapped, hemmed in all sides by bar stools and other patrons now crowding the bar.

His fingers wrapped around her upper arm. "No need to run off now. We're just gettin' to know each other."

He stepped closer and she matched his movement with a step backward, the edge of the bar now digging into her spine, the pain well worth it just to gain those last few inches of separation. She glanced to either side hoping someone, anyone, would make eye contact and come to her rescue.

Figures.

Her chest had been flashing like a lighthouse beacon all damn night and now when she needed a little assistance there was none to be had.

Oh, well. A good old-fashioned knee to the groin should do the trick.

She levered herself from the bar, prepared to strike, when all of a sudden the drunk's eyes went wide and he stumbled backward.

Chapter Two

WITH A FIRM grasp on the guy's shoulder, Michael yanked backward, setting the cowboy off balance. He wanted to do more. Seeing the wariness in her eyes was enough to make him want to pound the idiot's face in. But starting a bar fight wouldn't do his military career any favors. Not to mention it likely wouldn't make the best first impression either.

"Hey, beautiful," he said, placing himself between her and the drunk and quickly offering her a chaste kiss on the cheek. "Sorry I'm late. I saw your sister when I came in and she told me I'd find you over here." He searched her eyes, hoping she'd catch his hint and somehow sense that his intentions were honorable.

She glanced at the drunken wannabe-suitor and, perhaps deciding he was the lesser of two evils, turned her attention back to him. One corner of her mouth lifted in a smile. "About time you showed up."

Michael gave her a wink and felt a sense of accomplishment when that half-smile widened into a full-blown stunner. Emboldened by her playing along with his little act, he took the glass from her hand. "Whatcha drinking?"

"Margarita on the rocks. And it's terrible."

He kept his eyes locked on hers over the rim of the glass as he took a cautious sip. But before he was done, the idiot recovered, giving him a hard shove from behind, sloshing the drink all over Michael's hand and nearly down the front of his shirt.

"Who the hell do you think you are just shoving your way in here?" the man shouted. "We were talking!"

Michael calmly reached past her and placed the glass on the bar before facing the cowboy. "Oh, I'm sorry. Were you under the impression I interrupted something?" He turned slightly, talking to the bridesmaid over his shoulder. "Sweetheart, this guy seems to think you were interested in him."

Her expression became one of pure innocence. "I don't know what gave him that impression."

Again, the drunken cowboy gave Michael a forceful shove, tempting him to drop the idiot with a right cross to the jaw. "Don't do that," Michael warned as he reached back with his hand and guided the bridesmaid out from behind him. "Why don't you go find your sister," he said to her. The last thing he wanted was for fists to start flying with her pinned between him and the bar.

But instead of releasing his hand, she held on tight. "I'd rather you came with me."

He was considering doing just that, simply leading them away from the conflict, when a second drunken cowboy appeared from nowhere, making their exit a little more difficult. "There a problem here, Billy? This asshole hornin' in on your date?"

"I am *not* his date."

Michael looked over at the bridesmaid and grinned, impressed by her spirit. Despite her petite stature, he'd bet that with all the fury clearly coursing through her veins, she could single-handedly drop this guy like a sack of rocks. Which admittedly was one hell of a turn-on.

"Easy there, sunshine," he said to her.

The two cowboys, however, weren't as amused. Instead, they squared their shoulders in an attempt to appear more threatening and took a step closer. If there hadn't been a slight drunken sway to each of them, Michael might have been a bit more concerned. He could handle them if need be, but he found himself distracted by the gorgeous little thing that still held his hand.

Thankfully, backup arrived before things could get out of control. Danny and Ben strolled up, relaxed and at ease, each with a longneck in hand. "Everything okay here?" his brother asked.

"We were just excusing ourselves for a dance," Michael answered without ever breaking eye contact with Billy. "Isn't that right, fellas?"

The cowboys, quickly realizing they were outsized and

outmatched, took a look at the three of them and wisely chose to walk away without saying anything more.

Danny and Ben remained right where they stood, glancing back and forth between Michael and the bridesmaid, smug smiles on their faces as they obviously waited for thanks, introductions, something. Didn't matter since the music had transitioned back to a classic country tune and now he only had one thing in mind. "Thanks for the backup, guys. But I do believe they're playing our song," he said.

With her hand still in his, he led her toward the dance floor. But she stopped short at the edge of the parquet wood surface. "You don't really want to dance with me."

"Why is that?"

She glanced down to the strappy sandals on her feet. "Because I don't have the right shoes."

So of course he looked, his gaze traveling down shapely legs to see cute little toes painted hot pink. "You'll be fine."

"Okay, then." She lifted her face to look him dead in the eye. "I have no choice but to be completely honest." She took a deep breath and then spoke in a rush. "I have no idea how to two-step or country swing dance or whatever you want to call it."

It wasn't at all what he had expected her to say, but her not knowing how to dance wouldn't be enough to keep him from holding her in his arms.

"Well, then, no time like the present."

He tugged her onto the dance floor, and once they

were facing in the right direction Michael lifted her left hand and placed it on his shoulder. As a couple breezed past showing off their tight turns and fast spins, her jaw dropped slightly. With the tip of his finger, he lifted her chin so she'd look him in the eyes. "Don't pay any attention to them. You'll do just fine."

She smiled then. "Okay. You can't say I didn't warn you."

He placed his right hand just below her shoulder blade and pulled her close. "There's only three things you need to remember. One, relax. Two, step backward with your right foot to start. And three, the pattern is quick, quick, slow, slow. Got it?"

She gave a curt nod, then quickly circled her neck and rolled her shoulders. This woman meant business. "Start on right. Quick, quick, slow, slow. Got it."

As she repeated the pattern to herself over and over again, he started guiding her across the floor, keeping to the outside and doing his best to avoid colliding with any showoffs. After a couple of minor mishaps and several turns around the dance floor, she'd relaxed her grip enough that the blood flow had returned to his thumb. Despite her earlier hesitation, she was picking it up rather quickly. But after all, if copious amounts of alcohol could improve one's two-stepping skills it said something about the dance to begin with.

Midway through the second song, he guided them into an easy turn, and by the end of the third she was following his lead well enough for him to spin her.

Their first attempt was a bit of a fail, but the second she pulled off without a stumble. The smile on her face said everything he wanted to hear, and he'd never been so happy to spend time with a complete stranger in a country bar.

When the lights dimmed and the music slowed, several couples began leaving the dance floor and instinctively she tried to follow. But Michael kept hold of her hand. "How about a slow one after all that racing around?"

She glanced up at him, smiled, then lowered her eyes to the floor, hiding her expression. If the lights were up, would he see her cheeks flush pink? His hand drifted to her lower back and he pulled her even closer than before. Her hand slipped from his shoulder, coming to rest on his chest not far from his heart, and suddenly he became aware of how it raced beneath her palm.

The attraction was undeniable. He liked the way they fit together when they danced. He liked how she held his hand tight, unwilling to leave him to fight those cowboys. He liked that she was small, almost delicate, and yet he'd already seen her strong side. And on top of all that, she was very, *very* beautiful.

When she relaxed even further into his embrace, resting her head on the front of his shoulder, he knew that one dance, not even one night, with this woman would be nearly enough. Which was crazy since he didn't even know her name.

Fuck.

He didn't even know her name.

What the hell was wrong with him? This wasn't him. He wasn't the kind of guy to fall head over heels for some random chick in a bar. That happened to other guys. Younger guys. Fools who didn't know any better. And he definitely knew better.

And yet . . .

The song ended and he led her off the dance floor to the table where Danny, Bree, Ben, and Marie sat. And as timing would have it, just like a pied piper, Gibby returned with the entire bachelorette party following behind.

SAM CHARGED TOWARD her, arms outstretched, tiara and veil sitting slightly askew on her head. "Kacie! I rode the bull!" Her sister grabbed hold of her and swayed back and forth, the way happy, drunk people often do.

While she was glad her little sister was having fun, she really wanted to find out more about the mystery man who had so gallantly come to her rescue. Before she could pry herself from Sam's grip, he politely offered to buy her another margarita, then headed back to the bar without really waiting for an answer from her.

"So . . ." her sister said with a sly grin on her face. "He found you after all."

"He said you sent him looking for me. I wasn't sure whether to believe him or not. How do you know him?"

Sam laughed. "I don't!" She turned to point at another guy surrounded by bridesmaids. "That guy introduced me to him. Said that he's a nice, single guy who'd be happy to entertain you."

"What the hell, Sam?" Kacie shook her head in disbelief. "You sent some random stranger to babysit me?"

Her sister draped an arm around her neck and whisper-shouted in her ear. "I didn't send just anybody. You gotta admit he's damn good looking." They both looked up just in time to see the tall, blond hunk returning from the bar, a margarita in hand. "And lookie there. He bought you a drink."

Kacie couldn't believe it. Here she'd been thinking things were going pretty well, only to find out she'd been cast as the pity date. "Dammit, Sam. You sent the wingman after me?"

"Lighten up. Does he look like the wingman?" Sam turned and pressed her forehead to Kacie's, staring directly in the eyes. "I. Don't. Think. So. Anyway, this could be your lucky night. The night to break your dry spell."

Before she could say anything more, her little sister pulled away and ushered the other bridesmaids back onto the dance floor. Then, as he approached, the two couples that had been sitting at the table told him they were going to ride the mechanical bull, once again leaving the two of them alone.

"I asked for top shelf tequila. Hopefully, it tastes better than the last one." He handed her a fresh margarita and watched her closely, as if waiting for her reaction.

With the tip of her tongue, she quickly swiped salt from the rim and took a sip. It was definitely smoother than the others she'd had. She took another taste, all the while enjoying the view. The stranger had beautiful eyes. And a great smile, the kind that sneaks up on a person. More than once while dancing she'd caught herself smiling back at him without really knowing why. And then there was the fact that he *smelled* great. Not even a hint of Axe body spray or stale beer—just clean, manly man.

"Better?" he asked.

She nodded.

"What's your name, sunshine?"

"Kacie."

One corner of his mouth lifted, revealing a dimple in his cheek. "It's a nice name. It suits you. I'm Mike," he said, extending his hand.

Kacie felt as if she'd been smacked with a two-by-four. *Of all the names in the world . . .*

It was clear she hadn't done a very good job hiding her reaction; the guy slowly lowered his hand. "I take it you have a problem with that?"

"Just a lot of *very* bad memories attached to that name."

He folded his arms over his chest, his head tilting to one side as if trying to puzzle out a solution. "Okay, then, how about Michael? Normally, only my family calls me that, but for you I'd make an exception."

"Tomayto, tomahto." Kacie sighed in disappointment. It was just her luck that this guy shared a name with a man she'd put her life on hold for. Then there was the fact that her cousin, who had terrorized the hell out of her for years, also had the same name. Not to mention the kid down the street who'd spent his formative years in and out of jail. Almost every woman she knew had one name that sent chills down their spine, the kind that had bad juju attached to it. And for her, that name happened to be Michael. Mike. Whichever.

But like her sister said, he seemed like a nice guy. And it was silly to write someone off simply because of their name. She ought to give him a chance.

"What do you do, Michael?"

"I'm stationed at Hunter Army Airfield."

She felt her jaw drop. "You've got to be kidding me."

Just her damn luck. Not only did this guy share a name with her ex, but he was military, too? Could her night get any worse?

Kacie lifted her glass to her lips and drank the entire margarita down. She placed the empty glass on the table and wiped her thumb across her lip to brush away any salt. Of course, when she glanced over at him he was looking at her like she was nuts.

"Ex-husband?" he asked.

"I'm sorry?"

He leaned closer and spoke directly into her ear. "Who do I have the unfortunate distinction of sharing a name with?"

"He was only an ex-boyfriend, thank God. But he's a jarhead, too."

"Well, I hate to break it to you, sweetheart, but jarheads are marines. I'm army. Big difference."

"Oh, sorry," she said, raising her hands in surrender. "Civilian."

Thankfully, his friend picked that moment to return with a tray full of shots and lime wedges.

"Are you the rogue bridesmaid?" asked one of the guys.

"That would be me. Who are you?"

He smiled and offered her a shot. "Jeff Gibson at your service. Everybody calls me Gibby."

"Oh," she said with a smile. "Such a nice name." She glanced over at Michael and was slightly amused by the peevish look on his face. "And how do you know each other?"

"We serve together at HAAF."

Kacie shook her head.

"Try not to look so sad, sunshine," Michael said, handing her one of the drinks.

They clinked their glasses together and tossed back their shots. Once done, she immediately reached for a lime wedge and bit into it.

"Another?" Gibby asked.

She hadn't even recovered from the first when he placed a second shot of tequila on the table in front of her. Toast. Clink. Drink. The empties had barely hit the table when a waitress delivered a dozen more shots, intended for the rest of the bridesmaid group.

"So why aren't you out there with the rest of them?" Gibby nodded to Sam and her friends, all laughing and dancing beneath the bright club lights.

"Not really a fan of the Snow White and the seven dwarfs schtick."

"I'm assuming Snow White is . . ."

"The bride? Yes."

Both men laughed, then Gibby leaned toward her, pressing his shoulder into hers. "So if your sister is Snow White, what are the dwarfs' names?" Gibby asked. "They've gotta have names."

As she licked the juice from a lime wedge, Kacie studied each bridesmaid carefully. "Ginger," she said, beginning with the bridesmaid with long, red hair. "Sugar and Spice." She pointed to the sisters. "They're twins by the way. Followed by Angel, Brainy, and Texas."

Gibby grabbed hold of her arm. "Hang on a second. Twins?"

Kacie laughed at the way Gibby's eyes lit up. Silly men and their twin fantasies.

"Whether or not you like it, you're one of the dwarfs," Michael said, gesturing to the shirt she wore. "So what do they call you?"

She glanced down at her shirt, at the matching rhinestone uniform, and heaved a sigh before looking into those beautiful blue eyes.

"They call me Bitter."

Chapter Three

KACIE STEPPED OUT of the bathroom stall and went to wash her hands, enjoying the brief respite from the crowds and loud country music. As she held her hands beneath the tepid water, she studied her reflection. Reddened, tired eyes. Faint smudges of mascara and eyeliner beneath her lower lashes. The early signs of crow's feet. She was far from old, but wasn't young either.

The main door to the bathroom swung open violently, hitting the wall and nearly rebounding into the person entering. And of course, the drunken fool who'd just slammed it wide open was none other than her little sister, who was still parading around with that damn veil on her head.

"There you are!" Sam yelled. "I was wondering where you were hiding."

"I was hardly hiding. I was using the bathroom," Kacie replied.

"Well, I'm glad that I found you, because the limo is picking us up at . . ." Sam pulled her phone from her back pocket and squinted at the numbers on the screen. "One-thirty."

"Really?" For the first time, Kacie was hopeful this evening would end at a reasonable hour. "I'm surprised you're ready to call it a night."

"Nooo, silly." Sam pushed Kacie's shoulder as she walked past and stepped into an empty stall. "We're heading to the ice bar. It doesn't close until four."

Kacie leaned over the bathroom counter, letting her head hang. They'd been at this bachelorette stuff for seven hours now. No way could she handle another three. She just didn't have it in her.

"How's things going with you and the wingman?" her sister called from within the stall.

"I thought you said he wasn't the wingman?"

"Whatever. I've been watching him watch you. He's definitely into you."

Kacie turned and leaned against the counter, crossing her arms over her chest. "Stop it."

"You've shot down every guy I've introduced you to for the past six months for one silly reason or another. Too short. Too skinny. Too pale. I've heard just about every excuse. This guy is tall. Good looking. Have you talked to him much? Does he have a job?"

"He's military."

"Oh. Okay. Well, it's not ideal, but that doesn't automatically mean he's a douche."

"His name is Mike."

"I remember what his name was. But you made me promise to never say his name again. Remember?"

"No. The *wingman's* name is Mike. Or Michael. Same difference."

The toilet flushed and the stall door opened, allowing Kacie to see the amusement on her sister's face. "Well, if you two hook up at least you won't have to worry about accidentally yelling out the wrong name."

"Really, Sam?"

"Just trying to find the positives," Sam said matter-of-factly while squirting soap into her palm. "Come on, the guy out there looks nothing like your ex. He's a younger version of Brad Pitt and your ex was a short, 'roided out weasel that spent way too much time looking at himself in every reflective surface he passed by. It was obnoxious. I don't care that he could bench nearly four hundred pounds or that his biceps measured twenty-one inches in diameter or that he had five percent body fat, or any of the other nonsense he used to brag about, because not even on his best day did he come close to looking like Brad Pitt. I'm just saying."

"Please. Tell me how you really feel."

Sam smacked the faucet to shut it off. "Okay, then. Mike was an ass. And I'm glad you broke up with him."

"Technically, he dumped me."

"Only because you were too nice of a person and

didn't do it first." Sam ripped off a length of paper towel from a dispenser. "Listen, I'm not suggesting you marry this guy. I'm just suggesting you have a little fun. Seize the moment. He's got great dance moves. Aren't you even the least bit curious as to what he'd be like in bed?"

Kacie couldn't deny there was a little spark of *something* between her and Michael, but it would be silly to get involved with the guy. She'd never had sex without being in some sort of relationship. And it would be pointless to try and start one with this Michael since she was leaving town in a matter of weeks.

"Just consider it. It's either him or the ice bar. You've got an hour to make your move."

Kacie followed her sister back into the bar with a sigh. As they neared the table, Michael's eyes locked with hers and the butterflies in her stomach took a little tumble.

True, it felt like the universe had offered her all these signs in an attempt to warn her off from making a huge mistake.

But if he kept looking at her that way, she didn't know how much longer she'd be able to resist.

WITH EACH ADDITIONAL round of drinks and shots of tequila, the merged celebrations became rowdier and more raucous. And much to everyone's amusement, Kacie began calling him Joe—as in G.I. Joe. No big deal. He'd been called worse names over the years.

At one point she disappeared and he began to wonder

if she'd left without saying anything. A few songs later she returned, a shot of tequila in each hand.

"I owe you a drink," she said with a smile.

His fingers grazed her hand as he took the glass from her. She clinked her glass to his before they both threw back their shots. He opened his eyes just in time to see Kacie laugh and wiggle as she battled through the tequila aftershocks.

God, he loved her laugh. Throaty. Husky. Unlike any he'd ever heard.

She opened her eyes to find him staring at her. "Are you ogling me, Joe?" she yelled above the music.

"Not ogling," he said, closing the distance between them. "Appreciating."

Then, before he could second-guess himself, he wrapped his arm about her waist, pulled her against him, and covered her mouth was his.

Her response was immediate.

One arm wrapped around his neck as she arched her body to meet his. Somewhere in the distance, outside their alcohol-soaked bubble, the group began to clap and whistle. But he didn't give a damn about them anymore. Only her. He only cared what she thought.

He gentled the kiss, then finally pulled away just enough to look into her eyes, to see if the hunger he felt was reflected in hers. She smiled up at him, then said the three sweetest words he could have ever hoped to hear. "Take me home."

Before she could change her mind, before he thought

better of it, Michael took her by the hand and towed her out the front doors of the club.

"Please let there be a taxi," he chanted under his breath as they stepped out onto River Street.

As luck would have it, one had just dropped off its passengers at a nearby hotel. They quickly piled into the backseat and Kacie immediately gave her address. Seconds passed in awkward silence as the cab made its way through midtown until their eyes met across the empty space between them. He reached for her, his hand cradling her neck while his thumb stroked the curve of her jaw. The kiss began as a gently press of his lips against hers before trailing his mouth across her cheek to the tender skin of her neck. And when he nipped at her ear lobe, a soft moan escaped her lips.

She then cradled his face in her hands and guided his mouth back to hers. Through a series of kisses, she pleaded her case. "Just so you know," she began before playfully tugging on his lower lip with her teeth. "This isn't me." Another kiss. "I don't do things like this." This time her tongue teased his upper lip. "I don't pick up strangers in bars and take them home."

He chuckled at that. "I thought I picked you up." But her body stiffened beneath his hands and he drew back so he could look into her eyes. "If you've changed your mind . . ."

She stared at him what felt like hours but was likely only a matter of second before she finally whispered, "God, no," and covered his mouth with her own.

Within minutes the cab stopped in front of a large

historic home in Baldwin Park. Kacie flung open the passenger door and stumbled out, laughing as she fell into the soft grass just on the other side of the sidewalk. After handing the last of his bills to the cabdriver, he stepped out of the car just in time to see her standing on the driveway, her shoes now dangling from her fingertips.

"Hurry up, Joe!" she yelled before disappearing around the corner of the house.

He followed the blacktop to what once must have been a carriage house hidden beneath hundred-year-old live oaks draped in Spanish moss, and climbed the steps up the small porch to where the front door sat open.

"Kacie?" He took a tentative step inside.

"Shut the door," she commanded as her fingers grasped the hem of her shirt.

Michael did as told, closing the door behind him while giving a little nod of thanks to the Man upstairs.

He never would have pegged her to be the kind of woman to put on a private show, but he was more than happy to be her audience. To stand back. Observe. To sear the memory into his alcohol-soaked brain so he could revisit this moment again and again in the future.

Taking her time, she drew the top over her head and lowered her arms to her sides, the shirt slipping from her fingertips to land on the floor near her feet. The full moon's light streamed through the large picture window and served as a spotlight. Her breasts were luminous in the silver glow and a soft shine blurred the edges of her naked form.

Or maybe that was the tequila.

Either way, the visual effect was magnificent.

Despite the overwhelming need to have her, he kept his feet firmly in place. His mouth watered at the thought of tasting every seductive dip and curve of her body. His fingers itched to explore every inch of her skin. Blood surged through his veins. His dick stood at the ready, a sweet release its only demand. To hell with everything else.

But as strong a man as he was physically, he was even stronger mentally. In spite of the tequila, his brain took command and forced his traitorous body into compliance.

Her shorts fell to the floor next, along with her panties. His feet shifted restlessly beneath him.

Wait.

Wait.

Patience will be rewarded.

In the half-light of the room, her darkened eyes locked with his. Holding his gaze, she pulled the elastic from her hair and used both hands to shake it loose. Her sun-streaked waves, now unbound and free, tumbled over her shoulders.

Dear God she was beautiful. More beautiful than any woman he had ever known. For one fleeting second he double-checked his surroundings to ensure he wasn't suffering from heat exhaustion in the Afghan desert, that this woman wasn't just a mirage.

"Hey, Joe."

He brought his attention back to her and was now ninety-seven percent certain this was definitely not a mirage or a dream. No way would he ever fantasize a woman calling him by another man's name. Or in this case, a toy's name. But at this point, she could call him Dumbo, if she'd consider kissing his trunk.

He chuckled at his own joke. Jesus was he drunk.

"Joe."

His eyes snapped back to her face. *Focus, damn it.*

"You seem content to just stand back and watch, Joe."

He watched her lips and tongue form the words, a slight delay between sight and sound. Her voice was raspy, nearly hoarse, but the sound was so very seductive.

"You don't mind if I go ahead and help myself. Do you?"

He didn't answer. Couldn't if he tried.

Kacie sucked on the end of her middle finger and smiled at him as she pulled it from her lips.

Once again his dick surged at the front of his pants. Like a rodeo bull with a rider on his back waiting impatiently for someone to open that godforsaken gate so they could all go for one helluva ride.

The trail of wetness from her fingertip shimmered upon her skin in the moonlight. Over her chin. Along the column of her throat. Tracing her breastbone. Her hand moved to circle the outermost part of her breast, then worked inward to her nipple. Around and around and around her fingertips skimmed until it became a darkened, tightened bud. Not neglecting the other, she brought her other hand to her left breast, working it in a similar fashion.

Such a tease. Teasing herself. Teasing him.

Releasing one breast, her palm smoothed down her stomach, the muscles quivering beneath her own touch. Her hand stroked over one hip bone, then followed the crease at the top of her thigh, her fingertips disappearing into the shadowed area between her legs.

His control had frayed to the finest of threads. He took a deep breath, then another.

The way the moonlight highlighted some of her body while other parts remained in shadow was an erotic effect in itself. But now as she stood in front of him, completely uninhibited, pleasuring herself, he didn't know where to focus his attention.

Her head tipped back, eyes closed. The tip of her tongue caressed parted lips. Her breasts rose and fell heavily with each ragged breath. Her fingers taunted her nipples, alternating between soft caresses and pinches that made her wince in pleasure.

With her continued stroking, she drove herself closer and closer to bliss. And him closer to the edge of insanity.

Her body tensed, muscles quaked. A breathy moan escaped her lips.

The thread snapped.

He charged across the room and pushed her backward into an overstuffed chair. Her laugh, deep and husky, sounded of victory as he draped her legs over his shoulders and fell to his knees in worship.

Chapter Four

HER HEAD POUNDED. Her throat burned. Her body flashed from hot to cold. Kacie scooted to the edge of the bed and dropped one foot to the floor, a last-ditch effort to get the godforsaken room to stop spinning. Even that little bit of movement sent her stomach into panic mode and she had to take short shallow breaths to hold the nausea at bay.

There was only one option left—pray for death.

From beyond her bedroom door she heard movement in her small carriage house. Kacie stilled and listened closely, but pretty soon the breath holding thing only made her head pound worse.

If there was anyone in her place, and that was a pretty big *if*, it was most likely Sam since she was the only other person with a key.

Or it could be a serial killer.

Normally the thought would frighten her. But since she currently welcomed death, the prospect of meeting her doom at the hands of a serial killer wasn't necessarily a bad thing.

She closed her eyes and must have dozed off; for how long she didn't know, but when she woke a second time, she was absolutely certain there'd been a loud noise. Then she distinctly heard water running. Kacie grabbed the bottom edge of the curtain and drew it back, instantly blinded by the bright sunlight streaming in through the window.

It certainly wasn't raining outside.

And then the water suddenly stopped and she heard the sound of a shower curtain being thrown open.

"Holy shit!" she whisper-shouted to herself as she kicked off the remaining covers. Of course her phone wasn't on her bedside table where she typically left it to charge each night. She had no choice but to make a run for it.

Kacie stumbled out of bed, landing on her knees and wasting precious time before she made it to her feet. But just as she reached the hallway, the bathroom door flew open and a man stepped into the hall.

"Oh, hey," he said with a smile. "You're up."

Kacie stopped short in front of a mostly naked, beautiful man with a very familiar face. It took a moment for her to remember the deep blue eyes, the dimples. It wasn't long before her gaze followed rivulets of water streaming down his midline and pooling in his belly button a few inches above one of her brand-new coral pink towels wrapped around his hips.

"How are you feeling this morning?"

His words drew her gaze back to his face. "Joe?"

"Michael," he answered.

Kacie waved a hand to show she didn't really give a damn what his name was. She placed her palm on her forehand, hoping it would ease the throbbing so her brain could function. "What the hell are you doing here? And why were you using my shower?"

He just stood there staring at her, a lascivious smile on his face as he clutched the ends of the towel. He was hardly wearing anything and she was . . .

The air conditioner kicked on and a blast of cool air from the vents above her sent goose bumps racing across her skin. Kacie looked down at herself and realized that she was wearing absolutely nothing. Not a thing.

And he was standing there. Smiling at her. Just enjoying the view.

"Oh, Jesus! Turn around!"

His smile widened and a low chuckle rumbled from deep within him before he complied. "Would you like a towel?"

"Yes," she answered without hesitation.

And so he handed her his.

Which left her staring at a nicely shaped, albeit paler than the rest of him, ass.

He waved the coral pink towel in midair like a bullfighter waves his cape. "Are you still wanting this?"

Kacie yanked it from his grip and immediately wrapped it around her body. After tucking in the end, she looked up and found him peeking back over his shoulder at her. "Hey! Eyes to the front, buddy!"

He shook his head and laughed some more, all the while holding his hands up in the air as if she had a gun pointed at him. "Do you mind if I get dressed? Or would you rather I just stand here all day?"

"You still haven't answered my question." She gave his back an indignant little shove. "What are you doing here?"

"Kacie, come on." He peeked over one shoulder at her. "I'm here because you invited me."

Again, she rubbed a hand across her forehead, trying to remember the night before, and then it came to her.

Close the door.

"Dammit," she mumbled under her breath. Some of what happened the night before was slowly coming back. Her sister sending the wingman after her. The dancing. The tequila. Kacie groaned. There had been *a lot* of tequila.

"How about we both get dressed and I'll take you to breakfast?"

Her stomach twisted at the mention of food. "I don't know that's a smart idea."

"I promise that you'll be fine." His words low and soothing. "Take a shower. Get dressed. And then we'll go eat."

She'd never really been one who liked being bossed

around, but at the moment, she found it far easier to follow orders than to argue.

LEAVING HER TO get ready, Michael wandered into the bedroom where he gathered his clothes from off the floor and dressed.

For hours he'd lain awake in this room, in her bed, watching her sleep. After she'd passed out he knew he couldn't leave her alone because she could've become sick, stopped breathing, or choked on her own vomit. So he spent most of the night monitoring the slow rise and fall of her chest, listening to the soft huffs of her breath and occasionally checking the temperature of her skin.

Michael headed out into the living room, gathered Kacie's clothing from where it had been scattered about the night before, and carried her things back into the bedroom and placed them on the end of the bed.

He thought about going into her kitchen to make a pot of coffee. But in his mind that was a violation of sorts. He knew he didn't like women wandering through his place, going through his things, and more than one of his past relationships had ended as a result of it.

Nearly twenty minutes later she stepped into the living room, her hair still damp and twisted into a knot on her head. Her face was free of makeup, her green eyes bloodshot and lips pale, but she was up and moving.

"Are you ready?" he asked.

She took a deep breath and slipped on her sunglasses. "As I'll ever be."

Michael looked around as they stepped outside; he had a vague idea of where they were, but didn't really know the neighborhood.

"Is there a place within walking distance?" he asked. "One without tourists?"

She nodded. Gently. As if the slightest bit of mental exertion was painful. "There's a little hole in the wall a couple blocks away."

"I'll let you lead the way, then."

Again, she answered with a slight nod and started walking.

"So—"

Kacie immediately drew to a halt and showed him the palm of her hand. "Please, stop."

"I'm not—"

She shook her head. "I know you're just being nice and trying to make conversation, but I'd really appreciate it if we could just avoid any and all chitchat. At least until I have some caffeine in me."

"Sure thing," he said, stopping at that because he sensed if looks could kill he'd be lying dead on the sidewalk right about now.

Several minutes and a block and a half later, they stepped into the small diner, the bell above the door ringing loud enough that Kacie immediately flinched. It wasn't by any means a fancy place; the walls were covered in faux wood paneling and the booths were upholstered in green vinyl, with added touches of black duct tape covering what he could only assume were rips. A young woman, about college-aged, grabbed two menus from the counter and led them toward the back, winding their way past the counter bar stools and several tables in the middle of the room.

He immediately ordered two coffees, and when Kacie tried to wave off breakfast, he went ahead and ordered food for both of them, items that were sure to cure even the worst of hangovers. Essentially their breakfast consisted of carbs, more carbs, and a side of grease.

When the waitress returned with their coffees, he poured on the charm, gifting her a wink and smile just so she'd leave the full carafe. He was smiling victoriously when he looked across the table only to see his breakfast companion glaring at him through narrowed eyes.

Guess the means to an end wasn't appreciated.

Somewhere through her second cup of coffee, Kacie began to look somewhat human again. "Feeling better? You have a little more color in your face now than you did earlier."

She unwrapped her silverware, placed the paper napkin in her lap, then twiddled with the paper napkin ring, folding it upon itself over and over again as they waited on their food. "I shouldn't have drank so much. And yet, I did. Like a stupid college student."

He chuckled. "Or a bridesmaid at a bachelorette party."

"Still doesn't excuse the fact I know better than to drink round after round of tequila."

"True. I feel the same way about my dad's meat loaf."

Michael turned his attention to the coffee cup in front of him, adding a bit of sugar since the brew was on the bitter side of things. It wasn't until he took a drink and looked at her over the rim of his cup that he realized she was waiting patiently for an explanation.

"My dad makes truly terrible meat loaf," he continued, setting the cup down in front of him. "Has for as long as I can remember. But my brother and I, being growing boys and always hungry, we'd slather it in ketchup and choke it down anyway. Now, whenever we're home on leave, he makes meat loaf. And for those first few moments when I sit down at the table, especially after a long deployment and I'm hungry for anything not military-issue, my mind thinks, 'This looks so good. And it *smells* so good. This meat loaf is going to be the game-changer. It's going to be fantastic.' Three bites in, reality hits."

Kacie crinkled her brows and shook her head. "That is not anywhere close to being the same thing."

"Sure it is," he said matter-of-factly. "You just said it wasn't your first hangover and yet you continued to drink beyond your safety zone. Pleasant childhood memories of my father and the home I grew up in dulled the reality of his meat loaf. Just like the euphoric effects of inebriation outweighed the painful memory of every previous hangover. Same is said for childbirth."

"Oh, my God." She closed her eyes and cradled her head in her hands. "It's still too early for this."

By the third cup of coffee, the fog in her brain had lifted a little more. And yet, she still couldn't put all the pieces of the previous night together.

With her stomach having reached maximum capacity, Kacie pushed the remaining pancake to the edge of her plate with a fork, trying to find the right words. She glanced around the diner to make sure no one was eavesdropping on their conversation. Then she took a deep breath and forced herself to ask the question before she lost her nerve.

"I realize it's a little late to ask but . . . did you use something last night?"

She wasn't looking at him when she spoke. As a matter of fact, she only glanced up when he began to cough and sputter, having choked on his last bite of pancake.

He took a long sip of water before replying. "You don't remember?"

"No," she admitted.

His eyebrows lifted and he shook his head in disbelief. "If that isn't a shot to my ego, I don't know what is."

"You still haven't answered my question."

Yes, I used something," he said, keeping his words low so no one would hear. "All three times, as a matter of fact."

Now it was her turn to choke, only she didn't have the luxury of something to eat or drink as an excuse.

"Three times?"

"Yes, dammit." His words were stern and the muscles and tendons in his neck and forearms tensed and flexed. "And to be quite honest, I'm offended. Last night was probably the best single night performance of my entire life." He leaned on his forearms, bringing himself closer. "You really don't remember any of it?"

Well, this was certainly awkward. She couldn't do much more than stare at the inside of her coffee cup now.

Three times.

She'd had sex with the man across the table from her *three times* yet couldn't recall more than a few flashes of laughter and nudity.

Damn tequila.

She spun her coffee cup between her hands. "I remember coming back to my place. I remember standing naked in the middle of my living room. I remember you watching me. And then . . ." She stilled her motions, and finally met his gaze. "I'm sorry, but that's it. I don't remember anything after that."

His expression softened and one corner of his mouth twitched. "You don't remember because nothing happened. You passed out."

She felt her jaw drop as she tried to reconcile his words in her head. "Nothing happened?"

"I promise you," he said, raising his hand. "Scout's honor."

Kacie narrowed her eyes at him. "Something tells me you weren't a Boy Scout."

He laughed then and she was struck by his fantastic smile, one of the few things she recalled from the night before. "Okay. You've got me there. But really, I swear, we didn't have sex."

"But my clothes—"

"For the record," he said, pointing directly at her, "you did that yourself. I just carried you to bed. That's it."

She studied those deep blue eyes as she tried to decide if he was telling the truth.

He took a deep breath, then let it go as he shook his head, as if even he couldn't believe what he was about to say. "Sunshine, as much as I hate to admit it, I'm not twenty anymore. I promise you nothing happened. Even if you hadn't passed out, I had even more to drink than you did. So while my mind was oh-so-very-willing, well, let's just say the flesh couldn't hold up his end of the bargain anyway."

Small lines crinkled at the corners of his eyes as he held her gaze and took another drink from his coffee cup. He was obviously hiding a smile behind that cup. And for some reason unbeknownst to her, she couldn't help but smile back.

He cocked his head to one side, his smile no longer hidden. "There's the woman I remember from last night."

Damn, this guy was charming.

The waitress returned with their check and he paid the bill and generous tip before they walked the two blocks back to her place.

"I should probably let you get some rest," he said, stopping at the end of the driveway.

"Do you want a ride home?" she offered.

He shook his head. "Nah. My brother lives not far from here, but thank you. I would, however—"

Her phone chimed in her hand, and then two more times.

He gestured to her phone. "Do you need to get that?"

Kacie looked at the screen to see a message from her sister. She quickly typed her reply before shoving it into the back pocket of her shorts.

"Everything okay?" he asked, a little crease appearing between his brows.

"Everything's fine. Just my sister checking up on me. Wondering if I'm going to meet them at the day spa."

"Day spa, huh?" His face relaxed into a smile. "Like manicures and massages and stuff?"

"Yeah. But I told her I was too tired."

"You said no?" He folded his arms across his chest. "Seems to me that wouldn't be a bad way to suffer through a hangover."

For a moment she was entranced by his forearms and the strong, sculpted muscles and tendons. Nothing overworked like a bodybuilder, just . . . nice. Finally, she looked back into his eyes if only to stop ogling him. "I'm not really a fan of strangers touching me."

The corner of his mouth lifted in amusement and she struggled to not fidget beneath his gaze. Then, taking her by surprise, he closed the space between them, reaching out for her hand. His fingers loosely held her wrist, his thumb stroking the soft skin on the underside.

"You didn't seem to mind me touching you last night. The little bit I did get to touch you, that is."

With each brush of his skin across hers, everything inside her awakened. If she were smart, she'd pull her hand away before he realized how much he affected her. Or worse, before she did something stupid.

"Not the same thing," she said, pulling free and putting a little distance between them.

"It's not? Well, that's lucky for me, then, because I'd love nothing more than a second opportunity to have my hands all over you."

Kacie may have gasped in shock. One of them made a sound and she wasn't all that certain it was her.

Immediately realizing what he said, he scrubbed both hands over his face. "That didn't come out the way I meant it to. What I meant to say was that I'd really like to see you again."

Her first instinct was to say yes. To throw caution to the wind and just have some fun for once. But then her brain took over, listing all the reasons she should say no. Like the fact she wasn't the kind of woman to have casual flings, last night being the exception, of course. Or the fact she was moving in a matter of weeks and had a ton of stuff to do in the meantime.

"That's probably not a good idea."

He stepped closer but kept his hands to himself. "Is it because of the whiskey dick?" he asked, keeping his voice low. "Because I assure you it can happen to any guy no matter the age."

She chuckled at his honesty. "No. It's because I'm moving at the end of July and I don't really want to jump into a relationship knowing it has an expiration date."

His face brightened. "Okay, then. No relationship. Doesn't mean we can't still go out."

She shook her head.

"Friends with benefits?" he suggested.

"I don't even know your last name so we can't possibly be friends with benefits."

He held out his hand. "It's MacGregor."

She laughed and shook her head a second time. "Nice try, but no."

He took his hand back and shoved it into his pocket. "I have to say I'm greatly disappointed. Can I give you my number in the event you change your mind?"

She hesitated—only for a moment, but long enough that he noticed and raised one eyebrow in anticipation.

"I won't change my mind."

"Okay, then, sunshine. Best of luck wherever it is you're headed."

He gave a little half wave before he headed down the sidewalk, then crossed the street, finally disappearing as he reached the end of the block and rounded the corner.

And Kacie couldn't help but wonder if she just let a good thing walk away.

Chapter Five

COME MONDAY, MICHAEL found himself back in his normal stateside routine as battalion surgeon for the 1st/75th. After morning PT was sick call, where he spent several hours treating everything from upper respiratory infections to ankle sprains.

There was a lot to like about the job, but despite what many people thought, it wasn't always as exciting as it sounded. He enjoyed taking care of the men of the 75th. He liked working alongside the physician assistants and special ops medics and making sure they were well trained in battlefield medicine. He especially loved the unique challenges that overseas deployments presented.

Since many of their missions took place in remote areas far from the military hospitals or even forward operating bases, it was his responsibility to assign casualty collection points and establish temporary battalion aid stations for each operation. As battalion surgeon, he alone oversaw the medical treatment for the Rangers, a situation that forced him to react quickly and often fly by the seat of his pants.

But when 1st Batt wasn't deployed or training overseas, the majority of his time was spent completing administrative paperwork. Accounting for all the personnel currently receiving medical care. Noting any change in duty restrictions. Projecting estimated return dates for those on extended medical leave. And he was getting tired of it. Spending his day shuffling bureaucratic forms wasn't the reason he attended medical school or specialized in emergency medicine.

Later that day, Michael made his way to the office of Lieutenant Colonel Raymond Griffin, battalion commander of the 1st/75th. They'd served together at Hunter Army Airfield since Griffin took command nearly two years earlier. But come July, he'd be moving on to the next step of his military career and a new battalion commander would take his place.

With a shared weakness for Griffin's secretary's homemade snickerdoodles—and her willingness to indulge them—their meetings were fairly casual, at least when other administrative staff weren't involved.

Griffin kicked back in his desk chair, his booted feet propped up on the corner of his massive oak desk.

"Clayton has compound fractures of both the tibia and fibula," Michael said while retrieving a cookie from the small tin situated on the desk. "He'll make a full recovery, but it'll take six to ten months. He's got four left and doesn't want to reenlist."

"Another one and done." Griffin made a notation on the legal pad in front of him. "It's a shame not everyone's like your brother."

Unfortunately, where Danny was concerned, Michael and the commander did not see eye to eye.

Danny had been severely wounded while on a mission in Mali the year before, and Michael had ended up operating on him. His younger brother. His only brother. In the process Danny lost a kidney, a spleen, and a section of his small intestine, all things that Michael believed should have disqualified him from serving in regiment. In his medical opinion, his brother should have been issued his walking papers then and there. But somehow, some way, Danny convinced the top brass to give him one shot to prove he was still physically capable of doing his job.

"How is Danny doing by the way? I assume there weren't any issues during this last deployment?"

"No, aside from making sure we had additional meds for him."

Ray took a second snickerdoodle from the metal tin and dunked it in his fresh cup of coffee. How the hell the man could stand to drink hot coffee in the middle of a muggy, Savannah summer day was beyond him. But far be it from Michael to tell a man how to enjoy his afternoon snack.

"Look, I know you're still pissed about my agreeing to give Danny a chance to prove himself. But he'd earned that right. And your brother didn't ask for multiple chances, he asked for one." Griffin held up a single finger to emphasize the point. "And he met Ranger standards. As a matter of fact, his PT numbers were still far better than most of his counterparts."

"Yes, sir."

Griffin pulled his feet off the desktop, his boots thumping on the floor as he sat up straight in his chair. "Cut the bullshit, Mike. We've been friends for far too long." He leaned his forearms where his feet had been. "No one ever thought there'd be a conflict with you and your brother serving in the same battalion. After all, he doesn't report to you in any manner. It's unfortunate that you had no choice but to perform surgery on him. I can't imagine what that must have been like. There's a reason that shit isn't allowed in the civilian world."

Since there wasn't a question at the end of his statement, Michael knew the appropriate response was to keep his mouth shut.

The commander's posture softened along with his expression. "Have you spoken to anyone about that?"

Michael shook his head. "That's unnecessary."

More than once during the last year Ray had suggested he speak to an army psychiatrist and each time Michael politely declined. After all, they had their hands full treating hundreds of soldiers who suffered not only physical wounds but emotional ones. He sure as hell wasn't going to waste someone else's time whining about the higher-ups overriding his decision.

"You sure about that?"

"Yes, sir. Completely unnecessary."

Griffin laced his fingers together. This wasn't the first time Michael had been scrutinized by the commander and he sincerely doubted it would be the last.

"You were too close to the situation. If it had been anyone else, you know you would have been fine with giving them an opportunity to prove themselves. I mean, we've got several amputees serving in the Rangers. One even qualified for direct combat operations. Now I'm no doctor, but it would seem to me it's far easier to deploy overseas missing a kidney over missing a leg."

Again, Michael held his tongue. After all, any opinion he had regarding the matter was moot. Danny had proven himself to be physically capable of performing the duties his job required. End of story.

"Fine. If that's how you want things to be." Griffin grabbed a sheet of paper from his inbox. "It was brought to my attention that you will have fulfilled your commitment come November." He motioned to the paper.

"That's correct."

"Any plans on what you're going to do?"

"I'd planned on staying right here."

From the expression on Ray's face, that clearly wasn't what he expected to hear. "For how long?"

"As long as it takes," Michael answered. "Were you hoping to hear something different?"

"Just never would've figured you for the career military

type. I was fully expecting you to say you were already looking at civilian jobs."

"You don't think I should stay twenty and collect retirement?"

"You could do that. But I've seen plenty of guys reach fifteen years and decide they've had enough. It's not like you don't have options. I'm sure you'd be paid pretty well in the civilian world."

For the first time in his military career, Michael felt a sense of panic.

"Does HQ want me to leave?"

"Haven't heard anything of the sort. But come on, Mike," Griffin said with a shrug, "you told me yourself you never planned to be career military."

"I didn't realize I couldn't change my mind." Michael took a deep breath and tried his damnedest to sound convincing. Maybe he'd convince himself somewhere along the way. "I can say with absolute certainty, the 1st/75th is exactly where I need to be."

MICHAEL DROPPED INTO his desk chair, spinning it around to look out the window. Bright sunlight flooded the glass, the young trees planted outside no competition for the summer sun. All he could think about since leaving Griffin's office was the similar afternoon he'd spent with his mother, when he was ten.

His father had taken Danny shopping for new school shoes and for the first time in weeks Michael had his mother all to himself. No home health nurses or ladies from church around. No neighbors in the kitchen cooking dinner. For that one short afternoon, she was all his.

Despite the summer heat, she rested on a wicker chaise on the screened-in back porch so she could look out onto the backyard and admire her blooming garden. Michael placed the glass of lemonade and plate of cookies he'd brought her on a small side table, and she smiled and patted the cushion next to her.

Her head was wrapped in a bright colored scarf— as it had been for months since she lost her long brown hair to chemotherapy. Her skin was grayed and dull. Clear tubes pumping oxygen into her nose stretched across her face and tucked behind her ears. She was no matter the temperature outside, she was always cold.

A trickle of sweat ran down his spine as she hugged him close and he rested his head against her shoulder. His friends would make fun of him if they saw him now, especially since they were always stopping by, ringing the doorbell, and waking his mother, asking him to go to the beach or the pool or the park for a pickup game of baseball. But none of that interested him. He just wanted to stay with his mom.

"Are you ready for school to start?" she asked while her fingertips combed through his hair. "Fourth grade. I can hardly believe it. You're not a little boy anymore."

"I guess so." He shifted a bit, trying not to lean so much of his weight on her since she was having a hard time breathing, but she wouldn't allow him to move too far away. Proof she was still strong willed, although her body was weak.

"And Danny is starting school. He's so excited. Do you remember your first day of kindergarten?"

Michael shrugged. "I remember Bryan Carson puking during the Pledge of Allegiance."

His mom laughed, which made him feel like the king of the world. But then the laughter was replaced with uncontrollable coughing. He hopped up from the chaise and grabbed the glass of lemonade, steadying the bendy straw in case she needed a drink. But with one frail hand she waved it away and he was forced to just stand there, watch, and wait, while for several long moments she struggled to get air in her lungs.

When she finally settled and her breathing returned to as close to normal as possible, she patted the cushion next to her again and things went back to the way they had been before.

"Thank you for your help. You take such good care of me," she said softly, wrapping one arm around him as he leaned his head on her shoulder. "But I need you to take care of your brother, too. Watch out for him. Don't let your friends or other kids pick on him. Okay? He's so little. Take care of your brother."

"Do I have to go to school? Can't I stay here with you instead?"

"You don't want to do that. You like school. Wouldn't you miss your friends?"

He wrapped an arm around her middle, wanting to

hug her tight, except he was afraid of hurting her. "I'd miss you more."

He felt her body tremble and then heard her sniffle. When she reached for the box of tissues, he realized he'd made her cry.

"I'm sorry, Mom," he whispered.

She pressed a kiss to his temple. "You don't have anything to be sorry for."

HIS CELL PHONE vibrated against the desktop and Michael spun his chair away from the window to grab it. On the screen, a text message from his favorite sister-in-law.

Come over for dinner? I'm making enchiladas.

Not one to turn down a home-cooked meal, Michael quickly replied with a yes before turning off his computer and heading out the door. After a quick stop at his apartment to change clothes and another for a bottle of wine, he arrived less than an hour later on his brother's doorstep and was greeted by the heavenly scent of Bree's cooking. He rang the doorbell and immediately their newly acquired beast of a dog began barking his fool head off.

"Back up, Hank," Bree said as she fought to open the front door. "Come on in."

Michael wedged himself through the opening and was immediately assaulted by the one-hundred-thirty-pound French mastiff. Although their rescue dog was fully grown, he still acted like a baby, wasting no time shoving his nose right into Michael's crotch and wiping drool all over his shorts. "Nice to see you, too, Hank."

"Sorry about that. He means well, I promise." Bree grabbed his collar to pull him away. "Danny just called. He's right behind you."

For other men, killing time with their sister-in-law might prove awkward. Not so for him. Bree had grown up across the street from him and Danny; he'd known her all her life.

He moved around her as she finished preparing dinner, helping himself to the wine opener from one drawer and a wineglass from the cabinet. He poured her a drink and placed the glass on the island in front of her.

"What's this?" she asked with a raised brow. "Aren't you having some?"

Michael smiled and reached for the cookie jar instead. "I'd rather have a cookie."

Bree shook her head, but gestured with the wineglass in her hand. "Go ahead. They're peanut butter, made fresh today."

They spent the next few minutes chatting about her parents and the ten-state road trip they were taking the following month, as well as the wedding Danny and Bree were attending in Beaufort the following weekend. While they were talking, Danny arrived, greeting Bree with a kiss and Michael with a wave for him before heading off to clean up.

Bree handed Michael a stack of plates, napkins, and silverware. "So . . ."

He knew exactly what was coming next by the sly look on her face. She was on the verge of either prying into his personal life or suggesting a blind date.

"The answer is no," he replied, before turning his back and setting the table.

He heard Bree scoff. "I haven't even asked a question yet."

"Well, then, let me expand upon my previous statement and say, 'No comment.'"

"You're absolutely no fun," she muttered.

Just as Michael placed the last piece of silverware on the table, Danny arrived in the kitchen.

"So . . ." Danny began.

Michael wasted no time cutting him off. "Jesus. You, too?"

"What?" his brother asked with a smile that had been getting him out of trouble for as long as Michael could remember. "I was just going to ask what happened with Malibu Barbie."

Bree laughed as she placed the food on the table. "Oh, my God. That's an absolutely perfect description of her. She can be the Barbie to your Ken."

He loved his brother and his sister-in-law, but damn if the two of them weren't like peas in a pod. Oh, they were amusing as all get-out, until their tag-teamed sarcasm was directed at him. Then they were annoying as fuck.

"How much did have you to drink before I got here?" he asked, trying to get in a jab of his own. "I think it's time to cut you off." He jokingly reached for her wineglass, but unfortunately, he didn't intimidate Bree in the least.

"All we want to know about is the girl from the bar," she said matter-of-factly. "Any chance you'll be going out again?"

"Why does it matter?" Michael asked.

Danny chuckled. "Denied."

"But he said, 'No comment.'"

"Come on, sweetheart, you know men better than this," Danny said, wrapping an arm around his wife's shoulders. "That's guy speak. Clearly he was rejected. Because if they went out he'd say something like 'she was a psycho' if he never planned on seeing her again. And if they had plans to see each other, he'd tell you, if only to shut us up."

Michael had to try and save face. "We're going out," he muttered.

Danny shook his head, still laughing. "Too late. We already know you're lying."

Bree pulled the steaming hot dish from the oven and walked it over to the table. They all took a seat and began passing items around and spooning food on plates. Things were mostly silent for the next several minutes, the quiet disrupted only by compliments on the meal. But finally, he glanced up from his plate, accidentally making eye contact with her—and immediately he knew it was a mistake.

"I can't believe you're just going to let a little 'no' deter you. You know where she lives, right?"

Michael nearly choked on his last bite of food. "Bree!

A woman says no, that's the end of it. I'm not really interested in a prolonged vacation at the county lockup."

"What if you send her a little bouquet of flowers or a card or something with your phone number on it? That wouldn't be bad, would it?"

He shook his head. "That still feels like stalking, Bree. Besides, I offered her my phone number and she didn't want it."

Danny barked a laugh, then quickly covered his mouth when his wife shot him a dirty look. Which made Michael chuckle until she turned that look on him.

"What did you say to her?"

"I asked if I could give her my number."

Bree shook her head. "Nooo. I know you, Michael MacGregor. Everyone else might think you're a Boy Scout, but I know just how much of an arrogant ass you can really be. What did you actually say to her?"

If anyone else had spoken to him that bluntly, he'd have told them to fuck off. Instead, her reprimand made him want to hang his head in shame because she was right. So he shared the whole story, including the ugly fact he had suggested a friends-with-benefits situation.

Bree picked up a potholder from the table and smacked his arm with it. "Michael!"

"I know, I know."

He couldn't blame her for being upset. He sounded like an asshole even to his own ears. Lord knows what she'd have to say about the whiskey dick comment, but no way in hell would he ever own up to that. Ever.

"How can someone be so smart and yet say something so stupid? It's no wonder she didn't want to go out with you again. Heaven forbid a woman doesn't fall at Michael MacGregor's feet."

He set his fork on his plate and wiped his mouth. "Not much I can do about it now."

"Do you like her?" Bree leaned an elbow on the table, resting her chin on her hand.

"Of course I do. Did. It's why I asked her out." Michael shrugged helplessly.

"And I think it's great that you respect the fact that no means no," she said to him with a look of understanding. "But I can't help but wonder if you're using it as an excuse to avoid putting yourself out there."

Michael went to speak and Bree immediately held up a hand, silencing his rebuttal.

"Listen, all I'm talking about is a small gesture, a little something to apologize for being a bit of a jerk while letting her know you like her. Maybe, if you show a little interest in getting to know her instead of acting like you're just trying to get her into the sack, you might have some success."

Michael stared at his plate while he considered Bree's words. The truth was, he'd never had to work too hard with women. But was that really a reason to let this go? Just because he was used to being pursued?

Maybe, for the first time his life, this woman was going to make him work for it. And he ought to rise to the challenge.

Chapter Six

WITH HER LAST patient of the day gone, Kacie dropped into her chair and yanked open the bottom drawer of her desk, grabbing her secret stash of Ghirardelli squares. She quickly unwrapped the pink foil covering the dark chocolate and shoved it in her mouth. Before she even finished the first, she was unwrapping a second.

It had been that kind of day.

"If only there was a way to mainline those things."

Kacie froze, the chocolate's progress halted just inches from her mouth. She swiveled around in her desk chair to see her colleague Damien leaning against the doorjamb of the closet-sized office she shared with two other physical therapists.

"Counting down the days?"

"Mmm-hmm," she said, answering as best she could

around her mouthful of deliciousness. "Eighty-one days counting weekends and holidays."

"You have it down to the exact day? Do we need to make you one of those paper chains to hang up in here? You know, the kind schoolteachers use to count down to summer break?"

Kacie tipped back her chair and rested her head against the seat back. "I'd make room for it."

Damien laughed. "I bet you would." He nabbed a chocolate from the bag and departed with a grin, leaving her to finish her patient notes for the day.

Working in a standard clinical setting wasn't something she'd ever enjoyed. Occasionally she'd get those dedicated athletes who were working through their recovery, and she loved helped them to get back out to the competition. But the majority of her patients were middle-aged people who'd hurt themselves while trying to recapture their youth after spending twenty years on the couch, or whose bodies were simply starting to break down due to the aging process.

When she had chosen physical therapy as a career path, she'd always imagined working with the most challenging medical cases. Those who defied the odds, whose doctors said they'd never walk or run or dance ever again. Those were the patients she wanted.

But then she'd met a dreamy guy on spring break, and like so many of her friends, her focus shifted.

By the time she completed her doctorate in physical therapy, she simply wanted out of school, ready to move on with the next phase of her life. Since Mike had been deployed overseas at the time, she returned to her hometown of Savannah and took what she thought would be a temporary position—something to pay the bills until he returned stateside and they got married.

When he came home seven months later, Mike was assigned to a division only an hour away, in Beaufort, South Carolina. But there was no talk of marriage or even an engagement, so she remained in Savannah. Years passed, and what began as a short-term job became a long-term one. Meanwhile, her boyfriend was dispatched to places all over the world: Hawaii, the Philippines, Okinawa. As his career literally took off, hers stagnated.

When the relationship finally ended several months earlier, Kacie decided it was the perfect time for not only a more challenging career, but a change of scenery. She applied for and was awarded a highly sought after residency and research fellowship at Duke University. With the first step complete, all that was left now was to get through Sam's wedding, and the next phase of her own life would begin as well.

AN HOUR LATER, after a quick stop at the grocery store, she arrived at her place only to find all the lights on, a sure sign there was a certain uninvited guest in her home. As she shoved her way through the front door with an armload of groceries, she was greeted by her sister lounging on her couch, eating her food, and watching ESPN. While she loved Sam dearly, there were some habits of hers she would not miss. Showing up unannounced, and helping herself to whatever was in the kitchen, were two of them.

"You're out of honey-wheat pretzels," Sam said while waving the bag in the air.

"Well, hello to you, too." Kacie kicked the front door closed and dropped her bags on the small breakfast bar between the kitchen and living room. "That bag doesn't look empty to me."

"But it will be when I get done with it."

She was tempted to tell her sister to go home to her own place and eat her own food when Sam shouted, "There he is!" and cranked up the volume on the TV.

The face of Sam's fiancé—Bryce Elliott—filled the screen as he reported from Tuscaloosa, Alabama. A former quarterback for the University of Georgia and one-time first-round NFL hopeful, Bryce had suffered a career-ending cervical vertebrae fracture in what was his last collegiate game before entering the draft. With pro-football off the table and no desire to coach, Bryce moved into broadcasting, landing a job with a local news station in Savannah. Then, just eighteen months into his new career, ESPN came a-calling, hiring him for the SEC network channel.

He was a great guy and treated her sister like a princess, but Kacie couldn't help feeling a touch of resentment over the fact he would be taking Sam away to Atlanta within a matter of weeks. And from there, God only knew.

The close relationship she had once shared with her sister was now a shadow of its former self because of him; she'd been effectively and permanently replaced as her sister's best friend and closest confidante.

Before she even realized what she was doing, Kacie had torn into a fresh pack of Oreo Double Stuf cookies, cramming one and then another into her mouth. As her luck would have it, the report ended and Sam turned around just in time to catch her in the act.

"What are you doing?" her sister asked.

Unable to speak around a mouthful of dark chocolate cookie and vanilla frosting, Kacie could only shake her head in response and try to look as innocent as possible. Of course, Sam wasn't buying it and vaulted over the back of her sofa, making her way to the kitchen.

Why her sister found walking around the sofa too much effort, she'd never understand.

"What is going on with you?" Sam asked while searching through the various plastic bags holding her groceries.

"Nothing." Kacie smacked Sam's hand away from the bags, but her sister was undeterred.

"You've always been the epitome of health. And yet, what do we have here . . ." she began pulling items out. "M&M's. Ben & Jerry's Phish Food. That's in addition to the Oreos you are currently shoving in your piehole like there's no tomorrow." Sam held the pint of ice cream in front of her face. "If you keep this up, you won't fit into your bridesmaid dress."

"Pity," Kacie mumbled under her breath.

Sam snatched the pack of Oreos from her hands and shoved it in the bag with the other items. "I'm going to do you a favor and throw all of this crap away because this isn't you."

"It is now!"

Kacie made a play for the bag, but her sister was expecting the move, swinging her arm out wide to keep her from getting hold of it.

"Tell me what's wrong," Sam pleaded.

Kacie took a deep breath. "Nothing's wrong. I was hungry and craving chocolate while at the grocery store. Obviously, I went a little overboard, but it's not as if I was going to eat it all in one sitting."

It was true, for the most part—but Kacie was intelligent enough to realize that as her sister's wedding drew closer, her chocolate consumption was increasing exponentially.

Sam narrowed her eyes and Kacie fought the urge to laugh, because really, her sister couldn't intimidate a three-year-old. "You promise you aren't going to eat all of this the moment I walk out the door?"

Kacie swiped her index finger twice across her heart.

After staring at her a moment longer, her sister reluctantly handed over the bag of treats, then took a seat on a bar stool while Kacie put everything away.

"So . . ." her sister began. "You never said how the rest of your night went after you ditched the ice club."

Kacie opened the small pantry and set the box of Special K with chocolate on the shelf.

Damn. Maybe the problem was worse than she'd realized.

"Nothing happened," she answered. "He brought me home and I went to bed."

Her sister smiled. "Oh, I don't doubt that's *exactly* what happened."

Kacie huffed. "Did you miss the 'nothing' part of that sentence?"

"I didn't. I just choose not to believe you. Are you trying to tell me he walked you to the door, said good night, and that was it?"

Kacie reached for another Oreo, but caught her sister watching her. So she sealed up the pack, tossed them in the cabinet, and grabbed a bottled water instead. "He stayed the night, but I swear nothing happened."

Sam eyed her suspiciously. "What about the next morning?"

"We went to breakfast." Kacie shrugged. "He walked me home. Asked if we could go out again. I said no and he left. End of story."

"You said no?" Sam looked completely bewildered. "But why?"

"Because . . . I didn't want to go out with him."

"You're impossible." Sam folded her arms across her chest and shook her head in disappointment. "That guy was pretty damn hot. Don't get me wrong. I love Bryce and Michael was definitely too old for me—but he could've been a nice little rebound fling for you."

"Aren't there time constraints on what can and

cannot be classified a rebound? It's been over nine months. I think I've exceeded the limits." Kacie gulped down half of her bottled water, hoping to quench her thirst for chocolate. But it just wasn't working.

"You're purposely overthinking this," Sam said.

"He's military."

Her sister shrugged her shoulders. "I don't see the problem with that but obviously, you are finding one."

"Of course I am! They're all a bunch of overgrown boys who want to shoot guns and blow stuff up."

"That's a touch dramatic, don't you think? Not to mention untrue."

To hell with it. Kacie opened the cabinet and pulled the pack of Oreos back out. If she wanted to eat the whole damn thing in one sitting, she'd damn well do it. Because she was a grown woman who paid her own bills, her own way, and she'd do what she wanted. She didn't have to listen to anyone. Not even her sister.

"I'm moving in a few months," Kacie explained while peeling the pack open. "I don't want to start a relationship now."

"Nobody said anything about a relationship. Just a fling. A little summer fling. I think it would do you a lot of good."

"Why does it matter so much to you?" she asked around a mouthful of cookie.

Sam's threw her arms in the air. "Because you're substituting sex with chocolate."

Oh, hell, no.

"What on Earth does that mean?"

"You know exactly what it means," her sister said pointedly. "You're lonely and cranky and sexually frustrated!"

Kacie swallowed hard. "Am not."

But even as she heard the words come out of her mouth she knew they were nothing but lies. "I'm going to change my clothes," Kacie said, walking out of the kitchen and effectively putting an end to the conversation. She closed her bedroom door behind her, kicked off her shoes, and flopped down on her bed.

Her life at the moment was sorely lacking. She knew that. But she was on the road to fixing it. Once she moved to Durham and immersed herself in her new career, she'd be happy. And if she was happy with herself, she wouldn't need or want a man in her life.

Besides, everyone knew that soul mates showed up when you least expected them.

Everything she ever wanted out of life was waiting for her in North Carolina. She just had to be patient for a little bit longer.

Chapter Seven

MICHAEL RACED OUT to the medevac, shielding his face and eyes from the dirt and debris kicked up by the helicopter's rotors. The side door slid open and immediately the medic inside began talking to him. He could see his mouth moving, but couldn't hear what he was saying because the whomp-whomp-whomp of the rotor blades drowned him out. Frustrated, the medic shoved the litter Danny was lying on out of the helicopter, then slammed the side door shut as it lifted off the ground.

Michael screamed at the sky, at the medevac leaving them alone, then turned to the tent that was the battalion aid station and yelled for help. But no one came. He grabbed the handles of the litter carrying his brother and dragged it across the ground. Once inside, he lifted Danny from the stretcher and put him on the table. His brother stared up at him, eyes wide open, and as Michael *began cutting the clothes from his body, Danny began to laugh.*

"Shut up, Danny!" he yelled. "Shut up!" He couldn't think with him making all that noise as he tried to remember what he had to do next.

Danny continued laughing as Michael pressed the scalpel to his torso and within an instant the trickle of blood from his chest became a fast-flowing river of red. He shoved his hands into Danny's abdomen, hoping to find the bleeder. But there was too much red. He couldn't see anything as the river became an ocean . . .

Michael's eyes shot open and it took several seconds for him to realize he was at home, in his own bed, not back in Mali. He stared at the ceiling fan and took a deep breath, trying to slow his heart rate.

The nightmares had worsened since their last deployment to Afghanistan. This week, he had woken up every night with his heart racing and sheets drenched in sweat. It didn't matter if he cranked the air-conditioning way down or turned the fan on high before he went to bed. He still dreamed he was in that oppressing African heat and his brother was dying before his very eyes.

As far back as he could remember, Michael's worst fear had been something happening to Danny and not being able to save him. From the time his mother asked him to watch out for his little brother, he'd taken that responsibility seriously. He kept his eye on Danny for the next eight years until he graduated high school. Even after he went off to college, then medical school, he'd frequently call to check on his little brother. A dozen years passed and things always seemed just fine.

But Michael had grown complacent, and during Danny's freshman year at the University of South Carolina, things quickly went south. His little brother was not only kicked out of school, but he joined the army and somehow managed to become a member of the 75th Ranger Regiment, an elite special operations squadron that was known for leading the way into enemy territory.

In Michael's mind, there wasn't a question about what he needed to do next. And for the most part, he didn't regret becoming a member of the 75th. However, every time Danny's contract was about to expire, Michael would silently hope and pray his brother would choose not to reenlist just so he could breathe again. Those prayers always went unanswered.

Finally, sometime well before dawn, Michael climbed out of bed, dressed in his running gear, and laced his shoes. He wasn't really motivated to run, but what was the alternative? Spend another three hours staring at the ceiling wondering why he seemed to be the only person affected by the anniversary of Danny nearly dying?

When he'd spoken to his father the evening before, all they'd discussed was what a great round of golf the old man had shot earlier in the day. Danny and Bree were away for the weekend at that wedding. But even if they were in town would they be thinking of what happened a year before? Or were they both so happy with their lives now that they didn't bother reflecting on the past?

He simply had no option but to deal with it on his own.

The moment he hit the road and fell into a steady rhythm, Michael knew he'd made the right decision. Because if he hadn't gone for a run now, he'd be feeling guilty later. And if he felt guilty enough, he'd go running no matter the time of day or the heat index. It was best to just get it over with.

Of course, that's what Danny always used to say. Get it over with. Hangover or no hangover. Sleep. No sleep. Just get it over with.

He and Danny used to meet to run at five in the morning, sometimes earlier, just to avoid the worst of the oppressive Georgia summers. But since Danny and Bree moved out of the apartment complex and into their new house across town last fall, he and his brother rarely ran together anymore. Even though his little brother often made him crazy, and as much as he hated feeling responsible for him at times, there was no denying that he missed him.

And this particular week just amplified those feelings because Michael knew *exactly* how close he had come to losing Danny forever.

So he ran hard, faster than normal even, like he'd be able to outpace his demons. But three hours later, he was right back where he started, alone in his apartment with his thoughts.

After a quick shower and change of clothes, he grabbed

up his keys along with his golf clubs and headed back out the door. It had been months since he last played, weeks before their last deployment to Afghanistan as a matter of fact. A trip to the driving range was what he needed, something to knock the rust off his swing.

But first, breakfast. A quiet place to sit down with a hot cup of coffee and a donut.

And a peach fritter. Maybe a sticky bun, too.

THE CHORUS OF lawn mowers started early and were soon joined by the whine of a weed eater circling the perimeter of her small carriage house. It was only a matter of time before the leaf blowers got in on the act.

Since sleeping in wasn't a possibility, she gathered her backpack and headed down the street to her favorite café. Nestled between two larger buildings and behind a large live oak, the place was barely visible from the sidewalk. With limited seating and a cozy atmosphere, it was the perfect oasis. Lucky for her, a small table situated near the French doors leading to a lovely courtyard became available the moment she walked in. She quickly placed her order, then settled in for what she hoped would be a quiet, productive morning.

Kacie had been there nearly an hour when the bell above the door jangled, signaling the coming and going of another customer. For reasons she couldn't explain, she was compelled to look up. And just like a scene from a movie, she was struck dumb by the tall, well-dressed man who pulled his aviator sunglasses from his face and slipped them on the top of his head. Kacie's heart skipped a beat, immediately recognizing those dark blue eyes.

She slid down in her seat and held the textbook she was reading a little higher, angling her head just enough to peek around the side. Surely, he hadn't come here looking for her? She searched her memory, trying to recall if she'd ever mentioned this place or the fact she liked to come here on Sunday mornings. But he didn't appear to be the stalker type. And to be quite honest, if anyone was acting shady, it was her.

The door jangled again as a few more customers entered, and he stretched his arm out, indicating for them to go ahead. From the way he was taking up residence in front of the bakery case, it looked like he couldn't decide what to get.

A young woman behind the counter smiled flirtatiously at him and he politely smiled in return before turning his attention to the treats, one hand drifting up to his chin. He scrubbed his knuckles against his jaw almost in frustration.

The longer she watched him, the more he didn't seem like the same guy she'd had breakfast with. Instead of the confident, cocky man she remembered, he looked almost lost, uncomfortable. Before she knew it, she was rising to her feet and walking over to him. When she laid her hand on his arm, he practically jumped out of his skin.

"Hey there," she said. He turned to look at her, an unreadable expression on his face. Was he annoyed she approached him? Maybe he didn't recognize her. "I'm Kacie. We met at—"

"I remember." Then he smiled.

Oh, Lord. She'd somehow forgotten how pretty his smile was.

He cocked his head to one side. "It's really nice to see you."

She felt her skin heat beneath his gaze, forcing her to look away. What was it about this guy that made her feel like a blushing teenage girl?

She took a deep breath, hoping to regain some composure. To remind herself that she was a smart, professional, *grown* woman. But when she looked up and saw those deep blue eyes intently watching her, she damn near melted a second time.

Somehow, she found her voice again. "Are you meeting someone?"

His smile widened as he shook his head. "No."

Damn that smile. She decided right then and there it could be the end of her.

"Well, I have a table." Then, like an idiot, she pointed across the room to the empty table with her things piled on top, all because she didn't know what the hell to do with her hands. "You can use it."

Without warning, his smile disappeared. "Are you leaving?"

"No, uh . . . I wasn't planning on it."

His smile returned. "So you're inviting me to sit with you?"

"Um . . . yeah." Kacie winced at her response. She sounded like a nitwit even to her own ears. Then she went and made things worse. "The cruellers are really good. You know, if you're having a hard time deciding."

"Good to know." Michael gestured toward the counter. "Would you like anything? Need a refill on your coffee or tea or whatever you're drinking?"

"No. I'm fine. I'll just . . ." Like an idiot she turned and looked at the table as if there was a possibility someone would've walked away with it. "Wait. Over here."

"Sounds good. I'll be there." He leaned closer. "In a minute."

She took a few steps backward, maintaining eye contact until she nearly bumped into another table and was forced to watch where she was going.

Kacie shook her head as she returned to her seat. What the hell was wrong with her? She had only a matter of minutes to get her head straight, otherwise he'd be leaving here with the belief she was a total dingbat.

After shutting down her laptop and stuffing it in the protective sleeve of her backpack, she went about stacking up her books and papers until her pen rolled off the edge of the table. She leaned over to grab it, and when she sat upright she saw that Michael was now holding the textbook she had been reading in his hand.

"Neuronal Migration Disorders?" One side of his

mouth kicked up as he handed back her book. "Nothing like a little light reading on a Sunday morning."

She took the book from his hand and shoved it into her backpack along with the rest of her papers. "Just trying to get a little ahead on my required reading."

"So you're going back to school?" He settled into the chair opposite her with his coffee and tray full of pastries. "You said you were moving at the end of July. Where are you going?"

Considering the hangover he must have been suffering that morning, the fact that he not only listened to what she said but retained that information was impressive indeed.

"Duke."

Having taken a large bite from what appeared to be a jelly donut, he could only nod in response. And to be honest, she fully expected the conversation to end there.

"Are you going back to school to become a physical therapist?"

His question caught her off guard and she choked on a sip of her chai tea. "What would make you say that?"

He smiled while reaching for another napkin. "I might have noticed a physical therapy program brochure on your coffee table. But I swear that's all," he said while quickly swiping sticky glaze from his fingers. "No searching your bathroom or kitchen cabinets. No looking in your fridge or pantry. Not even a peek into your nightstand, although I was sorely tempted." He leaned across the table and lowered his voice. "Did I miss anything interesting? Blindfolds? Silk scarves? Furry hand-cuffs?" And then he winked at her.

Kacie felt her jaw drop.

Did he really just ask if kept sex toys in her bedside table? And shouldn't she be offended by such an impli-cation?

Except now she kind of wished she did have some-thing of interest in there.

Even more, if she'd had such a thing, she would've liked it if he *had* taken a peek.

She took another sip of her chai, which didn't help to cool her off any. She desperately needed to steer the conversation in a different direction, otherwise she'd implode right there in her chair.

"I'm already a physical therapist. I have my doctor-ate as a matter of fact. What I'll be doing is a pediatric PT residency combined with a neurodevelopmental dis-abilities research fellowship."

He didn't respond for a long time, just politely nodded while he continued with his next pastry and then washed it down with a sip of his coffee. If he was anything like her ex, he probably didn't have a clue what she was talking about.

"I have a friend from med school, an old roommate actually, who went into research instead of primary care. He's currently at Stanford conducting a large-scale clinical trial for a new medication intended for kids with Fragile X syndrome."

Now it was her turn to feel lost in the conversation.

Kacie gave herself a mental shake. "I'm sorry. Did you just say you went to medical school?"

"Mmm-hmm," he said around a mouthful of food. "Johns Hopkins."

"You said you were in the army."

"I am," he replied, once again grabbing a fresh napkin to wipe his mouth and chin. "I'm the battalion surgeon for the 1st/75th."

She couldn't believe what she was hearing. She knew what the 1st/75th was. Hell, everyone in Savannah knew who they were. They were the crazy guys who went to dangerous places and jumped out of airplanes in the middle of the night to chase down scary people. And when they weren't doing that, they usually took the city by storm with their nighttime training maneuvers.

"You're the medical officer for the Rangers?"

He smiled proudly. "Yep."

Kacie covered her eyes and shook her head. "For fuck's sake," she mumbled under her breath.

She heard chair legs scrape against the old wood-plank floors and footsteps walking away. If he was getting up and leaving without saying goodbye, she wouldn't be surprised.

A couple of minutes passed and the footsteps returned and her arm was bumped with something cold. Kacie looked up to see him standing there with a large glass in each hand.

"It's getting too hot to drink coffee so I got myself a lemonade. Got you one, too, if you want it."

Oh, man. He was such a gentleman. She looked at the large glass he set in front of her, then back to him smiling at her. "Are you kidding me about being a doctor? Please tell me you're kidding."

He handed her a straw and then unwrapped his own. "Afraid I'm not. Is there a problem I'm not aware of?"

"Yes. There's a big problem. Because here you were being all cute and charming and I thought I could overlook the fact you have the same name as my ex. And the military thing. But being a doctor, too?" Kacie threw down her straw on the table. "No way. I also swore off doctors—well, all medical professionals, really—on the very first day of my inpatient clinical rotation because I didn't want that kind of drama in my life. And you, sir, have hit the trifecta. You actually managed to tick off every box on my no-fly list."

"No fly list? That's funny." He took a long drink from his lemonade. "Do I get a prize?"

"Only if you score in the bonus round."

He smiled while rubbing his hands together like a cartoon villain. "Okay. I'm game. What's the last one?"

She leaned across the table to stare into his eyes. "Do you live with your mother?"

His smile slipped and he rested his arms on the table. "No, I don't," he said matter-of-factly. "Mostly because my mother died when I was ten."

Kacie gasped and her insides did a complete, anxious rollover. "Are you messing with me?"

He remained silent and took another sip of his drink.

"I'm sorry. I'm so sorry." Kacie folded her arms over the tabletop and buried her face. "God, I'm such an ass," she said into the scarred wood.

She felt his hand on her forearm and she looked up. "No, I'm the one who should be sorry. That was mean of me and I know you were just joking. Please don't worry about it."

Although he said it was okay, and the look on his face seemed sincere, she imagined her words had to sting a little bit at least.

"If it were me in your shoes, I would've bounced a long time ago. First, I acted like a lunatic. Then I was all smug and superior. And then I followed it up by insulting your dead mother."

He smiled again. Not that brilliant, hypnotic version, but a nice one just the same. "What are you talking about? You didn't insult my mother."

She couldn't keep from shaking her head in disbelief. "Why are you even still sitting there?"

"Because I like you." He reached across the table and took her hand in both of his. "I like that you're smart. I like that you're funny. I like that you don't take crap from anyone. I like that you have some dating standards, even if they are working against me at the moment." He gently stroked the back of her hand with his thumb. "But most of all, I like the fact that I've had one hell of a week and today wasn't going any better until you placed your hand on my arm and invited me to sit at your table."

They sat in silence for a long moment as Kacie let his words sink in. It was the single-most romantic thing anyone had ever said to her. Not even old-Mike came close to anything that nice, and he'd had seven years' worth of opportunities.

For a moment, she thought, maybe even hoped, he was going to ask her out again. And this time she would not have the willpower to turn him down. But just as he opened his mouth to speak, her cell phone buzzed in her backpack.

As she reached down to grab it, she caught sight of the textbook she'd been reading earlier. The one for her fellowship. In North Carolina. The fact she was leaving in a matter of weeks wouldn't change, and her previous reasons for turning him down the first time still applied now.

Kacie checked the text message. "I'm sorry, but I have to meet my sister for wedding shoe shopping in thirty minutes."

"You sound very unexcited. I thought most women liked shoe shopping?"

"Ordinarily, yes. But this shoe purchase requires bride approval."

Michael pointed to her phone on the table. "May I?"

She wasn't sure of his intent but allowed him to have it anyway, scooting it across the tabletop. He picked it up, swiped the lock screen with his thumb, and began tapping away. Within a matter of seconds he handed the phone back.

Kacie narrowed her eyes at him. "What did you do?"

"I put my number in your contacts. Under 'G.I. Joe' to avoid any potential confusion."

She stared at the phone she now held in her hand. "Why did you do that?"

"Just in case you change your mind and decide to disregard that no-fly list of yours."

He stood up from his chair and leaned across the table, placing a chaste kiss on her cheek. A kiss not unlike the one he gave her when he came to her rescue the night of the bachelorette party. "Thanks again for the company this morning, sunshine. I really needed it."

"You're leaving? Just like that?"

"The ball is in your court, Kacie. I hope to hear from you."

Of course he flashed her one of those dazzling smiles. Then, without another word, he turned around and walked out of the café.

Chapter Eight

KACIE REMOVED THE ice blue chiffon dress from its hanger and slipped it on over her head. It was a beautiful color her sister had selected for the bridesmaid dresses, not to mention the light, flowy fabric suited the hot Georgia summers. As far as bridesmaid dresses went, it was actually very nice.

There was a tap on the louvered dressing room door. "Are you ready to be zipped?"

"Yes, thank you," she answered.

The door swung open and a tall, willowy woman made her way inside and held out her hand. "I'm Della. Am I to understand you are the maid of honor?" she said in a slow, sugared, southern drawl.

"Yes, I'm Kacie," she said, shaking the woman's hand.

Kacie had to say Della was the epitome of southern

style. Her snow white hair was gathered into a sophisticated twist and her makeup was impeccable.

"Well, I must commend your sister on selecting such a lovely shade of blue. It's simply stunning with your coloring. I hope the other bridesmaids are as fortunate."

Instinctively, Kacie turned her back to the woman and lifted her hair up. Della gathered the two sides of fabric in one hand as she tugged on the zipper with the other. Almost immediately the dress felt uncomfortably tight.

"Oh dear, this dress seems a bit snug," Della said. "I hope I didn't give you the wrong one. Let me double-check." She unzipped the dress, peeked at the tag, and then excused herself to go look at her files.

Of course, Kacie knew exactly what she would find. That it was her dress, and they'd ordered the correct size. Her current situation was what Sam had predicted nearly two weeks earlier—that the chocolate bingeing would eventually bite her in the ass. And the waistline.

Twisting first to her left and then to her right, Kacie took a long hard look at her reflection in the floor-to-ceiling mirror. "Sam is going to kill me," she whispered.

Again, there was a light tap on the dressing room door and a slight pause before the door swung open. "I'm not certain what happened, but that's definitely the dress we ordered for you based on your measurements."

It was time to confess.

"It wasn't an error on your end. It's my fault."

Della gave her a look of sympathy. "I don't know that we could get a bigger size in time, but I do think a foundation piece that offers full control might be the best solution. We could have the seamstress attempt to let it out a bit, maybe a quarter inch on each side, but I'm afraid the fabric would show the original seaming. It's far easier to take in these dresses than to let them out."

Kacie took a deep breath, as much as the dress would allow, and let it all out in a rush, unable to hide her disappointment.

"Maybe you're just a little bloated today," Della offered.

"No. It's the chocolate. And the Oreos. And the Ben & Jerry's."

"I see." She placed her hands on Kacie's shoulders and looked at her reflection. "Is the bride your sister?"

Kacie nodded. "Younger sister. Whirlwind romance. He proposed four months after their first date. They're getting married on their one-year dating anniversary. Meanwhile I was with the same man for seven years and when I asked him what our future was he told me he didn't think he'd ever want to marry me."

She didn't notice the tears sliding down her face until Della offered her a box of tissues. Kacie dried her eyes and blew her nose as delicately as possible.

"I'm so sorry to hear that, dear. But would you rather

have found out his true feelings before or after you married him?"

As much as she hated to hear it, Kacie knew Della had a point.

"I understand though. I see a lot of joy in this business, but I see a lot of heartache as well."

Kacie nodded as the woman offered another sympathetic smile and gentle pat to her shoulder. "I'll see you out there. Take a few minutes if you need to."

As Della closed the door behind her, Kacie studied her reflection.

How had she become this woman?

It wasn't so much about the dress not fitting—though that was mortifying—as it was about the fact that the ill-fitting dress seemed to epitomize the current state of her life. She used to be fun. In fact, she used to be just like her sister, surrounded by girlfriends, always laughing and having a good time. Until she met Mike and made him the center of her universe. Then one by one all of her friends slowly disappeared from her life—and she became a shell of the person she used to be.

Kacie slipped on her heels and made her way into the salon, taking her place on the elevated platform so the seamstress could pin her hem. Thankfully, her sister and mom were busy trying different veil and shoe combinations and the seamstress worked quickly; she was done and undressed before they had a chance to notice the dress.

When Sam took her place on the fitting platform, there was an audible sigh from all the ladies in the room. Her sister was breathtaking, and her gown fit as if it had been designed specifically for her. She looked so very happy. And Kacie was happy for her. But never in a million years had she ever imagined her little sister would find her happily-ever-after first.

Kacie felt the burn of tears building in her eyes and within moments was crying for the second time in the span of an hour. Of course, everyone in the room was crying. Sam. Their mother. The few bridesmaids that were able to make it in for the fitting.

Thankfully, they'd never realize that she wasn't crying out of happiness for her sister, but out of sheer loneliness, heartbreak, and petty jealousy.

As she sat all alone on the tufted silk bench against a far wall, Kacie opened her handbag and proceeded to pull everything out. Her phone. Her planner. Her emergency makeup and period provision bag. She piled them next to her, all in the hopes of finding a rogue Hershey's Kiss in a bottom corner.

"What are you doing?"

Kacie looked up to realize Sam, along with everyone else in the salon, was staring at her. Perhaps her desperate hunt was more obvious than she'd realized.

Leaving her sister, their mother made her way across the salon to where Kacie sat. "Sweetheart, are you feeling okay?" she whispered as she pressed a hand to Kacie's cheek.

God bless the woman for giving her an out at that very moment, whether she realized it or not. "As a matter of fact, I'm not. I think I need to go home."

Her mother chewed on her lip, looking over her shoulder at Sam and then back to Kacie as she tried to determine how to best handle the situation.

Kacie patted her mother's arm. "You stay here. I'll call someone to give me a ride." Her mother had driven them over, but she couldn't ask her to leave the fitting just to drop Kacie home.

Relief washed over her mother's face. "That would be great if you could. I wouldn't want Sam to get upset if I left."

"It'll be just fine." Kacie tossed her things back into her handbag and kissed her mom goodbye. "I'll talk to you tomorrow."

She made her apologies and weakly waved to her sister and the other bridesmaids as she left the salon. But the moment she stepped out the front door of the bridal shop, she breathed a sigh of relief.

Her first thought was to try Damien, but then she remembered he was out of town for the weekend. Of course, she could always call a cab, but at this time, the wait might be long, and all she wanted was to get home as quickly as possible. As she scrolled through her contacts, she stopped at one listing.

G.I. Joe.

Her sensible side reminded her summer flings and meaningless sex just weren't her style. That she was a relationship girl through and through.

Kacie looked back inside. She recalled hearing her sister and her friends chattering away outside her dressing room door. How they teased one another and laughed and didn't take things so damn seriously.

As far as she could tell, she had two choices. She could keep eating her feelings, or let her hair down and have some fun.

The night she met Michael, she thought the universe was playing a practical joke on her. But maybe they had actually been sending her a sign? One that said, *here is a man just shallow enough to help you out of your rut.* After all, having sex with Michael wouldn't be a chore. The man was beautiful. And smart. And charming. As much as she hated to admit it, she liked the way he looked at her.

The door to the shop opened behind her, and she heard Sam laughing, a completely carefree sound. Just yet another sign. She couldn't remember the last time she had laughed that way, the exception being the night she spent with a certain army doctor.

Before she could talk herself out of it, Kacie typed out a quick message, hoping G.I. Joe was still willing to come to her rescue.

HAVING JUST COMPLETED a miserable round of golf, Michael was tossing his golf clubs into the trunk of his car when a text message from a number he didn't recognize popped up on his phone.

Hey, Joe. Any chance you could give me a ride? It's Kacie BTW.

And just like that, his day got a whole lot better.

But instead of texting, he chose to call her back. Keeping their conversation short and sweet, it amounted to nothing more than her asking for a ride home from a shop downtown to her place in midtown. Did he care that it was out of his way? No. He was just glad the woman he'd been fantasizing about for weeks was finally putting his number to use.

Fifteen minutes later he pulled into the parking lot of a fancy-schmancy dress shop and found her sitting on a white park bench outside, just as she'd said she would be. He parked in an empty spot just down the sidewalk from where she sat and climbed out of the car.

"Hey there, sunshine."

Kacie looked up from her phone and smiled immediately. The first thing he noticed was that she wore her hair down, her loose golden curls hanging past her shoulders. The second thing he noticed as she rose from her seat and made her way toward him was that she was wearing a summer dress with skinny straps over her shoulders and little flowers on it.

In the past few weeks, he hadn't fantasized about her in a dress, but now that he had the mental image, it was sure to become part of the repertoire. He liked how the skirt flared out over her hips and ended midthigh, showing off her strong, toned legs. The fact that she was backlit by the sun and her shape was silhouetted through the thin fabric was simply a bonus.

He also liked that she didn't try to hide that she was looking him over from head to toe as well.

"Thank you for coming to get me," she said, coming to a stop directly in front of him. "I hope I didn't interrupt any plans you might have."

"Nope. No plans at all."

She glanced at his car and then back to him. One corner of her mouth pulled up and he just knew she was going to rake him over the coals. "I wouldn't have taken you for a black Camaro kind of guy."

He folded his arms over his chest. "Really? What kind of car did you think I'd drive?"

"I'm not sure really. A red Porsche, maybe? Like you're overcompensating for something."

He chuckled. So this was how it was going to be with her.

"Did you forget I'm a military doctor, not a civilian one?"

She lazily lifted one shoulder as if to say she didn't care and he found himself momentarily distracted by the way one skinny strap slid across her skin.

"You just seem to fit the MO," she said, breaking his reverie. "Isn't that what all good looking, arrogant men drive?"

Purposely ignoring the "arrogant" part of her comment, he took the shoe box she carried under one arm and guided her around to the passenger's side, opening the car door for her. "Glad to know you think I'm good looking."

Since it wasn't a question, Kacie's only response was a shake of her head as she climbed in.

If he were a better man he would've looked away as she settled into the front seat. But he wasn't a better man. He liked how her skirt rose higher on her thighs as she slid across the black leather. Once she buckled her seat belt, she glanced up at him, and her eyes narrowed a bit, the expression on her face telling him she knew exactly how he'd been checking her out.

After handing her the shoe box, he closed the door and made his way around to the driver's side. She was quiet after she gave him directions, keeping her head turned to look out the passenger window. Nervous, too, if her fingers tapping the box she held in her lap were any indication.

Inside he was dying to know what made her change her mind about seeing him.

As he eased to a stop at a red light, he decided now was as good a time as any to ask.

"I'm curious," he began. He waited until she looked at him, although her eyes were disguised by her sunglasses. "Why did you call me?"

"I told you. I needed a way to get home."

Immediately, she went back to looking out the window, but was unable to hide the rapid rise and fall of her chest.

"You could've just as easily called a cab. Or a friend."

When she didn't respond, he decided to let her off the hook for the moment, focusing on the road. Another right. Then a left. Still, not a word from her by the time he pulled to the curb in front of her place. Only then did he realize he'd hoped for too much. She really only wanted a ride home. But as he shifted the car into park, she placed her hand on his arm and gave him a quick, almost shy smile.

"Would you like to come inside?"

KACIE DROPPED HER purse, keys, and phone on the kitchen counter and pointed to a bar stool. "Have a seat. Would you like something to drink? I'm afraid I don't have much." She moved from the counter and pulled open the refrigerator. "I have water. Pomegranate juice. Grapefruit flavored sparkling water."

"I'm fine for now." He took a seat on a bar stool and rested his arms on the breakfast bar. "Are you ready to tell me why I'm here? As much as I'd like to believe you've finally succumbed to my charms and looks, I doubt that's the reason."

Abandoning the refrigerator, she returned to where she'd been, the counter now separating them. Kacie took a deep breath, then let it all out at once with a rush of words. "I need to go on a diet."

He couldn't help but laugh. "What?"

A moment too late did he realize she wasn't kidding.

"You heard me," she said without an ounce of humor.

He reached across the bar and took her hand. "In my professional *medical* opinion . . . you're perfect."

Although she wouldn't look at him, a slight blush swept across her cheeks. "Well, it's lovely for you to say that and definitely earns you some brownie points." Kacie pulled her hand free from his grasp. "The real issue is I didn't fit into my dress."

Michael shook his head in disbelief. "Didn't I just pick you up from a dress shop? Buy a new one."

"It's my maid of honor dress."

Suddenly, he realized the gravity of the situation. "Oh."

"Exactly. And I have just over a month to drop the few extra pounds. Meanwhile, my sister believes I'm replacing sex with chocolate, and I think she might be right."

He couldn't believe what he was hearing. "So you're taking preventative measures?"

"Absolutely." Now she looked him directly in the eyes. "And that's where you fit in. If you're willing."

God, she was cute.

For two weeks he'd been fantasizing about this woman and now she was in front of him asking him for sex. A request he was more than happy to oblige.

But that didn't mean he wouldn't tease her a bit.

"Hmm . . . I might need some time to consider this." He leaned back and folded his arms over his chest. "How much sex are we talking here? Once every couple of weeks? Once a week? Once a day, perhaps?"

"Could you dial back your enthusiasm just a bit here? I don't think you realize how hard this is for me." She grabbed hold of her hair and pulled and tugged and twisted it upward until she had it piled on top of her head, then wrapped it several times with elastic pink elastic from her wrist. "This isn't normal for me. I'm responsible and punctual and sensible. All those things tend to make me less attractive, particularly to men who love the adrenaline-fueled life."

At first glance anyone would think she was a strong, confident woman, virtually unshakeable. But at this particular moment, the facade was starting to crack. Her gaze traveled from the countertop to the window, looking everywhere but at him. The longer the silence stretched between them, the more she began to fidget.

"Why don't we go out?" he suggested, his conscience getting the better of him. "Get something to drink. A beer or a coffee, whatever you prefer. Doesn't matter."

That brought her attention back to him and she stared up at him with uncertainty in her wide green eyes. "Don't you want to be here?"

"Oh . . . I most certainly do." He smiled at her in what he hoped was a non-leering nonperverted way. "I was just trying to give you an out if you wanted it."

The smile must have worked, because she visibly relaxed.

She braced both hands on the counter. "No out. I want to do this. I *need* to do this."

"You need *this*, do ya?" he asked, unable to stop himself.

Instantly those sea-glass green eyes flashed, darkening to jade as she pointed a finger at him. "Don't you get all smug there, buddy. This isn't about you. This is about me fitting into my bridesmaid dress. Remember that in those moments your ego is so inflated it's about to take flight."

He couldn't help but laugh. "Okay, okay, noted."

"Now for some ground rules." Kacie straightened her spine and came around the breakfast bar to stand directly in front of him. "One," she began, counting off her fingers. "No assumptions or expectations. If you assume I'm going to stay the night and I get up and leave, no getting pissy about it. If it's Friday night and you've got other things to do than hook up with me, I'm not allowed to get pissy about it. Actually, now that I think about it, no getting pissy at all because we aren't in a relationship."

By the time she was done, he was smiling so hard his face hurt. "You won't hear any complaints from me."

"Two: condoms. Always. Period. I'm on the pill, but that's not enough of a reason to go without because there will be no children in my immediate future."

"Condoms. Yes. You'll get zero arguments from me on that subject. Hell, I'll even buy ribbed . . ." Michael paused dramatically. "For your pleasure."

"Oh, dear God." Kacie shook her head with a groan. "Do not make me regret this."

He fought to hold in his laughter. "Just kidding. Continue."

"Three. No pop-ins. No showing up on my doorstep unannounced, especially not after a night out with the fellas. And vice versa."

Now shit was getting serious. Michael raised his hand. "Can I go on the record here as saying I have zero problems with the pop-in? I mean, a beautiful woman knocking on my door and demanding sex isn't a bad thing in my book."

Kacie rolled her eyes. "Fine. Duly noted. Item four. My ass is off-limits. Just imagine a big ol' sign that says DO NOT ENTER."

"What about—"

Her eyes widened and immediately she cut him off. "Nuh-uh. No way. No negotiation. Got it?"

"Okay, okay," he quickly agreed. And then he couldn't help himself. "Do you have rules regarding my ass? Because like the pop-in . . ."

Not only did the crinkle between her brows appear, she wrinkled up her nose, her entire face getting in on the act. It was quite the scowl.

"Seriously? What is wrong with you?"

To which, of course, he laughed. "Absolutely nothing. Or everything, depending on how you look at it."

He rose from the bar stool and seated himself on the sofa, stretching his arms out wide along the back. Earlier when his phone rang, he'd never expected his day to go like this. But now he couldn't wait to see what would come of tonight's encounter. Only one thing was for certain—this was gonna be fun.

"What are you doing?" she asked.

"Getting comfortable for the show," he answered. "I thought, just maybe, there would be a repeat performance of the other night . . ." He was still mostly teasing her. He couldn't help it. And in truth, those memories of her had been keeping him awake at night.

Her scowl was replaced by a look of shock. "Oh, no! That wasn't me."

"I'm pretty sure that it was."

"No." She shook her head violently. "That was the tequila. Believe it or not, I'm already pushing way beyond my personal comfort zone by even suggesting this. So if you're expecting Tequila Kacie all the time, you're going to be sorely disappointed."

"So not only am I being used, I'm expected to do all the work? I'm not sure I like the sound of this." Michael placed a hand over his heart as if her words had wounded him. "I've just never had this happen before. Don't get me wrong—women have definitely used me for my body—I mean, damn, just look at me. But I don't know that any have ever been so brutally truthful about it. I feel cheap."

He saw the exact moment she was completely over his bullshit. What had been just a small spark in her eyes roared into flames and she was ready to dish it back.

Kacie walked over, arms crossed, one leg kicked out wide. "I'm sure I can find someone willing to help me out who is not so damn sensitive. Like that other guy at the bar. What was his name?" she asked while snapping her fingers. "Was it Gibby?"

"Come on. There's no need for any crazy talk."

"Just remember I'm not twisting your arm here," she said, pointing at him. "You're either in or out. Which is it?"

He took a deep breath and feigned contemplation. "Do I have to choose? I'd like to be both."

"What? Both?"

That little crease between her brows reappeared.

"In. Then out. Then in again," he said matter-of-factly. "Don't you know how sex works? I never took you for a virgin."

"I'm not . . ." A pink flush crept across her skin. "And just . . ." She huffed. "Why do you do that?"

Michael rose from the sofa and closed the distance between until mere inches separated them. "I do it because you're fun to tease and I know you can dish it out as well as you take it. I also like seeing how your skin blushes and I'm fascinated by the way your eyes change color when you get a little fired up."

Her eyes widened in surprise for a moment, like he might have told her something even she didn't know, before she suddenly lowered her gaze to the floor. Although she was trying to hide her response, she couldn't disguise the rapid rise and fall of her chest or her pulse thrumming wildly in the hollow of her throat.

"To be completely honest, I just like seeing you, sunshine," Then, when he traced her arm with the tip of his finger, she trembled beneath his touch. He liked that he affected her because Lord knew she wreaked havoc on him, whether she realized it or not. "So . . . how soon did you want to get started?"

Her head fell back and she looked up at him with a smile. "No time like the present. Right?"

Chapter Nine

KACIE STARED UP into those dark blue eyes for what seemed like an eternity. With both of them sober, standing in her living room in the broad daylight, there wouldn't be any forgetting what was about to happen. She struggled to find her inner seductress without the tequila to reduce her inhibitions.

No need to be scared. Just touch him.

He's just a guy. You've seen him naked before. He's seen you naked before. No big deal.

You can do this. You can do this. You can do this.

She placed her palms on his chest, felt the contours of the muscles beneath his shirt as she closed the last few inches between them. His hands fell to her hips and the warmth of his touch soothed her and bolstered her confidence at the same time. Kacie rose up on her toes, pressed her nose to the base of his neck and breathed deep. For a man who'd spent the past several hours playing golf in the Georgia heat, he ought to stink to the highest heaven. But the combination of sweat and deodorant, and that something that was uniquely him, reeled her in.

Her hands coasted upward until she gripped his shoulders, and when she wobbled a bit, his grip tightened on her hips, bringing her body flush to his. With every rush of breath, her breasts rubbed against his chest and her skin began to heat.

"I'm all for getting this started." His words were barely above a whisper. "But if you don't mind, I'll just take a quick shower."

If she freed him from her clutches now, she feared the spell would be broken. It was hard enough to find her courage once. She didn't know if she could find it a second time.

"You don't smell so bad," she whispered against his neck. "As a matter of fact . . ." Kacie boldly touched her tongue to his skin and traced the part of his clavicle exposed by the open collar of his shirt. "Salty. I like it."

His laugh was a low and deep rumble from his chest. "And you say you're a good girl."

She lowered herself down and took a half step back. "I don't know what it is about you—" all the while shaking her head "—but I keep finding myself making questionable decisions when you're around."

A slow smile spread across his face. "Personally, I think you're making great decisions."

"It sure doesn't feel like it."

"In that case." He grabbed her hand and tugged until she was plastered against him again. "How about I make the next one for the both of us?"

Kacie nodded in agreement, anticipating a kiss when he placed his hands on her shoulders and lowered his face to within inches of hers. But instead of kissing her mouth, he pressed a kiss to her cheek, then jaw, then finally to the tender skin beneath her ear. He surprised her a second time when his hands continued down her back, sliding over her hips, and edging beneath the skirt of her dress. His fingers cupped and caressed her ass, before lifting her feet from the floor. Instinctively she banded her arms around his neck, wrapped her legs about his waist, her position now bringing them face-to-face.

"That's better. You're shorter than I remember," he said, smiling as he sauntered down the short hallway with her clinging to him.

"I'm five-seven and far from short," she countered. "But I will admit I was wearing wedges that night at the bar so I could see why you'd think I was taller."

The dimple in his cheek appeared. "I don't know what the hell wedges are, but okay, if you say so."

Once they reached the bedroom, he eased her to the ground, making certain she was steady on her feet before he took hold of the hem of her dress and lifted it off over her head. Since the bodice of her summer dress was lined and she didn't have much on top to begin with, she'd gone without a bra. Which meant she was left wearing only her panties.

He took his time having a nice long look at her. "Have to say I still don't see the problem here," he said, dropping her dress to the floor. "Clearly the problem must be with that bridesmaid dress, because, sunshine, it sure as hell isn't you."

She felt her skin heat beneath his gaze and any earlier hesitation she might have had about executing this prevention plan faded away.

Michael reached out to touch her and instinctively she took a step back. "Something wrong?" he asked.

Emboldened by his compliments and their playful exchanges, she lazily gestured toward him. "Quid pro quo, buddy. You've surveyed the goods and given your stamp of approval. It's only fair I get a chance as well. After all, I just might change my mind."

And just as she'd hoped, he shot her a cocky grin, his dimples on full display.

"Sure you will." He reached over his head, grabbed a handful of shirt, and pulled it off in one smooth motion. Then he held his arms out wide, putting his sculpted shoulders, expansive chest, and firm stomach on display, even throwing in a little spin.

Once he faced her again, she folded her arms over her chest, effectively hiding her breasts from his view, and nodded at his shorts.

"Oh, ho, ho. I see how things are now." Michael shook his head in disbelief, but grinned all the while.

"Shall I take it all off or do I leave a little something to the imagination?"

Kacie feigned indifference. "Whatever you're comfortable with."

He bit his lower lip, clearly fighting a grin. Reaching into the pocket of his shorts he pulled out an unopened pack of condoms and tossed them on the bed.

She eyed them skeptically. "Gotta say that's some confidence right there."

"Now hang on a second." Michael held up a hand. "I had zero expectations when I came to pick you up. It's just smart to be prepared."

"Do you always walk around with a pack on you, or did you stop on the way to the bridal shop?"

"I picked them up along the way," he said while removing his shoes and socks. "As a medical officer, I'm duty bound to practice what I preach. We get all these eighteen-, nineteen-year-old kids in regiment. Some of them have never been away from home. Some of them have never been with a girl. And God forbid their parents tell them anything. I lay down some rules for them. Guidelines, really." He went about loosening his belt and unfastening his shorts. "Buy your own condoms. Don't stash them in your car or keep them in your wallet since heat damages the latex. Don't be cheap and use one that has expired because it might cost you a hell of a lot more than three bucks in the long run."

Then he shoved his shorts and boxer briefs to the floor and stood proudly before her in all his glory.

The man certainly didn't lack confidence. And rightfully so. He was absolutely beautiful from head to toe. But damned if she'd tell him that. He already had the ego of five men combined.

"So." He looked down at his erection and then back to her. "What do you think?"

Her gaze traveled upward over the spectacular terrains of his body until finally meeting his eyes and that smug, smug smile.

Kacie narrowed her eyes. "Think about you, or the advice you're giving those boys?"

Michael scoffed. "About me, of course."

Kacie opened her mouth and faked a yawn, even patted her hand to her lips. "I guess you'll do."

"I'll just do, huh?" he muttered. "Well, we'll see about that."

He reached out and took hold of her wrists, pulling her body flush against his. She heard herself squeak in surprise, but the laughter bubbling up from within died the moment their bodies met. His flesh was hot to the touch, his muscles hard as stone. As were other parts of him.

With a slight tug, Kacie freed herself from his grasp, her hands now free to do a little exploring of their own. She trailed her fingers over the rise and valley of his ribs and couldn't help but smile when his breath hitched and little goose bumps erupted all over his skin when she found a particularly sensitive spot.

"How do you eat all that crap—the jelly donuts, the

peach fritters—and still manage to look like this?" She drew her hands together at his belly button, then ran them upward over his abs, his chest, finally coming to rest on the top of his shoulders.

He gave a little shrug beneath her hands. "Genes and a fast metabolism?"

Her exploration halted and she stared up into his eyes.

"I hate you," she said as a matter of record. "You realize that, right? I have no choice but to hate you."

"If you say so," Michael said, the corner of his mouth lifting.

Although he answered, it was obvious his attention was elsewhere. He reached out and pulled the pink elastic from her hair and dropped it to the floor, and then his hands were buried in her curls. He gently tugged her head back, tipping her face upward to his.

Never had she wanted to be kissed so badly in her life.

She licked her lips in anticipation and that seemed to catch his notice, his eyes darkening as he watched her tongue swipe across the plump flesh of her bottom lip. He lowered his face to hers, and just when she believed she'd won the battle, he hovered above her, his mouth inches away.

"You sure about this, sunshine? I just might ruin you for all other men."

She huffed a laugh because the man's arrogance knew no bounds. "Let me worry about that later."

And yet, he still made no move to kiss her.

Kacie pressed up on her toes in an attempt to reach him, but he dodged her advances. Finally, she caved. "Will you kiss me already, dammit?"

That was all it took.

In an instant, Michael wrapped one arm about her waist and lifted her high as his mouth crashed down upon hers. His kisses were not tentative or gentle. They weren't polite getting-to-know-you exchanges. They were the kind that said, "If you're looking for a summer of meaningless, no-strings-attached sex, I'm your man."

The kind of kiss that easily leaves a mark and could truly devastate a woman if she wasn't careful.

As they stroked and teased each other with mouth and lips and tongue, Kacie had no choice but to hold on to him for dear life. Not because she was short, but because he was so tall. And when it felt like they were losing their balance, he tumbled them onto the bed, careful to not crush her beneath his large frame.

Michael again tugged on her hair, demanding access to her jaw and neck. Her breath rushed in and out of her lungs as he nipped and kissed the length of her throat while running his hands all over her body. She wanted to touch him, too, to feel the strength and tension in his arms and shoulders, to feel his heart race beneath her palms, to make him feel as good as he did her. But he pulled her hands away from his body and raised them above her head, trapping them between one of his.

She opened her mouth to protest, only to be silenced with a kiss. One that left her breathless and dizzy and unable to remember why the hell she had a problem with what he was doing in the first place.

He released her from his grip, his fingers twining with hers as he eased down her body, pausing to nuzzle and suck her breast. As he toyed with her nipple using his tongue and teeth, his hand smoothed over her stomach and came to rest between her legs, his fingers stroking over the little bit of clothing she still wore. Which left her to question why the hell hadn't she removed her panties herself when given the chance? Because now he used that thin satin barrier as a means to torment her, to build the ache and tension coiling low in her belly all the while refusing to touch her in the way she craved. And then, when she was distracted by the teasing of his fingers, he bit down on her nipple, sending arcs of sensation shooting through her.

Time and time again he brought her to the edge of release, only to slow his pace or remove his hand completely. Somewhere around the third or fourth time, she realized the man was completely evil. And taking great enjoyment in driving her to the point of madness.

"Michael," she said forcefully. "I need you to get on with it."

He looked up from where he'd been kissing the soft skin of her hip, a puzzled expression on his face. "You can't be serious?"

"Oh, but I am. I really, really am."

That slow, smug smile returned. "But I planned on spending some quality time right about here," he said while taking hold of her panties and easing them down her legs. He pressed a kiss to the newly revealed flesh.

"Michael, we've got six weeks until the wedding. There will be plenty of time for that later."

She felt him laugh against her skin. At least she was a source of amusement for him.

Kacie flung her arms out wide on the mattress and her hand landed on the small cardboard box he'd tossed there while undressing. Grabbing hold of it like it were a lifeline, she tore it open. "What I need right now is for you to put this condom on and get inside me. Now." She threw a small square at him, bouncing it off the top of his head.

He laughed in surprise as he looked at the packet, then back to her. "To just look at you, no one would ever imagine you'd be so damn bossy."

"Like I told you earlier, I don't know what it is about you, but you bring it out in me."

"Sunshine, you certainly won't hear any complaints from me." Michael slid off the end of the bed and stood upright as he tore open the foil packet. "Now then, on your knees."

Her eyes widened in surprise. "Excuse me?"

His cocky smile returned. "You heard me. You want it now? Then get on your knees and back it on up to the edge of the bed," he said, waving his hand, directing her.

But she wasn't in any hurry to move.

"Trust me, Kacie." His tone was notably softer this time. "You're short. I'm tall. And this will be a helluva lot more fun than missionary."

He grasped her ankles, waiting a moment to make sure she was game before he playfully tugged her to the end of the bed. "I swear to God, Michael," she said, while rolling over and pressing up on her hands and knees like he suggested. "You better not get any ideas about spanking my ass. Or making me call you 'sir' or 'daddy' or any other crap like that because it is *not* going to happen."

"I wouldn't dream of it."

At first his strong hands caressed her thighs and butt. Then, with his palms spanning the width of her back and his thumbs followed the gutter of her spine, he smoothed his hands upward until he reached where her hair draped over her shoulders. With one hand, he gently gathered the strands and brushed them to the side. His other hand continued upward over her shoulder, down the front of her arm as he leaned over her, bringing his body flush with hers. He placed kisses across her shoulder and to the curve of her neck, nuzzled her ear, then gently nipped her lobe, igniting an involuntary shiver that raced through her body.

"Is this okay?" he asked.

Already her body hummed with desire and forming a coherent thought provided difficult. As a result her reply was something along the lines of "gnuh."

She felt his smile against her skin as his hands re-traced their path, this time skimming along the underside of her arms alighting every nerve. He continued to take his time, cupping and molding her breasts in his palms, using his fingers to pinch and pluck her nipples. Meanwhile his erection remained nestled between her thighs, so close to where she wanted him and yet . . . not.

Kacie shifted restlessly beneath him, trying her damnedest to get him into position on her own. Finally, he got the message.

"Hang on, sunshine," he whispered as he positioned himself, then eased inside her.

Although her body was more than ready for him, he took his time, working himself deeper with slow, measured strokes until he was seated to the hilt.

"Two weeks I've been thinking about you, about doing exactly this to you," he said, no longer moving slowly or otherwise. "Just so you know, Kacie, I refuse to race toward the finish like a horny teenager. At least, not this time. I'm gonna savor this no matter how much you might want me to get on with it."

As far as she was concerned, two could play at this game. "Is that so?" she asked while simultaneously contracting her muscles and squeezing him tight.

Somewhere in the middle his low chuckle transformed into a groan. "Someone likes to fight dirty."

He started to ease in and out of her and she let her head hang languidly from her shoulders. As his hands roamed her body, he whispered how great she felt, how soft her skin was. How she drove him crazy and he had a million and one ideas of things he wanted to do to her.

Then, without any warning at all, he gripped her shoulders and pulled her upright so that her back was nearly flush to his chest. And directly in front of her, in the full light of day, was the reflection of the two of them in the mirrored closet doors.

Her insecurities got the best of her and she tried to pull away, but he wouldn't let her go. "Don't run away. Just give it a second and watch the two of us."

Watching him was easy to do. Watching herself, however, was something completely different. But now, trapped in his embrace, there was little she could do. Her eyes tracked his movements in their reflection as his left hand caressed her breast and his right skimmed down her stomach to between her legs. Although she knew his intentions, she still gasped at the first stroke of her clit. Then, within a matter seconds, he'd found the perfect rhythm, his fingers moving in counterpoint to his thrusts, playing her body like a highly skilled musician.

And just like that, he seduced her. With words and touch. With how he moved with her instead of just using her for his own satisfaction. It was a feeling she could at the very least become accustomed to. At worst, she might have found a new addiction.

"God, you are beautiful," he growled in her ear. "Look at you."

She studied their reflection in the mirrors and even she had to admit he was right. As she watched their bodies move in unison, despite the wildness of her hair and the smudged makeup around her eyes, she was beautiful. And the fact her maid of honor dress didn't fit was all but forgotten.

Kacie lifted up one arm and draped it around his neck. When she turned to look up at him, his lips crashed down on hers, his tongue diving deep into her mouth, tangling, twisting around hers. His hand fell from her breast to grip her hip tighter as their movements became more hurried. He groaned into her mouth and worked her body harder, causing the tension to ratchet higher and higher until she shattered beneath his touch. She gasped for breath as Michael relentlessly raced toward his own finish, finally coming with a muffled groan.

As Michael draped his arms about her waist a tiny bead of sweat trickled down her breastbone and disappeared against his skin.

"I guess we're both sweaty now," she said.

He nuzzled her ear, then took a quick taste of her neck with his tongue. "Mmm. Salty. I like it."

Kacie laughed. "And here I thought you were a good boy."

"Sunshine, I can assure you no woman has ever put those two words together in the same sentence when they were talking about me." He stared back at her with those dark blue eyes and the one corner of his mouth hitched up. Again, a little shiver of excitement coursed through her body.

Michael released her from his embrace and lowered her back down onto her hands and knees. After he eased himself from her body, he leaned over and pressed a kiss to the base of her spine. And then, once her eyes met his in their reflection, he followed it with a playful smack to her ass.

She swung around to look at him. "Hey!"

"Sorry, but I couldn't resist," he said with a laugh as he headed for the bathroom.

Kacie fully collapsed onto the bed and pulled the sheets up to cover herself, her body still humming with satisfaction.

And then, like a man who knew his own sexual prowess, he strode back into her bedroom wearing nothing more than a smile.

"So . . ." Michael fell into the bed next to her, not bothering to cover himself with the sheet. "Did that meet or exceed your standards?"

Oh, this arrogant, arrogant man. He knew damn well that performance was one for the record books.

Kacie smiled and patted his forearm. "I think you'll do."

Chapter Ten

MICHAEL RETURNED HOME a few hours later, leaving Kacie exhausted yet satisfied. He would have been happy to stay the night in the event she had a middle of the night craving that required an intervention, but he didn't want to wear out his welcome.

It was still early evening though, and he spent the next couple of hours sitting on his couch, surfing through the channels, unable to find anything that held his interest. What he really wanted to do was text her, to ask what she was doing the following day and whether or not she'd be interested in seeing him. But he found himself uncertain of how to proceed since Kacie clearly held all the power in the situation. She had established the guidelines. She had set the end date. He was merely along for the ride.

He picked up his phone from the table and scrolled

through the messages she'd sent earlier in the day. What the hell for, he sure didn't know. Was he searching for some deep and hidden meaning in her words? She'd been nothing but straightforward from the get-go about what this was and was not between them. And theoretically, he should be adhering to that age-old guy rule that said he should wait two days before initiating contact. But waiting in this instance could result in missing a window of opportunity.

Fuck the rules.

His fingers flew over the screen as he typed, then quickly hit Send before he could change his mind.

Any plans for tomorrow?

He stared at the screen several seconds, anxiously waiting her reply.

"Goddammit." Michael tossed the phone to his coffee table. "Don't be pathetic."

He should go out. Drink some beer. Do manly things, whatever that might be.

Finally, he headed into the kitchen, yanked open his refrigerator, and stood there staring into the barren space. When his phone rang, he practically killed himself dodging the breakfast bar and his reclining chair to reach it. But the dream died the moment he turned over the device and saw his father's name on the screen.

Dammit.

Michael swiped his thumb across the screen and dropped into his recliner. "Hey, Dad."

"You should've seen this shot I had today," his father began.

No pleasantries or easing into the conversation. No "Hey, how are you, son?" Michael kicked up the footrest and made himself comfortable, knowing this would likely take a while, especially since Mac MacGregor was known for two things: his undying devotion to his late wife, Lily, and his gift of gab. And gab he did. Ever since Danny married, their dad never wanted to "disturb the newlyweds" during the evening hours. As if people never had sex during the day. But the fact his dad sure as hell didn't have any problem calling him on Saturday night said a lot about his lack of social life. His. Not his father's.

His father was always quite busy; although he'd been considered one of Myrtle Beach's most eligible bachelors for nearly twenty-five years, he'd never been captured by his female pursuers. Oh, he'd happily escort women to the occasional social event (weddings, company parties, charity events, even a concert here and there). He likely did more than that, although Michael never let his mind wander in that direction. But his dad always made it known his heart was, and would always be, taken.

"Are you coming down this weekend?" Michael asked when Mac finally took a breath in the midst of his storytelling.

"Not this weekend. The fellas and I are playing in a charity four-man scramble down at Caledonia."

Michael was hit with a twinge of jealousy. Caledonia was one of his favorite places to play golf and he hadn't been there in years. But the feeling only lasted until his phone beeped notifying him of an incoming text message.

Not much. Going for a run in the a.m.

He found himself smiling at the screen, happy she'd responded even if it did take her thirty-two minutes. Not that he was counting.

"Michael?" came the voice from his phone. "Michael? Are you still there?"

Shit.

He quickly lifted the phone to his ear. "Yeah, Dad. Sorry about that. It's just that I've got some messages coming through and I really need to answer them."

"Sure thing. You go do your doctor thing," his father replied. "And by the way, son, I'm proud of you."

"Thanks, Dad. I'll talk to you tomorrow. Love you."

The moment he ended the call he, of course, felt guilty as shit, ditching his old man for a text conversation with a woman, while his dad believed he was off to save lives or something of the like.

Eh. What he didn't know wouldn't hurt him.

Was planning the same. Want to run together?

Again, he stared at the screen in anticipation.

Depends. What time do you go?

0600

OMG. Did you just military time me?

Sorry. 6:00 a.m. Better?

Not really. Enjoy your run.

Dammit. No way was he going to let her get off that easily.

What time works best for you?

9:00

Jesus. Michael shook his head as he typed.

Half the day is gone by then.

I'm not the one begging for a running partner.

Fine. You win. I'll meet you at your place at 0845. Sorry, 8:45.

Okay.

BTW. I promise to go easy on you.

Michael stared at the screen, just waiting to see what she'd say in response.

You just did not?!!?

Michael laughed as he read his screen.

I'll have you know I run a seven-forty mile, she added.

Good. You shouldn't fall too far behind.

While Kacie might not have been amused, Michael found himself smiling as he went to bed that night and again in the morning when he woke well before sunrise. And at a quarter to nine, he was knocking on her door.

It swung open to reveal a woman who was clearly not a morning person, even minus the hangover.

"Should've known you'd be prompt," she grumbled. "Come on in." Kacie stepped back and waved him in. "I still need to get my shoes on."

He waited just inside the door as she headed down the short hall and disappeared into the bedroom. He had half the mind to follow her in there with ideas of how to brighten her mood, but thought better of it.

She returned within a matter of minutes, shoes on and apparently ready to go as she tugged her hair into a pile on top of her head and secured it with an elastic.

"Ready?"

He smiled at her. "As I'll ever be. After you," he said while opening the door for her.

She gave him the side-eye as she passed by him, and maybe he was hearing things, but he would've sworn he heard a low growl come from her as well. He closed the door behind them and moved out of the way as she pulled the coiled key holder from her wrist and locked the dead bolt.

Again with the side-eye. "Are you always so damn chipper in the morning?"

"I'm a morning person," he said unapologetically.

Then he heard it again, that low, throaty growl. Not unlike the warning from a feral cat telling you to back the fuck up because you're about to get the claws.

He followed her across the small lawn and down the narrow driveway past the main house. "How far do you normally run?" he asked while stretching halfheartedly.

Kacie pulled up her leg and pressed the sole of her shoe to her backside, stretching her quad. "Usually I run to Daffin Park, circle it three times and come back. Works out to about five miles." She dropped her foot and switched to the other. "Is that too much?"

Michael scoffed. "Sunshine, I run twice that before most people get up in the morning."

Kacie shook her head and mumbled something that sounded along the lines of "God help me" as she continued on with her stretching.

Meanwhile, he really needed her to hurry the hell up through the whole warm-up routine, because despite the fact she wore baggy running shorts and a tank top that looked like it had been picked up from off the floor and pulled on over her faded purple bra top, she was still sexy as hell. And watching her bending and stretching and stuff, well, it was giving him some dirty thoughts.

Very dirty thoughts.

"Aren't you going to stretch?" she asked while looking up at him as she leaned over to touch her toes.

"No need."

"You do realize improper stretching is one of the main reasons for injury, right? Surely they taught you that in medical school—or is there some mystical belief that your ego is a superpower that somehow prevents injury?"

Now she lowered into a lunge, stretching her calf, which meant her shorts rode higher up her toned, muscular thigh. If she didn't get a move on, he wouldn't be physically able to run, much less walk. At least, not until he'd had his way with her.

"I appreciate the concern, but I can assure you I'm completely warmed up and ready to go."

She narrowed her eyes at him. "You've already run today, haven't you?"

"Sure didn't," he lied. "I saved all of this for you." Michael clapped his hands together, then pointed down the sidewalk. "Can we go now? Or are you purposely trying to drag this out until the sun reaches the highest point in the sky?"

"Fine."

And of course the single word answer was said in such a way it meant she was anything but.

Michael followed her lead down the narrow sidewalks until they finally reached the park where there were proper trails that allowed enough room for them to run side by side. He allowed her to set the pace, which was still slower than his average, but faster than what she'd said hers was the night before. When she suggested they do another lap around the park, and then another, adding three miles to their run, he got the feeling she was testing *his* endurance. Much to his delight he'd learned that Kacie was competitive, and damn if that wasn't one hell of a turn-on.

Their pace that final half mile from the park back to her place slowed almost to a crawl as the weekend traffic picked up and they encountered one stoplight after another, block after block. Such was the downside of running in town.

They walked in silence down the narrow drive that led to the carriage house in the back, and the uncertainty of what would happen once they reached her front door overtook him. Never had he been thrown so off balance by a woman.

Kacie unlocked the door and pushed it open wide, leaving it open in invitation behind her. Michael followed and closed the door behind him while Kacie was already opening cabinets and pulling out two large glasses. After filling them both with ice water, she handed one to him, then relaxed back against the counter. Michael drank down the first glass and quickly refilled it, then took his time with the second as he watched her over the rim.

Her eyes were closed as she drank, affording him the opportunity to thoroughly observe her. He found himself entranced by the flushed color of her cheeks, the short strands of hair that curled at her nape, the droplets of sweat that raced the length of her neck only to pool in the hollow of her throat.

Long, damp lashes fluttered open and suddenly those sea-green eyes were staring back at him.

Fuck it. Just because she called the shots didn't mean she had to initiate everything.

His glass hit the counter and in two strides he was towering over her, his mouth crashing down on hers, his fingers tangling in those damp curls at the base of her neck. Her lips and tongue were chilled from the water, her hands cold from the glass. Michael lifted her from the floor and set her on the counter, stepping in between her legs and pressing his body flush to hers. But still he couldn't get close enough, and wouldn't be until he was inside her.

The soft gasp that escaped her mouth was quickly followed by another kiss. Then she whispered, "I should shower."

In his opinion, she smelled amazing. But her words flicked on the proverbial lightbulb in his head because, damn, if that wasn't a fantastic idea.

"Okay, then," he said, sliding her off the counter. "A shower, it is."

"Together?" she asked, clinging to him like a koala to a gum tree.

He carried her through the living room and down the hallway. "I'm all about water conservation."

"But are you sure you want to shower together? I'm not sure that's safe." Kacie tugged on his lower lip with her teeth, then offered another teasing kiss. "All that tile. It's so slippery."

Michael groaned. "If that's your best argument as to why we shouldn't, you're saying all the wrong things."

She ground her hips against his as her breathy words feathered across his lips. "It would seem to me I'm saying everything just right."

AFTER THEIR SOAPY interlude, Michael and Kacie both collapsed into her bed and dozed for a bit, their bodies desperately needing rest. When he woke, Michael was immediately struck by a sense of déjà vu. But this time, instead of worrying about alcohol poisoning and monitoring her breathing, he just relaxed and enjoyed the view.

She slept on her side, facing him, her hands tucked beneath the pillow she rested her head on. Her hair was damp in places and dry in others, the sun-streaked waves spread out in all directions. He liked how the strands weren't straight but weren't really curls either, wavy enough they twined around and clung to his fingers like vines. Her hair alone gave the impression she belonged on a California beach or a deserted island.

He liked the faint freckles that dotted her nose and cheeks and the golden undertones in her skin. He liked the pale pink color of her nipples and how they darkened with arousal.

Speaking of which . . . Michael tugged on the yellow-dotted bedsheet covering her body, shifting the thin cotton fabric just enough to expose her breasts to his gaze but not disrupt her sleep.

And that was a tactical mistake.

Because now that they were on display in front of him and not merely an image burned into his brain, he wanted to touch her and taste her.

"Quit ogling my boobs."

Her eyes were closed but there was a smile on her face. He'd been busted by his not so sleeping beauty.

"What makes you think I was looking at your breasts? And even so, I'm a doctor. You've seen one breast, you've seen them all."

She opened her eyes and stared at him with a look that said he was a lying liar who lied. And he couldn't really argue. Kacie grabbed hold of the bedsheet and pulled it higher she snuggled into her pillow.

"So . . ." He playfully tugged on the sheet again. "There's one topic we didn't discuss earlier."

"Oh, God. Do I even want to hear this?" She pulled the sheet free from his fingertips. "You're not one of those guys who has a bag of toys in his closet, are you?"

"I could be. Does that interest you?" He bounced his eyebrows at her and she decided to make a break for it. But since she was worried about modesty and tried to take the sheet along with her as she vaulted out of the bed, he was able to catch her before she got very far. She squealed and squeaked as he dragged her back, finally straddling her body and pinning her wrists to the mattress.

"Oh, damn," he said as he hovered over her, his mouth just inches from her lungs as they worked to catch their breath. "It appears you've lost your bedsheet."

Kacie narrowed her eyes. "What do you want?"

He lowered his head and traced her jawline with the tip of his nose. "I want to know if I can take you out to dinner sometime."

"Dinner implies it's a date. And dating makes it a relationship." Her breath hitched as he pressed kisses to the tender skin beneath her ear. "You need to remember this isn't a relationship."

"What if I suggest dinner just because I'm hungry?" He gently tugged on her earlobe with his teeth, then soothed the bite with his tongue. "And what if you just happen to be at the same place? We can split the tab if it makes you feel better."

"I'm not adverse to food. I'm just against going out."

"And why is that?" he asked while moving to the other side of her neck.

"Because I wouldn't be able to do this."

Taking him by surprise, Kacie wrapped her strong legs around his waist and reversed their positions so that she now straddled his hips and held his wrists in her grip. That beautiful, wild hair fell in a curtain around them, and the scent of her shampoo tickled his nose. She stared down at him with a mischievous twinkle in her eyes and one corner of her mouth hitched up in a smug smile. "How about we do things my way?"

She locked eyes with him as she kissed and licked her way down his sternum, the strands of her hair tickling his chest and stomach as she headed south past his belly button. Much to his delight she showed no signs of stopping.

"Sunshine, one thing is for certain. I will never complain about the way you do things."

Chapter Eleven

A WEEK INTO Kacie's "diet" and things were going well for the most part. After jumping into the deep end of the whole friends with benefits, no-strings sex, whatever others might call it, she was feeling pretty happy about life in general. And as much as she hated to admit it, a lot of the credit went to Michael.

Although they spent most of the previous weekend together, they didn't tire of each other. Instead, they ended up seeing each other every night after work. A couple of times he picked up dinner along the way since she still refused to go out.

When she was with him, she often laughed until her sides hurt. There was no talk of failed relationships, ill-fitting dresses, or jealous tendencies. There was no pressure to introduce him to her friends, coworkers, or family and vice versa. When they were together it was as if they existed in their own little bubble and the rest of the world just faded into the background.

He'd become her little secret and it surprised her how much she liked having him all to herself.

But instead of planning another rendezvous with Michael, she and Sam were driving west on I-16, headed for Atlanta, to attend a bridal shower Sam's future mother-in-law was throwing in her honor. Their mother was also supposed to make this trip, but had come down with a terrible summer cold; she hadn't wanted to spend her weekend sneezing and coughing on a roomful of strangers, so Kacie and Sam went on without her.

For the three hours they drove the tree-lined divided highway, Sam and Kacie sang along to the radio, laughed about old boyfriends, and shared stories about the kids they grew up with. Occasionally, the flow of conversation was interrupted by her sister and Bryce trading text messages back and forth, but for the most part, it was just the two of them. One last little hurrah between sisters before they both went their separate ways.

They wove their way through Atlanta, taking one Peachtree-named street after another until they reached the exclusive suburb of Buckhead. Kacie knew Bryce's family likely had money. Just how much was something she hadn't really contemplated—not until she drove her little Honda Civic down streets filled with Land Rovers, Mercedes, and BMWs.

"Not this driveway," Sam said, pointing to her right, "the next."

Unlike many other homes on the street, the gates sat wide open in invitation. Kacie stomped on the gas pedal, helping her car up the steep incline to reach the paved circular drive. She was so focused on avoiding the water fountain and the cars worth two years of her salary, she didn't really take in the house itself until she parked and stepped out the driver's side door.

"Holy shit," she whispered to herself.

But obviously Sam heard her because she leaned on the roof of the car and whispered back. "I know, right?"

One of the massive mahogany front doors opened up and Bryce made his way across the drive to them, his arms stretched out wide to greet his bride-to-be. Sam wasted no time, running to him and leaping into his arms.

Kacie loved seeing her sister so happy and there was little doubt that Bryce was head over heels for Sam. But without warning, that little pinch of jealousy she hadn't felt at all the past week returned.

Right at that moment, her phone buzzed in her pocket.

Make it okay?

Just pulled in. And holy crap this house is massive.

Kacie looked up from her phone to see her sister and future brother-in-law still playing kissy face, so she seized the opportunity to snap a picture of the front of the house and send it to Michael. A few seconds later his reply came.

You weren't kidding. Be sure to turn on your GPS and keep your phone on you. That way if you get lost I'll have coordinates for a rescue squad.

LOL. Will do, she answered. **TTYL.**

Just as Sam and Bryce came up for air, Kacie tucked her phone into her pocket and popped open the trunk. Ever the southern gentleman, Bryce took their bags from the car and led them into the house. His mother, Gwen Elliott, greeted them at the door dressed to the nines and promptly began with the gentle hugs and air kisses.

"Don't you girls look just lovely," Gwen said. "I'm so sorry your mother wasn't feeling up to coming."

"Mom sends her apologies," Sam replied. "She was really looking forward to it and just hates that she's sick."

Gwen took hold of Sam's hand and patted it gently. "Better she's under the weather now than during the wedding, dear. We'll have your parents another time."

With suitcases in hand, Bryce led the way up the wide spiraling staircase and down a long hall to their room for the weekend.

"I hope you girls don't mind sharing a room," Gwen said. "I was going to give Kacie her privacy, but the air conditioner went out in the pool house and it's just too warm to expect anyone to sleep comfortably out there."

"Well, if Kacie doesn't want to share, Sam is always welcome to stay in my room." Bryce waggled his brows, causing Sam to giggle like a schoolgirl as the corners of his mother's mouth turned downward.

"Now, Bryce . . ." his mother chided, but the two lovebirds disappeared down the hall before she could say any more. As she watched them rush out, she gave a slight shake of her head, before turning to Kacie. "I was going to tell them lunch is ready downstairs but they'll figure it out. Also, there's plenty of time for you to rest or enjoy the pool this afternoon if you like. Most of the guests won't arrive for another few hours at the earliest."

"Thank you, Mrs. Elliott," she said.

"You're more than welcome, Kacie. And please, call me Gwen." She turned for the door but stopped short. "Before I forget, there's extra towels in the bath. The TV remote is in the nightstand along with an index card that has the Wi-Fi passcode." She smiled sweetly. "I'll see you downstairs, dear."

With the bedroom door closed, Kacie looked around the room that was nearly the size of the carriage house she rented. Decorated in a serene color palette of blues and whites, it was elegant, but not fussy. One side of the room, with its oversized linen sofa and a wall-mounted flat panel TV, served as a sitting area. Across from it was a massive king-sized four-poster bed with layers of bedding and a mountain of pillows.

Again, she couldn't help herself; she snapped a pic of the bed and messaged it to Michael. She then wandered into the bathroom, where touches of black set off large expanses of Carrera marble. She snapped the oversized shower, complete with multiple body sprayers and a rain head showerhead.

Her phone vibrated.

That place is giving me all kinds of ideas. The bed especially.

Pervert.

Takes one to know one.

Kacie laughed, shoved her phone in her pocket, and headed downstairs for lunch. Later that afternoon, with the bride and groom missing in action, she entertained herself by sending Michael more pictures. The first was of her reflection in the mirror showing off her new swimsuit. He, of course, asked her to take another— minus the clothes. The next was the view from her patio lounge chair, showcasing her cute pedicure and the turquoise waters of the swimming pool beyond.

When the time arrived to shower and change for the backyard barbecue Bryce's parents were hosting, she sent another selfie of her wrapped in a towel. Followed by one of the towel on the floor.

Now you're just being mean, Michael replied.

She was smiling as she stepped in the shower and had the same look on her face when she finished. As she dried her hair and applied her makeup, there was a knock on the bathroom door. Kacie opened it to find

Sam standing there with her shower stuff bundled in her arms and a sheepish look on her face.

"Sorry I just kind of abandoned you this afternoon," she said. "We went to the condo to see how the renovations were coming."

Kacie couldn't resist teasing her. "How *do* things look?"

Sam blushed. Her hair was mussed and there was a bit of stubble burn on her collarbone. There was little doubt of what she and Bryce had really been up to for the past several hours.

"Things are right on schedule," she said while placing her things on the counter. "They should be done in time for us to move in before the wedding."

Kacie nodded. "That's great. You'll come back from your honeymoon and be able to jump right into your new life."

Sam turned on the shower and grabbed a towel from the linen closet. "It's crazy to think, isn't it? That in just a matter of weeks, I'll be living in Atlanta, with my *husband*, in a place we can decorate however we want because we own it."

"Sure does." Kacie grabbed her things and headed for the bedroom. "I'll finish getting ready out here."

"Kace?"

She stopped short in the doorway and looked back at her sister, almost certain this would become one of those tender moments between siblings where Sam would tell her how much she was going to miss her when she moved away.

"Can you undo my zipper for me? I have a hard time with it."

Disappointed and a little hurt, Kacie pasted on a smile until Sam turned her back and lifted her hair. After lowering the zipper, she made a hasty exit, pulling the bathroom door closed before her emotions got the better of her.

Was she only upset by her sister's behavior because she didn't have someone to call her own? Kacie tried to think back to previous years when she was happy and in love. Did she make time for her sister then? Or had she used Sam to conveniently fill in the gaps when Mike was deployed or otherwise busy?

She didn't have much time to mull it over since Sam showered quickly, and they headed downstairs, where her sister spent the first half hour introducing her to members of Brycc's extended family and some of their college friends that lived nearby. But eventually she was called away and Kacie was left to wander the crowd alone.

She did her best to socialize and enjoy the evening, but it wasn't long before she realized nearly everyone in attendance, minus a few elderly relatives, were part of a couple. If they weren't married, they were engaged, or at the very least appeared to be deeply in love.

By the time dinner was finished and the desserts were brought out, Kacie was feeling pretty blue. And much to her despair, there was a tower of chocolate cupcakes that called her name. She pulled her phone from the hidden pocket in her skirt and snapped a picture of it, then sent it to Michael. Almost immediately her phone buzzed.

There was no hiding her smile as she swiped her thumb across the screen. "Hey."

"Can you not go one night without supervision?" he asked. "Dammit, Kacie. Step away from the cupcakes."

She snort-laughed in response, and when Bryce's grandmother gave her a puzzled look she quickly apologized. "You're absolutely right," she said while grabbing a glass of ice water before making her way across the pool deck to a quiet spot far from the rest of the party. "I'm walking away as we speak. How was your day?"

"Mine? Well, I started the day off with a run. Then I went to the grocery store. At the moment I'm doing laundry and watching a *Man vs. Wild* marathon."

"Sounds exciting."

"You have no idea. What better way to spend a Saturday night than folding underwear and watching Bear Grylls drink his own piss?"

Again, Kacie barked a laugh as Michael's low-rumbling chuckle filled her ear.

It'd been less than twenty-four hours since she'd last seen him. Only a matter of hours since they lasted exchanged text messages. But the man was addictive. He had a way of changing her mood in a heartbeat.

"Oddly enough, I think I'd much rather be doing that than being the third wheel here."

"That bad, huh?"

Kacie sighed. "Yeah. Which is why those cupcakes are looking pretty damn attractive."

"Sounds like an intervention is necessary."

"And how are you going to manage that?"

"Fortunately—" his voice dipped to a lower register "—my mind is a beautifully dirty thing."

And suddenly, she found it difficult to breathe.

It didn't take much imagination on her part as Michael proceed to tell her, in graphic detail, just exactly what he would be doing to her if she were with him at this very moment. His words scraped across her skin, alighting every nerve just as if it were his touch instead. As he painted an erotic picture in her mind, her heart raced, her face heated. She pressed the ice-filled glass of water against her neck, hoping it would cool her, but she didn't anticipate the sharp contrast in sensation to coil the tension in her body tighter.

"Fuck, Kacie. Just the thought of you . . ."

Through the earpiece she heard a low groan followed by the phone being shuffled a bit, then a soft grunt.

"Michael. Are you doing what I think you're doing?"

"Hell, yes. Care to join me?"

If her face was flushed earlier, she had to rival a beet at this point. "I'm standing about fifty feet away from a boatload of Bryce's family."

"Okay, then. But you're out of earshot, right? So you talk."

"Michael, I—" As much as she hated to admit it, she was a thirty-one-year-old phone sex virgin. Hell, she was more of a text message girl to begin with, one who had never sexted either. So the fact she was even carrying on a phone conversation, much less engaging in phone sex? The pressure was just too great. She couldn't formulate a complete, seductive thought much less put it into words. "I just . . . I can't."

His breath huffed in her ear. "Do you want me to stop?"

Kacie looked across the pool at the crowd of guests and her eyes just happened to lock with Bryce's grandmother's.

This was wrong. So very wrong.

She turned her back to the party and whispered into the phone. "Don't stop."

His low groan sent shivers down her spine and once again she was entranced. By the sound of his erratic breathing through the earpiece, by him repeatedly whispering her name. As his pace picked up, so did the rate her heart pounded in her chest. And when she whispered his name into the phone, it was just enough to push him over the edge.

For the next several seconds, both Kacie and Michael tried to catch their breath, their collective exhales overlapping. Somehow through the residual sexual haze, her brain recognized the approaching sound of high heels on the pool deck and Kacie turned just in time to see her sister headed straight for her.

"I gotta go," she said, disconnecting the call before even hearing his response.

Sam folded her arms across her chest. "Who were you talking to?"

"Damien," Kacie answered while shoving the phone back into her pocket. "From work."

Her sister's expression was skeptical at best.

"Why would he be calling you about work on a Saturday night?"

"It wasn't about work," she said brightly. "He was just calling to tell me he ran into a former patient of ours."

Kacie took a long drink of her water, hoping it would temporarily halt her sister's questions or at least delay the next until she had a grip on things.

Sam narrowed her eyes. "Why is your face flushed?"

"Because it's hot?" she said with a shrug. "Or it might be the wine."

Her sister pointed at the glass Kacie held in her hand. "You're drinking water."

"Now I am. Because I drank too much wine earlier."

"Sam!" Both sisters turned toward the gathering to see Bryce waving her over. "Come here, sweetheart. I need to introduce you to someone."

Sam took one last look at Kacie and gave a slight shake of her head before walking away. Kacie knew she'd been saved by the proverbial bell and could only hope her future brother-in-law would keep Sam occupied for the rest of the evening.

The phone in her pocket vibrated with a message.

With trembling fingers, Kacie removed it from its confines.

Call me when you get back to your room.

Why?

She held her breath as she stared at the screen, already knowing what he was going to say.

You're next.

Chapter Twelve

"ALL RIGHT, ALL right. I'm coming," Michael yelled to the person threatening to break down his front door at nine o'clock on a Sunday morning.

He flipped the dead bolt and yanked it open, fully expecting it to be the old guy from maintenance that was hard of hearing and always wanting to check the plumbing for any leaks. Instead, he found his sister-in-law standing with a bright smile on her face, the very picture of innocence.

"Something's wrong with your phone."

"You know damn well there's nothing wrong with my phone," he grumbled. But he stepped out of the way to allow her inside.

"It's one thing for you to ignore Danny's texts," Bree said while marching past him and into his living room, dropping her handbag on his recliner. "But to ignore mine? I'm crushed."

Damn her and her guilt trips. He was immune to most of the games women played but Bree had next-level talents.

Michael flung the door shut and folded his arms over his chest. "What do you want?"

She blinked up at him with doe-like eyes. "You know exactly what I want."

That he did. For the past two days he'd effectively ignored his brother's text messages, asking if he were going to attend C-Co's family picnic. In the past, it was nothing more than a round-robin softball tournament and more food than you could shake a stick at. But this year it happened to fall on Memorial Day weekend, which meant an even bigger event with more people in attendance than years past.

"Given how things ended last year, I wasn't sure it was a good idea."

Michael headed into the small kitchen and opened his refrigerator, pulling out two bottles of water. When he turned around, Bree was standing at the breakfast bar.

"I told Danny that's why you weren't answering his texts."

He opened both bottles and slid one across the counter to her. "Brawling in the parking lot at a family event is pretty bad. Brawling with your own brother makes things even worse."

Bree shook her head. "Don't be silly. If what hap-

pened last year is anyone's fault, it's mine. Besides, everyone is expecting you. I think they're counting on you to
umpire."

"Figures," he mumbled. Of course they only wanted
him there to offer some kind of service.

"What else are you planning to do today? Sit here by
yourself and watch TV?"

If he had his way, he'd spend the day exchanging
texts with Kacie just like he had done the day before.
But he wasn't about to say that to Bree. And anyway, he
knew she'd likely be busy with the bridal shower most
of the afternoon. At best, he'd hear from her tonight.

Bree made her way around the counter, placed her
hand on his arm, and stared up at him with her big
brown eyes, just like she always had when she was a
kid. "Pretty please?" she asked so sweetly. "I've made a
batch of my mom's oatmeal-chocolate-chip cookies and
I know Marie made some of those orange-cranberry
things you love so much."

His stomach growled in anticipation. "You two don't
fight fair."

Her bright smile returned to her face because she
knew damn well she'd just won the battle.

"Fine," he scowled. "I'll go."

"Yay!" Bree clapped her hands. "I have to go get
Danny, and pick up a few things along the way. Do you
want to come with me back to the house and then we
can all go together? Or do you—"

"How about I meet you guys there?"

She pulled her car keys out of her handbag. "You promise you're going to show up? You aren't lying to me, right?" she asked, pointing at him with the key.

"I'll be there. I promise."

Michael walked her to the door, and after a few more assurances that he would indeed be at the picnic, she finally left him in peace.

He immediately grabbed and dropped into his reclining chair, scrolling through the text conversation with Kacie from the day before, pausing on the selfie of her in her bikini. She looked fantastic, as always. She wasn't wearing any makeup and her wild hair was piled on top of her head. And her green eyes seemed to pierce right through him.

Part of him wished she was in town so she could go to the picnic with him. But that would mean Bree and Marie would be all up in their business asking questions neither he nor Kacie would want to answer. No, it was far better to keep her all to himself. That way, when their arrangement ended and Kacie headed off to Durham, he wouldn't have to deal with any of the pitying looks or long-winded advice about relationships.

Michael glanced at his watch. Surely she'd be up by now, even if he had kept her up late last night with their phone rendezvous. After a moment, he quickly typed out a message.

Have fun today.

He was quite proud of himself for keeping his text

short and sweet, despite wanting to know when she'd be returning to Savannah.

His phone vibrated in his hand.

As far as I'm concerned, this weekend won't end soon enough. Hoping to cut out early if I can.

His heart leapt in his chest as he stared at her words on the screen. If there was even the slimmest of possibilities of seeing her tonight, it was worth going for it.

Should be home by dinner if you want to stop by, he replied.

Duly noted.;)

He waited several seconds for another text, a photo, an emoji. Anything. But that seemed to be the end of their conversation for now, so Michael tossed his phone onto the couch and walked away from it.

When she first laid down the rules, it had been easy to agree because historically his relationships never lasted long anyway. But now, only one week in, her rules were becoming a source of frustration. He wanted to take her out, wine and dine her. He wanted to show her off. For once in his life, he wanted more from a woman than she was willing to give.

Perhaps that was the attraction? The fact she didn't cater to his every whim. The fact she always left him wanting more.

Whatever it was about her, he needed to figure it out soon just so he could get the hell over it. Otherwise he'd make a damn fool of himself when this thing between them came to an end.

With a sigh, Michael headed to his bedroom to get ready for the picnic.

By THE TIME he arrived the park was filled with people, and as he stepped out of the car he was greeted with the sounds of laughter and squeals from the kids jumping around in the bouncy house. The scent of hot dogs and burgers on the grill made his stomach grumble in hunger. Then there was the ping of the aluminum bat meeting a softball. As always, someone was taking the round-robin matches quite seriously and he wouldn't be surprised if he later learned his little brother was the one out there warming up.

He popped open the trunk and pulled out his large medical bag. The likelihood of using even a Band-Aid from it was slim to none, but if he didn't bring it, he could damn well bet someone would likely lose a limb out here today. Always better to be safe than sorry.

He was heading through the parking lot when someone called out to him. He turned to see Lucky James, one of the 1st/75th's special ops medics, coming toward him with a very beautiful, very pregnant redhead leaning on his arm.

Nearly a year earlier Lucky had left the military to attend college with hopes of going to medical school. Then, much to everyone's surprise, he returned to the 75th several months later, this time with a fiancée and baby on the way.

"Major. I wanted to introduce you to my wife, Rachel." Lucky extended his hand to Michael but kept one protective hand wrapped around her waist. "This is Major Mac-Gregor. He's the battalion surgeon for the 1st/75th."

She flashed him a smile. "Are you the one who recommended my OB/GYN?"

"That would be me," Michael said warmly. "However, that information really comes from collected responses over the years from 1st Batt wives. After all, they're far better equipped to tell me who to recommend."

Rachel laughed. "I take it you're not one for stirrups?"

Lucky's eyes widened. "Jesus, Rach. Don't say that to him. He's practically my boss."

"Oh. I'm sorry." Rachel looked first at her husband and then at him. "I'm still trying to figure out this whole military thing."

Michael chuckled as he waved off her apology. "There's little doubt you'll fit right in with some of the other wives. My sister-in-law, for one." Rachel's brows crinkled in confusion. "Have you met Bree Mac-Gregor?" he asked.

Her face instantly brightened. "I have! I went to lunch with her and Marie . . ." She turned to look at Lucky. "How do you say her last name again?"

"Wojciechowski," he and Lucky said at the same time.

She pointed at the two of them. "That's it! I love the two of them. So much fun!"

Michael and Lucky shared a look and shook their collective heads, because both of them knew there was absolutely no good that could come from those three being friends.

Two hamburgers, a bratwurst, some watermelon, two cupcakes, and a piña colada snow cone later, Michael stood behind home plate umpiring the final game of the day. And just as everyone would've predicted before the tourney began, the team captained by his younger brother was battling Captain J.T. Anthony's team for the championship.

Danny donned his batting helmet and glove for what would likely be his final at-bat. His team was down by one and they were going into the bottom of the final inning. Anthony, who was playing catcher, turned to look at Michael.

"Doc, I shouldn't have to tell you how important this game is to me," he said with a huge smile that vacillated from threatening to charismatic. "I'm trusting you to call this game fair."

Although J.T. was one of the nicest people Michael had ever met, he also wasn't someone he wanted to accidentally piss off.

Anthony was a big guy, an intimidator, and definitely not built like the typical Ranger. While he was the same height as Michael, his arms were as large as most men's thighs. He was the kind of guy who looked like he should be playing defensive end in the NFL instead of squatting behind home plate at a family picnic in Savannah.

Before Michael could even answer, Danny did so for him. "No need to worry, Cap. If anything, the fact you're playing my team is in your favor, not working against you." He smiled, then turned at looked at Michael. "Or have you not met my big brother."

Michael shook his head and pointed to the chalk outlined box on the ground. "Get your ass in the batter's box."

His brother was still chuckling when he fouled off the first pitch into the chain-link backstop. The second he sent foul down the first base line. Danny stepped out of the box, tapped his cleats with his bat, then took a few extra swings.

"You're just delaying the inevitable, MacGregor," Anthony chirped from beneath his catcher's mask. "My trophy is waiting."

"Whatever you say," Danny answered with a smile, showing a great deal of restraint.

Because at the end of the day, Anthony was his commanding officer and could make his life a living hell if he really wanted to. Not that he would ever do it.

The final pitch was a freaking watermelon right

over the middle of the plate. Danny's swing connected, sending the neon yellow ball sailing to deep centerfield, but landing just inside the fence. Danny dropped the bat and took off running, watching as the outfielder made his way to the ball. As his brother rounded second, Michael already knew what would happen next. And sure enough, ignoring Gibby's signals to hold up at third, Danny skidded around the corner and headed home.

The cutoff man made a strong throw, one-hopping it to Anthony, who grabbed it bare-handed and steadied himself for the tag. Danny lowered his shoulder and Anthony held his position until they both collided just left of home plate. Once the dust settled, Anthony sat up from the carnage of limbs showing Michael that he still had the ball in his hand. Michael then called his brother out and a string of expletives streamed from Anthony's mouth celebrating the fact.

But once the excitement wore off, the expletives became pain-related. Two of his fingers were now pointing in unnatural directions.

"Goddammit, Danny." Michael immediately took hold of Anthony's hand as his brother stood wide-eyed, shocked by what had transpired. "We should probably X-ray these, J.T."

"You should listen to him," Danny said. "No need to make things worse by staying. No stupid trophy's worth it."

Anthony gave Danny a steely look. "Not. A. Chance."

Then the hard look transformed into a wide smile, making Danny swear under his breath as he headed back to the dugout.

"Your brother was their last best chance and he knows it. So just pop them back in, Doc. I've got a game to win."

Michael shook his head.

Typical Rangers. Of course, many of them had suffered far worse injuries over the years.

"Deep breath," he ordered as he took hold of the first digit and manipulated it back into position.

"Whew." Anthony shook his head, then grinned again. "One down, one to go."

Michael then took hold of the second finger and manipulated it as well. By the time he was done, both fingers were swelling, but Anthony ignored his advice to go put ice on them immediately.

Thankfully, the pitcher made quick work of the last two batters and Anthony got his prized trophy. Which was presented to him by the previous year's winner—Danny. And, of course, his little brother garnered lots of laughs as he swore vengeance would be his.

Thirty minutes later, after he had taped a bag filled with ice to Anthony's hand, he finally had a chance to check his phone.

Couldn't take another minute. On my way home.

The message had come at four-thirty, which meant she would be back in Savannah around eight. Which meant there would be plenty of time for them to hook up. But in that moment he knew he didn't want her to show up for a quickie and then leave again; he wanted to actually spend some time with her.

Fuck it. Couldn't hurt to ask.

Michael took a deep breath and dove straight into the deep end.

Or you could come to my place, stay the night, and we get up and go for a run together tomorrow morning?

It felt like hours passed as he stared at the screen, waiting for a response, when really it was only a few minutes.

idk

He stared at the three letters on the screen.

"Idk? What the hell does that mean?

He didn't realize he'd asked the question out loud until his brother who was standing a few feet away chirped up. "I don't know," Danny replied.

Michael turned to look at him. "What?"

"IDK means 'I don't know.'" Danny shook his head. "And you're supposed to be the smart one of the family."

As his brother walked away, he was almost certain

he heard him mumble, "Idiot." If that wasn't a perfection description as to how he felt at the moment.

"In for a penny, in for a pound," he muttered to himself while typing out his address.

Just in case, he added.

Then he shoved his phone in his pocket and tried his best to forget about it. And he did. At least until the picnic was over and he returned to his empty apartment without hearing another word from her.

Low-level irritation simmered in his gut. He grabbed a can of beer from his fridge, popped the top, and was about to take a drink when a knock sounded at the door. Michael flipped on the small outside light and yanked open the door to find Kacie standing in front of him, staring up at him with those beautiful green eyes and a bright smile.

And even better, a large duffel bag in her hand.

Like the saying went, Rome wasn't built in a day. And if he had to win this woman over one day at a time, one hour at a time, he'd never consider a moment wasted.

Chapter Thirteen

———————————————

THE DRIVING RAIN and booming thunder matched Kacie's mood as she spent her evening curled up on her couch, binge-watching *Grey's Anatomy*, and wallowing in her own misery. In the past when she felt this terrible, she'd soothe herself with a take-out order of mashed potatoes and gravy, then chase it with three Midol and a pint of Ben & Jerry's. However, due to her pesky little dress problem, two items from her treatment plan had to be excised. But no way in hell was she going to have salad twice in one day, so dinner was a cold bowl of cereal.

As the summer thunderstorm raged outside, she queued up season two on Netflix. It was her failsafe because no matter how bad she felt or how things were currently going in her life, it was always far worse for the employees of Seattle Grace.

Several episodes into her misery marathon, Kacie rolled onto her side and hugged her pillow a little tighter. Of course it was only once she'd achieved maximum comfort levels that someone knocked on her door. She froze in place, her eyes darting to the clock on her wall. It was well after nine at night, far too late for it to be a salesman, even if the weather hadn't been horrible. Hell, most solicitors never even noticed her little carriage house hidden far from the street. Hopefully, whoever it was, they'd just go away if she ignored them.

A second knock came and her heart began to race. She peeked over the back of the couch and stared at the dead bolt, hoping she'd truly locked it when she came in and hadn't just given it a ceremonial flip.

"Kacie, if you hear me, you better open the goddamn door before I break it down."

Recognizing the voice, she shot up straight in the couch. "Oh, no, he didn't," she growled.

Fueled by anger she marched across the room, turned the lock, which had been fully engaged, thank you very much, and yanked the door open.

"We agreed no pop-ins!" she yelled at the giant shadowed figure standing on her small front porch.

"Glad to see you're alive." A damp and dripping Michael pushed past her, then slammed the door shut behind him. "The least you could've done was return my texts."

Once he was inside she could see his eyes were filled with rage.

Well, two could play at that game.

"Aren't you supposed to be busy with some night training thing? Jumping out of airplanes or something like that? Because you're certainly dressed for it."

Michael glanced down at his rain-soaked military-issue clothing, then sarcastically pointed to the door. "Did you happen to notice the raging thunderstorm? Kind of makes night jumps impossible."

"Of course I did," she dished back. "I'm also noticing you're leaving a puddle on my floor."

When she looked up from his combat boots to meet his gaze, she noticed his eyes were focused on her chest. Only then did she remember she was wearing the thinnest of T-shirts. With no bra. Kacie looked down to see what he was seeing and, just as luck would have it, her nipples were oh-so-happy at his appearance they were practically waving.

She folded her arms over her chest, obstructing his view. "What are you even doing here?"

"What am I doing here?" he parroted while shaking droplets from his hair like a wet dog. "How about the fact the last message you sent me was stating how terrible you were feeling. So bad, in fact, that you were leaving work early. Throw in the weather, a million car wrecks, and then—" Michael tossed his hands in the air. "Fucking radio silence."

Kacie winced, realizing he was here dripping on her floor because he was actually worried about her.

"My phone died on the way home and when I came

in I just stuck it on the charger." She grabbed a towel from a neatly folded stack of laundry on her small kitchen table and offered it to him. A peace offering of sorts. "I didn't think to turn it back on."

He removed his digital camo print jacket and hung it on the back of her dining room chair before taking the towel from her hand. "I texted to make sure you got home okay. Asked if you needed anything. No reply." He tossed the towel over his head and began rubbing his scalp violently. "I texted again." His words were muffled. "Still no reply, so I tried calling. And calling. And calling."

By the time he draped the towel over his shoulder and took a long hard look at her, she was feeling a bit guilty. There was denying the concern in his eyes.

"I'm sorry, but it never crossed my mind that you'd check up on me. After all, you said you wouldn't be able to see me this week because of army stuff. And now you know I'm just fine."

Michael studied her thoughtfully as he swiped an errant drip from his ear. "How about since I'm here, you consider it a house call. Tell me what's wrong."

That was not a conversation she wanted to have with him, doctor or not.

"Thank you for asking, but don't worry about it."

"Damn, woman." He propped his hands on his hips and stared down at her. "Do you know how many people try to take advantage of the fact I'm a doctor and can give them free medical advice? Would you please quit being so stubborn and let me help?"

And . . . now she was ticked again. Who the hell did he think he was to barge into her pity party of one and start demanding answers from her? Worried or not.

"Well, you can't help. It's just that time of the month. Happy now?" She opened the front door. "Thank you for coming by to check on me. I appreciate it. But you can just go on home and I'll send you an all clear message when we can resume. Until then, you can entertain yourself elsewhere."

The high winds gusted rain through her front door and all over her floor, yet she continued to hold it open for him. Michael shook his head and made like he was going to leave, but instead pushed the door shut again. With him still inside.

"Do you really believe I wouldn't want to spend time with you because of your period? Do you think I'm such a self-centered asshole?"

If she thought he was upset before, he seemed even more so now.

But two could play at that game. "Go home, Michael." She tried to shove him out of the way so she could open the door again.

Michael took a firm hold of her shoulders and looked down at her with those dark blue eyes. She watched as the anger dissipated from his gaze and softened into a look of concern. Like two kids having a staring contest, she wanted to outlast him. Wear him down. Wanted to hold on to her anger and end this little standoff by tossing him out on his arrogant ass. But the longer he watched her, the more her resolve weakened. And when she took a second to think about it, she was just too tired to argue more.

As if he sensed the moment the fight left her, he pulled her into his embrace, smoothing one strong hand up and down her spine.

"What can I do to help? What are your symptoms? Cramps? Body ache? Fatigue?"

This was one hell of a bedside manner he had, his words as gentle and soothing as his touch.

"You forgot irritability," she mumbled against his chest.

Taking hold of her shoulders, he eased back just enough to meet her gaze. The corners of his mouth quirked up and the dimple popped in his cheek. "No, I didn't forget. That one's obvious."

She gave a weak punch to his arm and he laughed, pulling her close once again, almost curling his body protectively around hers. As his arms held her tight, his warmth seeped through his worn cotton shirt and into her body like an oversized heating pad.

"I'm gonna ask you again, what can I do to help?"

"This," she mumbled into his chest.

"Okay, then. How about we call it a night? It's been a long day."

Kacie eased away from his embrace to look into his eyes. "You want to stay the night? With me?"

"If you don't mind." He gave her a half smile. "I'll have to leave pretty early, especially since I'll need to go home and get my gear before I head into work. But I'd like to stay. If you'll let me." As he spoke he carefully pulled the elastic from her hair, raking his fingers across her scalp and through the strands in slow, comforting motions.

Suddenly, she found it difficult to swallow around the lump in her throat.

As if his words and kindness weren't enough, he had to go and make everything worse by being tender, too.

For the past week and a half she'd been telling herself Michael was only interested in one thing. And that the attention he paid her was only a means to get that one thing. But this? Coming over in a thunderstorm to make certain she was okay? Wanting to know what he could do to make her feel better? This was not the Michael she was accustomed to.

As he held her tight, as his breath fanned across her skin and he pressed light kisses to her hair, she realized the arrogant, self-proclaimed sex god had disappeared and been replaced by Michael from the coffee shop. The man who had shared his secrets and bought her lemonade and kissed her on the cheek as he said goodbye.

And while it was possible she could've walked away from the first one when the time came, she wasn't sure she could with the second.

THANKFULLY, KACIE GAVE up the fight. Her eyes closed and her entire body went lax as he gently stroked her hair. From the weight of her body leaning into his, it was quite possible she'd fall asleep where she stood if he kept it up.

"Sunshine," he whispered, and her eyes fluttered open to look up at him. "Do you want me to leave?"

"No." Her answer was barely more than a whisper.

While he would've preferred a more enthusiastic response, it was far better than her trying to throw him out.

"Are you ready to call it a night, then?"

This time she responded with a simple nod against his chest and he pressed a kiss to the top of her head.

"Okay, then. Why don't you head off to bed and I'll lock up."

There was no argument, just a soft groan as she centered her weight on her own two feet and powered herself down the short hallway to the bedroom.

Michael removed his combat boots and stacked them side by side, then used a couple of paper towels to dry the puddles of rain and mud he'd tracked inside. As he worked his way around her small carriage house, locking the front door, turning off lights, shutting off the television, his heart rate slowed and his anxiety eased. He was smart enough to realize even as he raced across town in the driving rain that his worries were likely unfounded. He knew he'd find Kacie safe and sound in her house, and yet, he couldn't stop himself from panicking. And now what he needed most to settle himself was to hold her.

When he made his way to her bedroom, he found her already snuggled up in bed, well on her way to being sound asleep. He couldn't contain his smile as he noticed she'd situated herself on what had become her side of the bed, facing the space she'd left for him, the covers thrown back in invitation.

As he quietly stripped down to his boxer briefs, neatly folding his clothes and placing them where he'd be able to find them in the early-morning darkness, he looked at her, her body curled into the fetal position with that mass of wild hair spread out behind her.

Is this what would it be like to have a wife or a girlfriend to come home to every night?

What would it be like to come home to *her*?

Michael slid into bed next to her, careful to not bounce around on the mattress too much as he adjusted the blankets. But just as he settled, she lifted his arm and scooted toward him, bringing her body flush to his as she rested her head on his shoulder.

"I'm sorry if I woke you," he whispered.

"You didn't."

They spent the next few minutes rearranging themselves, both of them restless and struggling to find the sweet spot. After all, this was atypical behavior for the two of them. But eventually, he found himself perfectly comfortable, on his back near the center of the bed, with Kacie's body draped over his, her palm resting over his heart and her head tucked beneath his chin.

Michael covered her hand with his, and used the other to stroke her spine. While the motion seemed to relax her, there was no denying it soothed him as well.

And after the evening he'd had, this is what he'd desperately needed.

For the past year, he'd found himself to be more and more on edge. Ever since he packed his brother onto a medevac, not knowing if he'd survive the plane ride to Germany. And if the anxiety he felt after that wasn't bad enough, he lost four men and one woman just six months later. The IED blast had done so much damage that even if he'd been standing just out of the blast radius, ready and waiting to treat them, they still wouldn't have survived. For those five there was nothing he could have done. He knew it. His superiors knew it. Everyone knew it. And yet, he couldn't help but feeling he'd failed them.

As a doctor, he'd been trained to deal with matters of life and death. However, the things they taught him in medical school, the things he saw during his residency in Texas, couldn't prepare him for the things he had seen in Afghanistan.

And they sure as hell hadn't prepared him for that one hot afternoon in Mali, when he ripped the clothes from Danny's near lifeless body.

His mother's death had made him want to be a doctor, but it was his brother's brush with death that had made Michael a little less cynical, a little more caring, and a lot more scared.

Ever since that day, when someone offered him a hug he held them just a second longer. When he spoke to his father, he was always sure to tell him he loved him before ending the conversation. And now he'd gone and added someone else to that ever-growing list of people he felt responsible for, whom he cared for.

Kacie mumbled something unintelligible in her sleep and wriggled off him, ending up on her side, facing the edge of the bed with her back pressed against him. He turned to his side, mimicking her position, curling his body around hers. His arm slipped over her waist, and whether she consciously did it or not, Kacie took hold of his hand and held it in hers against her chest.

Beneath his palm he felt the slow, steady beat of her heart. Once again, he buried his nose in her hair, and the last bits of tension seeped from his body.

Somehow, in just a matter of weeks, this woman had become extremely important to him, whether she realized it or not. Whether he wanted her to be important to him or not.

For the first time in a long time, he found someone who soothed his soul and he didn't know how he'd ever let her go.

Chapter Fourteen

LATE ONE FRIDAY afternoon, Michael found himself sitting at his desk in the relative quiet of battalion headquarters staring at the planner laid out in front of him. In two weeks, Battalion Commander Griffin would hand over command of the 1st/75th during Fourth of July celebrations.

Two months after that, having fulfilled his service obligation to the military Michael would be eligible to resign his commission. Everyone knew the army regarded doctors as a hot commodity, so resigning would be easier said than done. Thankfully, his medical degree combined with combat experience afforded him far more negotiating power than most. If he chose to stay another six years, he would reach his twenty and be eligible to collect his full retirement.

Griffin hadn't been wrong when he questioned Michael's decision to stay in the military; Michael had said more than once he was only going to stay the length of his commission, retirement money be damned.

But now, Michael felt his decision hinged on whether Danny reenlisted in the next six weeks. If he could convince his brother to leave the army, then he'd be free to move on.

However, if Danny reenlisted and stayed in 1st Batt, then it was where Michael needed to be.

It wouldn't be the first time in his life he changed plans because of his little brother. Within minutes of receiving Danny's email stating he'd graduated from the Ranger Indoctrination Program, was being assigned to the 1st Batt, and deploying to Iraq within the week, Michael picked up the phone and called his superior, asking what he needed to do to become a battalion surgeon for the 75th. Gone were any thoughts of becoming an oncologist, of simply serving his time at Walter Reed or some other stateside hospital. Every day for the next five years, he prayed to God to keep his little brother safe, at least until he made it to regiment and could take over from there.

But it would only be a matter of time before the army required him to move up in rank or move out. He'd been fortunate enough to have landed the 75th Regiment gig in the first place, and it was highly unlikely the brass would allow him to retain his position indefinitely.

Then there was the added wrinkle of his non-relationship with Kacie.

Although her sister's wedding was a little over a week away, she had yet to say anything regarding the two of them. Would she end things before or after the wedding? Or would they continue to see each other during her final month Savannah? Truth be told he wasn't ready to say goodbye to her just yet.

So many life-changing decisions and he felt he wasn't in control of any of them.

Michael grabbed a yellow legal pad, flipped to a clean page, and started a list.

First, he needed to research career alternatives. If he wasn't allowed to remain at the 1st/75th, where would he like to go?

He skipped a few lines down the page and wrote a single word—Kacie.

If he stayed here, would they be able to manage a long-distance relationship? Would she even consider it? It wasn't like he could head to North Carolina for the weekend whenever he wanted to. And she likely had work requirements of her own due to her fellowship. Even if they somehow made it work over the next year, he had no idea of her plans beyond that. Did she want to stay in Durham? Did she plan on moving back to Savannah? Or was she open to going wherever the job offers took her?

Either way, they could find themselves in the exact same position a year from now.

Maybe things with him and Kacie were a case of wrong place, wrong time. Maybe they just weren't meant to be.

His thoughts were interrupted by a knock on the door. He looked up to see his brother standing in the doorway dressed in civilian clothes. Although he looked perfectly fine to the naked eye, Michael couldn't stop the feelings of panic coursing through him. "Everything okay?"

"Everything's fine," Danny said with a smile. "I'm not interrupting, am I?"

"Just doing a little paperwork. Nothing urgent." Michael turned the legal pad facedown on his desk. "What brings you by?"

With a look of surprise on his face, Danny dropped into one of the chairs on the opposite side of the desk. "Did you not notice the date?"

Michael looked back at the open calendar on his desk. June 21. He'd been so busy creating a plan of attack for the next several weeks he hadn't paid any attention. He scrubbed a hand over his face. "I don't know how it could've slipped my mind."

"You're busy. It happens."

His brother was kind to give him an out and Michael couldn't be certain that if the tables were turned he'd be so forgiving. After all, what kind of man forgets his mother's birthday?

"Is that your only reason for coming by?"

"I thought maybe we could go grab a drink."

"What about Bree?" For the past eighteen months Danny rarely went anywhere outside of work without his wife.

"She thought it'd be better if just the two of us went."

Michael's gut warned him this was more than his sister-in-law wanting them to spend some brotherly time together.

"Give me a few minutes to wrap up a couple of things?"

Danny rose from his chair. "Meet you at Murphy's in thirty?"

"Sounds good."

With a nod, he headed out of the office and Michael turned the legal pad back over. He scribbled another note, then underlined it for emphasis.

He'd spent most of his life without his mother and damn near lost his younger brother. He would do everything in his power to keep Danny safe.

THE BELL ABOVE the door gave a cheerful tinkle as Kacie entered the bridal shop. What an amazing difference five weeks made. When she last left this place, she had been swamped by feelings of hurt and jealousy and loneliness. And now as she walked through the door, she felt like a stronger, more confident, far happier version of herself.

As she stood in the showroom in the midst of all the bridal gowns, it didn't matter that she wasn't married herself or engaged or even in a serious relationship. Because Michael, whether he realized it or not, had helped her come to see that a man alone couldn't bring her happiness. If anything, she needed to be happy with herself in order to make a relationship work.

"Well hello," Della said in her syrupy sweet southern drawl. "I was so excited to see you on the schedule today. Are you back for your final fitting?"

Kacie caught her tone, that subtle way of politely questioning whether the dress would fit.

"I am pretty sure this will be my final fitting," she said, unable to contain her happiness. "I even remembered to bring the heels I'll be wearing." Kacie gave a little wave with the shoe box in her hand.

"Excellent. Your dress is already waiting for you." Della led her to the dressing rooms in the back and directed her to the one with her gown hanging in it. "I'll just give you a few minutes and then I'll be back to zip you up."

And with a little wink and a smile, off she went, closing the door behind her.

Kacie dropped her things onto the small padded bench and went about undressing. All the while she stared at the ice blue dress. She'd come to think of as her nemesis these past few weeks, but standing here now, staring it down, she knew without a doubt that not only would the dress fit, it would look fabulous.

I wish Michael could see me in this dress.

The thought took her by surprise, because that wasn't what she and Michael were about.

For the past month and a half, they'd managed to keep their relationship mostly superficial. Of course there was the morning they ran into each other at the coffee shop and she told him of her future career plans and he shared that his mother died when he was young. Then there was the night he showed up on her doorstep in a raging thunderstorm because he was worried about her. But those occasions were anomalies. For the most part, their conversations generally revolved around brief rundowns of their work day, what kind of food they wanted to order in, and what sexual position they should try next.

Kacie felt her skin flush warm.

Okay. So things between them were quite intimate in that sense. He knew just how and where to touch her to make her come completely undone. But at the end of the day, she didn't really know much about him.

And yet, if there was one person she'd like to take as a date to Sam's wedding, it was Michael.

One, because he wouldn't allow her to get all mopey about her unmarried status. He wouldn't let her sit in the corner and watch everyone else have fun. No, he was the kind of guy who'd drag her out into the middle of the dance floor and have everyone watching them by the time the song ended.

Two, his presence would reduce, if not eliminate, any awkward questions her relatives might have about the breakup with her ex. Having him run interference with all the nosy busybodies would be reason enough to extend an invitation.

Three, with Michael by her side there would be no pity faces. Because no way could any woman take a look at him and think Kacie had somehow lowered her standards or missed out on something better. As fantastic as he looked in a golf shirt and shorts, she could only imagine how he'd look all dressed up in a suit and tie.

Or, if he went without a tie, she could peek at the hollow of his throat, lean in close as they danced, and smell the warm scent of his skin.

Yes, that would be much better. Nice suit. Starched white shirt. Open collar.

With her mind made up, Kacie went about slipping the dress on over her head, careful to not catch the delicate chiffon on anything for fear of making the fabric run. As she studied her reflection in the mirror, she imagined how people might react to the sight of them. She imagined them on the dance floor, him pulling her close with one hand low on her back and the other holding her hand over his heart.

A knock on the dressing room door startled her from her daydream. "Are you ready to be zipped up?"

"Yes, please," Kacie answered. "Come in."

The door swung open and right away Della smiled. "This really is just the most wonderful color on you," she said while taking hold of the two sides and easing the zipper upward.

Unlike last time, Kacie could breathe normally. It definitely wasn't too tight now.

"So far so good," Della exclaimed. "It fits you like a glove. Just as it should be. Now let's check the length."

Kacie pulled on her heels and followed Della out to the main room where she stepped onto the raised platform. As she turned in slow circles, Della studied the bottom. "Well, I must say I'm pleased with the results. What do you think?"

She had never been one to stare at herself in the mirror, but Kacie sure didn't mind looking now. Because, just as Della had said, the color looked fantastic on her. The sculptured bodice fit snugly, but still allowed her to breathe and move comfortably. The off-the-shoulder piece that draped from front to back, designed as a faux sleeve, accented the dress perfectly. "I think it looks lovely. Please tell the seamstress thank you for all her hard work."

Della waved off the compliment. "My dear, the hard work was your part. We have brides and bridesmaids in here all the time saying they're going to drop that extra ten or fifteen even fifty pounds before their next fitting. And you are the only one in recent memory who actually pulled it off. Not that you had much to lose to begin with." Having noticed a thread hanging from the hem, Della lowered down to one knee and carefully snipped it off. "But more importantly, you are positively glowing."

"You think so?" Kacie studied herself in the mirror.

"Absolutely," Della exclaimed as she rose to her feet and clutched her scissors to her chest. "As a matter of fact, I'd say you have the look of a woman in love."

Kacie's stomach dropped and her heart began pounding in her chest.

It couldn't be, could it? She hadn't screwed up and fallen in love with Michael, had she?

She was happy because she was short-timing at a job that left her unfulfilled. She was happy because she'd just made a deposit on a great place to live in Durham. She was happy because her life was moving toward something instead of just sitting idly, stagnating.

Michael wasn't responsible for any of that. Only she was. *She* made her own happiness.

Besides, they didn't really know each other. Aside from that first night at the bar, she'd never spent time with his family. Never met any of his friends. She didn't know whether he wanted to stay in the military until he retired. She certainly didn't know if he saw a wife and family in his future.

As far as she knew he was the consummate bachelor and would continue breaking hearts for years to come. He was just a short-term fling, not the kind of guy she could ever have a future with.

No, on that note Della had to be wrong.

Chapter Fifteen

THE WAITRESS PLACED their order of hot wings and cheese fries in the middle of the table, along with two small plates and a pile of napkins. "Anything else I can get you? Would you like another Guinness?" she asked, directing her questions specifically to Michael.

"Another round would be great," he answered.

The brunette patted his arm, even batted her eyelashes. "I'll be right back with those."

Although he was shoving a handful of fries into his mouth, it wasn't enough to muffle Danny's laughter. Of course his brother found it amusing, especially since their waitress hit on him first. Only by putting his wedding ring on full display was he able to get her to stand down.

Michael piled food onto the small plate, his way of laying claim to it. They were, after all, brothers first.

And no mercy would be shown to Danny if he chose to dawdle instead of eat.

"Do you ever wonder how different our lives might have been if Mom hadn't died?"

Danny's question came from so far out of left field that Michael actually paused in the act of reaching for a hot wing. His brother wasn't known for being the introspective type, at least not before he and Bree were married. Just further proof of how their relationship had changed him for the better.

"Different how?"

"Would you have become a doctor? Would I have been such a screwup in college? It's likely Dad would've been tougher on me and I wouldn't have gotten away with a quarter of the shit that I did," he said with a shrug while shoveling a pile of fries onto his plate. "If so, then Bree and I could have been married ten years and had a couple of kids by now instead of being married one year with zero possibility of kids."

It would have been easy to tell his brother that everything happens for a reason. But it was hard to believe the universe was justified in taking their mother away when they were young, or taking away Bree's ability to have children.

Committing what their mother once deemed a cardinal sin, Michael placed his elbows on the table while studying his little brother. "Where is all this coming from?"

"Just lots of decisions I need to make. Do I reenlist? Do I get out?" Danny never looked up from his plate, just pushed the food around with his fork as he talked. "And if I do leave, where do I go? Government work? Private security? It's not like I have a ton of marketable skills."

Michael's jaw dropped, stunned his brother was even considering, for the first time ever, leaving the military. "I think you have far more skills than you're giving yourself credit for."

Danny shook his head while staring into the bottom of his glass. "Not really. But I might have to figure out something in a hurry."

"You're seriously thinking about not reenlisting?"

"If Bree asked me to leave the army, I'd do it in heartbeat," he said without hesitation. "No questions asked. I'd do anything for her."

Michael couldn't believe his luck. If Danny were to leave the military, then he could resign his commission and not feel guilty about it. And then, maybe he could convince Kacie to give them a real shot.

"So . . . what about you? You'll have fulfilled your commitment this fall, right? Have you decided what you're going to do?" Danny pointed at him with his fork. "It's not like you need to stay in and do your twenty. I bet you'd make pretty decent money out in the civilian world."

"I think I'd do okay. Are you wanting me to leave the 75th or just trying to get rid of me completely? Tired of your big brother hanging around?" Michael asked with a laugh.

But there wasn't any amusement in Danny's eyes as he washed down his bite of food with Guinness. "I don't want to get rid of you. I like that we can grab a beer anytime we want. But I wouldn't mind if you left the army. It'd be one less thing I'd need to worry about."

"You worry about me? What the hell for? I'm not the one kicking in doors and shit."

"How can you be so fucking smart and so fucking stupid at the same time?" Danny huffed in frustration. "You're just as likely to step on an IED or be killed in a rocket attack as I am. And let's not even talk about what could possibly happen if you came face-to-face with an insurgent."

Figures his brother didn't think he could handle himself. "You know, the army issues me a gun."

"Yeah. And I've seen your handiwork at the range." Danny laughed. "It's a damn good thing you're a doctor because you'd fucking suck as a soldier."

Well, he couldn't really argue with Danny on that point.

He was on the verge of telling Danny he'd sleep better at night if he followed his own advice, when Danny's phone vibrated on the tabletop and Bree's face appeared on the screen. His brother wasted no time in answering, and as the two of them chatted, the things Danny mentioned earlier about not having kids circled around in Michael's mind.

He knew his brother regretted the ten years he and Bree spent apart and the unfortunate fact that by the time they did marry there was no chance of kids. Throw in his career choice and her past cancer battles and adoption would be highly unlikely, if not impossible.

The moment his brother ended the call, Michael spoke up. "Danny . . . what you said about kids? I thought you two were fine without?"

"It's fine. It's just . . ." His brother struggled to find the words. "Sometimes I watch Bree with Ben and Marie's kids. Or like at the picnic, I saw her staring at Rachel's belly, and there's a sadness in her eyes. I want to give her everything, but I can't."

"Do you two talk about it?"

"We do when she's feeling down about it. Which isn't very often, and she handles it like a champ. But . . ." Danny shook his head.

"It feels like a missed opportunity."

"Yeah. But don't worry about us, we're good. Really good." Danny drank down the last of his beer and set his glass heavily on the table. "Bree, however, is quite worried about you. She thinks you're isolating yourself."

That made him choke on his drink. "Excuse me? I'm doing what?"

"She's worried you might be depressed. Nothing serious, just kind of low-level stuff."

He studied his brother and there wasn't a single ounce of amusement in his eyes. He was absolutely fucking serious. "And why would she think that?"

"Because you rarely go out anymore. And you keep refusing her dinner invites."

Michael held up a hand in protest. "I do not refuse invitations to dinner. I do, however, refuse to let her and Marie play matchmaker."

Danny chuckled. "Can't say as I blame you there."

"It's not funny."

"Of course it is. Just not to you." Danny signaled to the waitress. "So what do you want me to tell her?"

The way Michael saw it, there were two ways he could handle this. He could lie and dig a deeper hole and worry his sister-in-law more. Or he could tell the truth and get the monkey off his back, so to speak.

"If it will make her feel better, tell her I've been seeing someone."

"Nope. Not gonna do it." Danny paused momentarily as the waitress placed two more beers in front of them. "I'm not going to lie to my wife for you."

"I didn't ask you to. I've been seeing someone for a while now."

Danny looked at him skeptically. "That seems pretty convenient. I can't just take your word for it. I need proof."

Michael thought on it a bit. No way in hell would he show their text messages as evidence. Instead, he scrolled through the photos Kacie had sent, selected one, and slid his phone across the tabletop.

"What the hell is this? It's a picture of a woman's feet and a pool." Danny shoved it back. "You're gonna have to do better than that."

Michael scowled and then pulled up the selfie of Kacie in her bathing suit. He started to hand the phone back, then yanked it away from his brother's grasp at the last second. "I'm only showing you this as proof. But I swear to God, if you give Bree any specifics about the woman in this picture, I will break your face. Got it?"

"Jeez. Okay."

He swore under his breath and reluctantly handed Danny the phone.

"She's cute," was his brother's first response. And then he took a closer look. "She looks familiar. Who is she?"

"Remember the bachelorette party the night we went out for Bree's birthday?"

Danny's head shot up and he stared at Michael with wide eyes. "Holy shit! It's Malibu Barbie!"

Michael snatched his phone back and pointed at his brother. "Break. Your. Face."

Danny scoffed, then took another drink of his beer. "Why all the cloak and dagger bullshit?"

"Because it's not a relationship. We're just . . ." He wasn't sure how to finish the sentence because he wasn't even sure how to describe whatever it was between the two of them.

"Fuck buddies?" Danny supplied.

Michael's blood started to boil. "Don't. Do not. I fucking warned you."

Intrigued, his brother sat up a little straighter in his chair. "You like her."

"Fuck off."

Danny laughed then. "Oh, you *definitely* like her."

Michael signaled the waitress for the check.

"So what's the problem here?" Danny asked, still grinning.

"She's moving to Durham next month for a fellowship at Duke. It's a pretty big deal."

The waitress appeared with the check and Michael quickly handed her his card.

"What the hell is it about North Carolina, huh? First Bree and now . . . what's her name?"

"No way. I've told you too much already."

"Well, big brother, the way I look at it, you've got a little over a month to somehow convince her to stay."

"I don't see that happening."

The waitress dropped the check and Michael doubled-checked the receipt and added a generous tip, ignoring the fact she'd written her name and phone number on the customer copy.

"Why not? I stopped Bree from taking that job in Greensboro."

"What stopped Bree from leaving was the fact you were shot up and nearly died." Michael signed his name with a flourish and closed the folder. "Call me crazy, but that seems a little drastic at this point."

"Whatever," Danny said with a shrug. "It worked for me. It could work for you."

Unfortunately, he'd never been a grand-gesture kind of guy. And if that's what love required of him, maybe he wasn't cut out for this relationship stuff after all.

WHEN KACIE LEFT the bridal shop, she wasn't really in the mood to just go home and sit alone in her place. If anything, she wanted to celebrate her success. But she hadn't spoken to Michael since he'd left early that morning.

She pulled out her phone and was on the verge of texting him. But then she remembered what he'd said that first afternoon in her apartment—that he wasn't opposed to the idea of her showing up unexpectedly at his door—and she decided to see if he really meant it. After one quick stop at the drugstore for a provisional box of condoms, followed by another at the little bakery he often talked about, she was on her way.

If anyone asked, Kacie wouldn't be able to explain her actions. There was just something about him that made her want to try anything and do everything.

She parked in the guest lot and followed the walkway to Michael's place. As she lifted her hand to knock on the door, she suddenly realized the music echoing through the breezeway between the two buildings was coming from inside his apartment. Not accustomed to hearing him play Elton John, she took a step back and double-checked the building number.

Certain she was at the right door, she knocked a little harder than usual. When he didn't answer by the count of three, she was tempted to run away and pretend she'd never even been there. Instead, she took a deep breath and knocked one last time, and the door opening unexpectedly beneath her hand.

His expression quickly shifted from one of annoyance to happiness. "Hey there."

"I . . . figured I'd pop in."

She hadn't thought it possible, but his smile widened even further, those charming dimples appearing in his cheeks and his eyes darkening as the meaning of her words sunk in.

Kacie held out the small white pharmacy bag and pink bakery box as she took in his appearance. His hair was wet and he wore a towel wrapped low on his hips. Droplets of water were scattered across his shoulders and chest, some of which occasionally lost their grip and raced down the firm planes of his stomach.

Michael pushed the door open wider and took the things from her hands, setting them on a small table. But the moment she was inside, the door slammed shut behind her and she was being pressed up against it as his mouth tasted hers and his hands roamed her body.

"You don't mind that I just showed up?" she asked as his lips skimmed the length of her neck.

"God, no."

With both hands he tugged down the top of her strapless maxi dress to reveal her breasts. After only a split second to visually appreciate them, he plumped one in his hand before taking her nipple in his mouth. Emboldened by his reception, she grabbed hold of his towel and, with one swift tug, freed it from his hips and tossed it aside. The moment she took his erection in hand he groaned low in his throat. It wasn't long before he pulled himself from her grip, then reached beneath her dress to grasp her panties, yanking them down.

She knew what would come next, or at least hoped.

And of course Michael didn't disappoint; his hands grabbed her ass and lifted her from the ground as excitement coursed through her. Instinctively her legs wrapped around his waist as he leaned her heavily against the door. The soft cotton fabric of her dress was shoved high around her hips, and he used his fingers to tease between her thighs.

"The bag, the small white bag," she said breathlessly.

He shifted her weight in his hold and she heard the rustle of the bag. He tore open the box with his teeth and offered it to her. "Take one, put it on me."

She wasted no time following his orders, tearing the small package open, slipping the condom free, rolling it onto his length. She'd barely released him before he was inside her. With his hands behind her knees, he lifted her higher against the door, holding her there with his body as he moved with an intense urgency.

His breath was hot in her ear, rushing from his lungs as he worked their bodies in a hurried rhythm. She clutched his shoulders, her nails digging into his skin as he shifted his feet, changing the angle as he drove deeper, harder, into her.

If anyone were walking past his apartment door, there would be little question as to what was happening on the other side. And if they were still uncertain, her cries as he brought her to the edge of orgasm and quickly tossed her over would've been confirmation enough. Never mind the string of expletives that came from his mouth as he followed her over.

"Well, that was quite the welcome." Kacie smoothed her hands over his shoulders and back as he leaned heavily against her. "I should pop in more often." She felt his laugh against her neck as they both struggled to catch their breath.

After a few moments, he withdrew, lowered her to the ground, and made certain she was steady on her feet before kissing her tenderly.

"It's nice to see you." Then he flashed her a grin while picking up his towel from the floor. "Make yourself at home."

She watched him go until his naked butt disappeared around the corner and into his bedroom. Then she put herself back to rights and wandered over to the entertainment center. Just as she'd suspected, the source was an old turntable she'd noticed when visiting his place previously. He had told her then that most of the records in his collection once belonged to his parents, and when his father no longer had an interest in them, Michael swiped them.

She picked up the white album cover and was reading the back when he returned wearing black running shorts and an ARMY T-shirt.

"I wouldn't have taken you for an Elton John fan," she said, holding up the cover.

"He was my mom's favorite. She listened to him all the time." Michael picked up a remote from the coffee table and lowered the volume. "Today's her birthday so I was feeling a bit nostalgic, I guess."

Although the corners of his mouth were upturned into a smile, the sadness in his eyes weighed it down.

"How old was she when she died?"

"Thirty-three."

"And how old were you?"

"Ten," he said matter-of-factly. "I was ten. Danny was five and had just started kindergarten."

Kacie shook her head in disbelief. It seemed inconceivable that his mother, any mother, could die at such a young age. Even more surprising was that she had only been two years older than Kacie when she died.

"Was it an accident?"

Michael shook his head. "Lung cancer. Both she and my father smoked. She started as a teen and used to smoke those long, thin cigarettes with menthol when I was a kid. Such a distinct smell. For a long time she had a cough that just wouldn't go away, always saying she thought it was a cold or the flu. She'd have times where she got better or didn't seem to cough as much and so she'd put off going to the doctor."

He took the album cover from her hand and filed it with the others on the shelf, then gestured for her to take a seat in the couch.

"I think she knew what it was and was scared to find out," he continued without any prompting as he sat down beside her. "By the time she finally went to a doctor and X-rays were ordered, they found the cancer in her lungs. It wasn't much longer before they discovered it had metastasized to her brain and liver."

"Does your dad still smoke?"

Again, he shook his head. "Nope. He quit cold turkey the day they diagnosed my mom."

"I'm so sorry, Michael." Kacie reached out and placed her hand upon his. "I didn't mean to dredge up bad memories."

He shook his head. "I was thinking about them anyway. And it's okay. It was a long time ago."

Neither of them spoke for a long while; instead, they just sat next to one another listening to the music.

"Do you have a picture of her?" she finally asked in a pause between songs.

Immediately, he went to the bookshelf and pulled down an age-worn photo album, one filled with yellowed Polaroids and faded school pictures. He quickly flipped through the pages, landing on a studio portrait. "This was taken of my mom and dad just a few months before she was diagnosed."

He gave her time to look at it, then turned several more pages. "This is my favorite," he said while staring at the picture. "Although you can't see her face very well, you can *see* her."

Unlike the previous photo, this one was a candid shot taken at a carnival of some sort; little Michael was in the picture, shoving a cone of cotton candy into his mom's face.

"It looks like you both were having a lot of fun."

"She was a lot of fun. Always laughing." He turned and looked at Kacie intently with those dark blue eyes. "You remind me of her."

She glanced at the photo again, knowing he wasn't talking about looks. After all, his mother had dark brown hair and blue eyes. "Is she why you became a doctor?"

Michael continued flipping through the pages of his childhood. "Yeah. It's kind of predictable, right? I didn't want any other kid to lose a parent like that."

"I'm surprised you didn't become an oncologist, then."

He shrugged his shoulders. "That was the plan when I first went to medical school. Plans change though."

Now her curiosity was piqued. She knew his medical school was paid for by the military and his service now was part of his repayment. But it didn't explain a few things.

"Did you always plan to go into the Ranger regiment?"

"No." He answered without hesitation.

"How, then?"

One corner of his mouth hitched up. "Basically it was a pissing contest. Although we're five years apart, Danny and I have always been competitive. Probably because I never let him win as a kid."

"Sounds like typical oldest sibling behavior to me. Of course you wanted to be better."

"No, I wanted *him* to be better."

Kacie arched one eyebrow, waiting for him to explain.

"After our mom died, most people went easy on him. Teachers. Coaches. Our dad. No one was willing to be hard on him except me." He continued turning pages until he came to a page that had photos of both of them in uniform. "He had a baseball scholarship to South Carolina, but got into some trouble his first year and lost it. He enlisted as an infantryman for regiment. Went through RIP, Airborne, next thing I knew he'd been deployed to Iraq. When 1st Batt returned home, he was sent off to Ranger School. When he finished, he sent a picture of his tab. Basically, he threw down the gauntlet."

"He didn't think you could do it."

A smile overtook his entire face. "Exactly. He said I was too soft."

"So you never intended to do all of this when you joined the army?"

"Nope. Not really. I assumed I'd end up working in a VA hospital or a base hospital treating running noses and stuff. But what can I say? I'm competitive."

Without any warning, Michael tossed the photo album onto the coffee table, and retrieved the pink bakery box. He lifted the lid and smiled the moment his eyes landed on the cannoli dipped in chocolate chips and dusted with powdered sugar. "I'm really glad you came over."

She felt herself smile back. "Me, too. And I wanted to share my good news with you."

"And that is . . ." He plopped back down in the couch next to her and immediately pulled one of the desserts from the box.

"I went for my final fitting today and my dress fits perfectly."

"Do you have it with you? In your car, maybe?" he asked around a mouthful of cannoli. "I want to see you in it."

"Why on earth . . ."

"Because I had a hand in it. I helped whip you into

shape." He licked the powdered sugar from his fingertips. "That's like letting a man train a horse to run but not allowing him to watch it race the Kentucky Derby."

Kacie snorted because he was just so ridiculous sometimes. And he knew it.

"Well, I'm sorry to keep you from your derby. You can, however, be my date at the wedding if you want."

She froze, suddenly realizing the words that had just left her mouth. Although she'd been considering it at the bridal shop, she hadn't decided definitively to invite him. But it was too late to take it back.

"It's no big deal or anything, but you might have fun. Maybe. Probably not. On second thought, just forget I said anything at all."

He put a hand over mouth, shushing her. "Sunshine, I'm looking forward to it."

Then he flashed a mischievous smile and held the cannoli out to her. "Do you want a bite?"

"That kinda negates all my hard work, doesn't it?" She backed away from the temptation but he just kept coming at her. "Just because I fit into my dress today, doesn't mean I'll fit into it next week if I go hog wild."

Her answer didn't deter him. Instead, he leaned even closer and skimmed her lips with the tasty dessert.

"I think you'll be just fine," he whispered. "After all, I know a great way to work those calories off afterward."

Chapter Sixteen

IT WAS A typical hot and humid summer day in Savannah as Michael made his way down the palm-tree-lined street, suit jacket in hand. When he reached the front of the historic Methodist church, he shrugged into his coat and straightened his tie as he climbed the front steps to the entrance. The moment he stepped inside the heavy wooden doors, he was greeted by a man quite a bit younger than him but several inches taller and nearly double his size. Since he was wearing a tuxedo and offering a program, Michael assumed he must be one of the groom's friends.

"Are you a friend of the bride or the groom?" the man asked.

Michael took the program from his hand. "I'm a friend of the maid of honor actually."

"Sam's sister? Nice," the guy said with an approving

nod and smile. "Do you want to sit up front with the bride's family, then? There are a few spots left."

Michael glanced around the sanctuary. Despite his arriving twenty minutes early, the church was nearly full. "I'll just grab a spot in the back, thanks."

As he started for an empty seat the usher quickly stepped in front of him. "I really think I should show you to the family seats up front. I wouldn't want Sam to be upset you ended up all the way in the back."

"I can assure you, it won't be a problem," he said, keeping his voice low. "I've never even met their family."

Michael waited for the guy to step out of the way; instead, his eyes widened in surprise.

"You mean to tell me you're meeting the entire family for the first time today?" The guy smacked Michael's shoulder with the back of his hand. "Have to say you're braver than most. Or crazy. One of the two."

"Great. Thanks," he said without humor. "I appreciate that."

The guy finally moved, allowing him to make his way to an empty seat in the back row on the aisle. As the preservice music from the massive pipe organ reverberated throughout the church, he sat quietly, hands folded in his lap, much like his mother taught him when he was young. Of course, after she died, they rarely attended church, aside from going to Christmas Eve and Easter Mass with Bree's family.

As he took in the chapel's Gothic architecture and elaborate stained glass, he wondered if this was the church Kacie had gone to growing up, or if her sister booked it because it would look pretty in the wedding photos. How odd that as much time as he and Kacie had spent with each other, he really knew very little about her. He knew how she liked her coffee and he knew how to make her come, but he didn't even know if she was a practicing Methodist. Then, upon realizing he was thinking about sex with Kacie while sitting in church, he immediately offered a prayer of apology and asked for forgiveness.

Obviously, that small Catholic boy in him hadn't vanished completely.

It wasn't too long before the groom's parents made their way down the aisle, followed by the same usher he spoke with earlier now escorting the bride's mother. He'd be lying if he said he didn't feel a twinge of nervousness knowing he'd be meeting her entire family following the service. Especially since he couldn't remember the last time he'd met any woman's family. And then there was the fact she likely hadn't told them anything about him, just as he'd said very little to Danny about her. However, he'd been promised one hell of a party afterward and that was reason enough for him to attend. Which was a complete and total lie. But if anyone asked, that's what he'd say to avoid looking like some lovelorn puppy.

From a side door, the minister entered along with the groom and his groomsmen, all of whom made the usher look small. Then the doors in the back were opened and one by one came the dwarfs from the bachelorette party, wearing different styles of dresses in the same pale blue color and carrying white flowers. A few smiled at him as they passed and he wondered if they recognized him from the night of the party. Or maybe they regarded weddings the same way many single groomsmen did—a prime hookup opportunity?

Either way, there was only one bridesmaid he was interested in. And it felt like a lifetime before she appeared through the double doors. But when she did, she simply took his breath away. Her hair was piled on top of her head, minus a few curly tendrils. The dress she had complained about, cussed, and nearly convinced him was the handiwork of Satan himself looked absolutely gorgeous on her. As if it was made for her.

He continued watching her, patiently hoping she would look in his direction. Not until she was right in front of him did she notice him standing there. But once her gaze locked with his, he gave her a little wink and her cheeks flushed pink in response.

What he wouldn't give to take her in his arms and kiss her right there in front of God and everyone. It had been three days since he'd last tasted her, touched her, held her. Stupid last-minute wedding preparations and family stuff. Instead, he was forced to settle for smiling at her before she continued down the aisle, finally taking her place across the way from the groom.

Although the music changed, signaling the entrance of the bride, he couldn't take his eyes off her. He even found himself frustrated when his view of Kacie was blocked by Sam and their father as they made their way down the aisle.

As the minister began to speak, Michael's mind began to wander. Would he get to have Kacie all to himself once the reception was over? He'd made provisions just in case that were to happen. What kind of food would they serve at the reception? Would there be an open bar?

"Do you, Bryce Edward Elliott, take this woman, Samantha Renee Morgan, to be your lawfully wedded wife?"

Something about the groom's name piqued his curiosity, so Michael pulled out his phone and as discreetly as possible did a quick Google search. Sure enough, Kacie's new brother-in-law was a former Heisman Trophy–nominated quarterback and, at one time, the pride of Georgia. At least that explained why most of the groomsmen looked like an offensive line standing at the front of the church.

Thankfully, the ceremony was short and sweet and before he knew it the organ was blaring a cheerful tune as the newlyweds practically skipped down the aisle. They were followed by the entire wedding party, the parents, the grandparents, until the guests began filing out. But instead of following, Michael remained at the back of the church just as Kacie had suggested so she'd know where to find him afterward.

Five minutes later, she tapped him on the shoulder. "Waiting for someone?" she asked.

"As a matter of fact," he began, turning to find her staring up at him with those green sea-glass eyes and that bright smile. "One of the bridesmaids asked me to meet her here. Hopefully she won't be too long."

Kacie narrowed her eyes at him. "Very funny."

"I thought so." Since they were alone in the church, he placed one hand on her hip and tugged her closer, wanting to kiss her. But she quickly lifted her flowers between their faces.

"No, no, no. You can't ruin my lipstick. There are still pictures to be taken."

Michael grumbled under his breath and she took hold of his hand as she lowered her bouquet.

"I'm glad you came through," she said, her thumb caressing his knuckles. "Thank you for being my date."

"Anytime, sunshine." Lifting her hand to his mouth, he pressed a kiss to her palm and another to the underside of her wrist. "You look beautiful by the way."

"And my dress?"

Still holding her hand, he guided her in a slow turn, appreciating her, not the dress, from all angles. Then, once she faced him again, he leaned closer and whispered in her ear. "I think it'd look better rumpled up on the floor."

With a laugh she shoved at his shoulder, putting some distance between them. "We're standing in church in case you've forgotten."

"Kinda hard to miss."

Her gaze followed the arched ceilings to the front.

"It's beautiful, isn't it? We weren't big churchgoers growing up, but Bryce's family are devout Methodists. So he and Sam compromised and agreed to have the wedding in Savannah as long as they were wed in a Methodist church." Kacie turned back to look at him. "The minister actually baptized Bryce when he was little."

"Speaking of, you never once said who your sister was marrying. It was a little surprising when all these guys who look like they could bench-press a car walked in."

"I know, right? Sam said they're the reason they decided to go with a buffet at the reception. I'll be surprised if there's any food left. But they're all really nice."

He folded his arms over his chest. "Are they now?"

"And very young," she quickly added.

"As opposed to . . ." He arched an eyebrow, baiting her.

"Being very old?" She laughed, then gave his hand a tug. "Come on. Let me introduce you to my parents."

AS THE PHOTOGRAPHER went to work, Michael returned to a seat near the back of the church so it wasn't long before the bridesmaids spotted him sitting all alone in the mostly empty sanctuary. As soon as the wedding party was dismissed, the whole flock of them moved in his direction to say hello.

Kacie kept one eye on the situation at hand and was vaguely reminded of the Discovery Channel. The sharks were circling and Michael was the chum.

"Who is that in the back?" her sister asked.

"That's Michael."

Sam craned her neck, even squinted her eyes as if that would help her get a better look.

"Remember G.I. Joe?" Kacie added, keeping her voice low. "The guy I went home with the night of your bachelorette party?"

"Seriously?" Her sister's words were a harsh whisper. "Why would you invite him to my wedding?"

Slight irritation churned in her gut. She hadn't just invited some random guy to be her date, she'd invited Michael. And he was nice. And fun. And sexy as hell. But even if he had just been a random guy, why should that bother her sister?

"We ran into each other at the coffee shop and shared a table. Since then we've become friends."

The photographer directed them to all look at her and Kacie struggled to relax her face and give a genuine smile.

"You're friends now. Really?" Sam asked, as the photographer added more family members to the group.

"We go for runs together. We hang out."

"You *never* just hang out," Sam said accusingly. "Is that who you were really talking to when we went to Atlanta?"

Kacie nodded.

Sam leaned closer and whispered in her ear. "Are you friends who have sex?"

"Will you knock it off?" Kacie glared at her sister. "It's nothing serious. He knows I'm moving to Durham next month. We're just having fun."

She didn't think it was possible, but Sam's eyes nearly bugged out of her head. "Oh. My. God. Are you kidding me?"

"Isn't that what you wanted me to do?" Kacie answered in a harsh whisper of her own. "'Let your hair down, Kacie. Have a fling, Kacie.' Hell, you're the one who sent him after me!"

"Hey, sweetheart?" They both turned to look at Bryce. "The photographer is wanting the two of you to quit arguing and smile for the camera."

They both apologized profusely, then gave their best smiles as the photographer took his final shots. Finally, they were dismissed and Kacie headed toward the back of the church, prepared to fight her way through a sea of dwarfs. But Michael saved her the trouble, politely excusing himself and meeting her halfway down the aisle.

Kacie looked past him to the crowd of women now watching their every move. "Looks like my fellow bridesmaids kept you company. Were you having fun?"

"Not really." He stepped into her line of sight, forcing her to look up at him instead. And when their eyes met, he flashed her that charming grin, the one that allowed him to get away with almost anything. "Can I give you a ride to the reception?"

She had to hand it to him—the man was smooth.

"I just need to grab our things from the bridal room first."

He offered to go get the car and meet her by the side entrance, and she headed downstairs, where she exchanged her heels for a pretty pair of sandals. There was no way she'd make it through the reception wearing sti-lettos. She stepped out the side entrance just as Michael pulled into a spot along the sidewalk. Ever the gentleman he popped the trunk and quickly hopped out, taking her things and stowing them away.

"You shrunk," he said while opening the passenger door for her.

Kacie lifted the hem of her dress and revealed her new shoes. "Traded heels for comfort."

"Smart cookie," he said with a wink.

Once she and her dress were safely tucked inside, he closed the door and circled around to the driver's side. Instead of shifting the car into Drive, he leaned on the center console, staring at her with those dark blue eyes. "Would it be okay if I mess up your lipstick now?"

Kacie laughed. "Absolutely."

He reached for her, cradling her cheek in his hand as he pressed a tender kiss to her lips, followed by another and another. There was no rushing him as he teased her with the gentle kisses, then coaxed her lips open and savored her with his tongue. It was the sort of kissing that made her heart race, made her feel dizzy, and left her wanting more.

But the spell was broken when a police car sped past, siren blaring.

Michael watched to see where it went, and when he finally looked back at her, she noticed the smudge of lip-stick on his face. Using her thumb, she carefully swiped away the little bit of pink.

"Is it not my shade?" he asked, his eyes full of amusement.

"Not really."

She couldn't help but smile as she continued touching him, tracing the edge of his lip and caressing his smoothly shaved chin.

"I have to say I've really missed you these past couple of days."

From the way he looked at her, she knew he was telling the truth. He wasn't being funny, wasn't implying that he'd missed their sexapades.

And suddenly she realized she felt the same way.

"I've missed you, too."

He smiled and pressed one more kiss to her lips.

"Ready?" he asked while buckling his seat belt.

"As you are," she replied.

But as he pulled away from the curb and they headed across town, she wondered if she really was ready—ready to either admit her feelings for him and effectively changing their relationship or ready to let him go for good.

Chapter Seventeen

ONCE THE DINNER was served, the wedding cake sliced, and the first dance for the newlyweds complete, the guests filled the dance floor. But Kacie headed across the ballroom to the French doors that led outside instead, in the hopes of claiming a spot in the gazebo near the water's edge and stealing a moment with Michael, who was at the bar getting them drinks.

"Kacie."

She jumped, then winced upon hearing the familiar voice behind her. Her heart began to race as she turned around, hoping all the while that her mind was playing tricks on her.

Unfortunately, it was not.

Her ex had never been one for subtlety, so it shouldn't have surprised her that he'd shown up here, uninvited, wearing his dress blues, putting all his ribbons and medals on full display.

Mike extended his hand to her. "May I have this dance?"

"I'd rather not." Kacie took a step back, not going as far as placing her hands safely out of reach behind her back, although she really wanted to. "What are you doing here?"

"Why don't we talk? Outside, perhaps?" He gestured to the French doors that led to the place where she was supposed to be meeting another Michael. A better Michael.

Not wanting to make a scene, she politely nodded and led the way. In her mind, the sooner she talked to him, the sooner he'd leave. But irritation surged through her when he placed his hand low on her back and guided her through the door. Marking his territory, laying claim to her.

The door had barely closed behind them when she stopped in her tracks on the patio.

"Why don't we talk over there?" He gestured to the gazebo at the water's edge. "It's more private."

Whatever he was selling, she wasn't buying and she refused to go any farther than the lawn. "What are you doing here, Mike?"

Surprisingly he didn't argue; instead, he just tucked his hands in his pockets. "I've been doing a lot of thinking these past few weeks, ever since that reminder you put in my phone about Sam's wedding showed up on my calendar."

Great. Her own organizational skills had come back to bite her in the butt.

"I think we should reconsider our separation." He pulled his right hand from his pocket and held it out to her, a small black velvet box in his palm.

Kacie shook her head in utter disbelief. "What? *Why?* Why on Earth would you want to get back together?"

"It's simple, really. We worked well together. My friends think you're beautiful, my superiors like you."

Her instincts told her there had to be another reason for this sudden change of heart. "What else?"

"You know me so well," he said with a sheepish grin. "It might have been suggested to me that being married—being seen as a family man—would help with my career advancement."

Kacie had dreamed of Mike's proposal for years. Of him wearing his dress blues and asking her to marry him while she stood in front of him in a pretty dress and music played in the background. And not once in all her imaginings had the proposal ever included job talk.

"Now, I'm not suggesting we get married right away," he said while easing the lid open, revealing the solitaire diamond ring nestled inside. "I thought a long engagement would probably be better. That way you have time to move, find a new job, and settle in before you start making our wedding plans."

And here these past few weeks she thought Michael was arrogant. He couldn't possibly hold a candle to her ex.

He took hold of her left hand. "So . . . what do you think?"

Kacie fought the urge to laugh and cry all at the same time. "You know what, Mike? I think I'll pass," she eased her hand from his grip. There was no need to point out that not once had he mentioned loving her. Missing her. Needing her.

His brow wrinkled. "I thought this is what you wanted?"

"It is." She swallowed around the lump in her throat. "But not with you. Not anymore."

"You need to be sure, Kacie." He gave the box a little shake. "Think long and hard because I won't ask twice."

He truly expected her to change her mind. And it as possible that six months ago, she would've said yes the moment he pulled the box from his pocket.

But thankfully, she was no longer that woman.

"I won't change my mind."

The hinged box snapped shut and Mike stared at her in disbelief. "Your loss," he said, before he finally turned and walked away.

Thankfully, he decided to follow the path along the perimeter of the building instead of cutting back through the ballroom. Kacie breathed a sigh of relief as she made her way to the gazebo where she and Michael had planned to meet. She stared out across the water and at the historic riverfront on the other side, hardly believing what had just happened. Why had she wasted so much time with a man who always put his career before her? Who never really worried about her or cared for her?

And how could she have thought Michael was anything like him when they first met?

They were nothing alike. Not even close. And tonight only proved it.

AFTER A LENGTHY wait at the open bar, Michael found Kacie standing in the gazebo near the water's edge, just where she'd said she would be. As she looked out over the river, the warm summer breeze played with the soft fabric of her dress and the loose tendrils of hair at her nape.

"I hope you're in the mood for a Chatham Artillery Punch."

Happy to see a smile on her face, Michael handed her the signature drink, a potent combination of wine, rum, tea, and champagne garnished with an orange wedge and maraschino cherry.

"Why aren't you drinking one of these? Are you trying to get me drunk so you can take advantage?"

At least she wasn't so upset she couldn't make a joke.

"No. I just figured maybe you could use a strong drink." He flashed her a smile, then took a long pull from his longneck.

Kacie didn't smile back, having caught the full meaning of his words. "You saw Mike, didn't you?"

Michael nodded and leaned heavily against the gazebo's waist-high railing, his beer dangling from one hand as he watched one of those riverboat cruises drift by. "I was just about to step out onto the back deck when I saw him take hold of your hand. I decided to give you some privacy."

What he'd really feared in that moment was that she'd accept her ex if he asked her to take him back. Not knowing the particulars of their breakup, not knowing if she had lingering feelings for him, he honestly hadn't known how she'd react.

"Why do men have to do crap like that?" she said, shaking her head.

"Crap like what?"

"Like what he did. Showing up here in his dress uniform." Kacie mimicked his stance and stared down into her glass. "I'm sure everyone noticed him in that ballroom and that's exactly what he wanted—to be the center of attention. He knows my phone number. He knows where I work, where I live. He could've made that gesture any time, any place, and yet he chose to do it tonight."

She took a drink of her punch, then kept on drinking, finishing nearly half the glass before she stopped to catch her breath.

"I'm sorry, sunshine." Using his finger, Michael turned her chin to face him. "Maybe he thought you wanted a grand gesture like that. There's plenty of women who probably would."

"I don't doubt there are women who would like that.

If anything, his little stunt just proved how big a bullet I dodged." As she looked at him the little crease between her brows appeared. "But I can't believe you saw him and didn't do anything. Would it have killed you to kick his ass? At least threaten a little bodily harm?"

Michael chuckled. "I was kinda hoping you'd do it. Because that would've been hot."

Kacie shoved at his shoulder and laughed. "Your sexual turn-ons will never cease to amaze me."

"I know. Me either," he said, wrapping his arm around her shoulders and tucking her close to his side.

"You know, we've never talked about him." His fingers skimmed the length of her arm, from shoulder to wrist and back again. "How long were you with this guy I have the unfortunate distinction of sharing a name with?"

"Do you really want to do this? Do you want to talk about my ex?"

"Sure. Why not?" He took a fortifying sip of his beer. "Let's start small. How long were you together?"

She leaned heavily against him, resting her head on his chest as they watched the sun slowly sinking over the horizon.

"Seven years." She sighed.

Thank God she couldn't see his expression because . . . wow. There would be no way for him to hide his surprise. After all, his longest relationship had been almost two years nearly a decade ago, and even that relationship was on life support months before he ended it. "The only people I know who've been together that long are married."

"Exactly."

Normally, he didn't care about a woman's past, but he was curious about hers since this guy had made his own pursuit of Kacie more difficult.

"I know he's a marine. What does he do?"

"He's a fighter pilot."

And the surprises just kept coming. He took another drink of his beer, a longer, much needed drink. One that damn near polished off the bottle in his hand.

In his mind, he'd made her ex out to be just another jarhead, a grunt. Maybe someone who worked in the motor pool and spent his day performing routine vehicle maintenance for the brass. He sure as hell didn't think he'd be an officer, too. No wonder she didn't want to have anything to do with him in the beginning.

"How did you two meet?"

"My roommate in grad school invited me to her parents' condo for spring break. He was in flight school in Pensacola." Kacie took a sip of her punch. "I don't think I want to tell the rest of this story because it's not one of my finer moments."

"Why? Did you give him an ultimatum about getting married?"

He was half joking when he suggested it, but when she pulled away from his embrace he knew he'd hit the nail on the head.

"I did." Kacie shrugged her shoulders, not bothering

to sugarcoat it. "My sister and Bryce had dated all of four months before he proposed and I got jealous. Here I'd spent seven years of my life in a relationship with this guy and not once had he mentioned any kind of future together. But I was the idiot, don't you see? We never even lived in the same town. It was always long distance. There were times we were closer than others, but the most we ever saw each other was when I visited him on the weekends he wasn't deployed. The exceptions were those times he would come stay with me for a week or so while on leave, or we went on vacations with his friends."

She pushed the loose strands of hair back from her face and swiped the skin beneath her eyes with her fingertips. She wasn't on the verge of tears, just visibly frustrated. If there was one thing he'd learned about her over the past seven weeks, she was harder on herself than anyone.

Something he easily recognized, since it was a trait they had in common.

"It wasn't wrong of you to have expectations, Kacie. If anything, this guy was a dick for stringing you along like he did for all those years."

She didn't say anything in return. Just pursed her lips and gave a slight shake of her head.

"Sunshine, you gave him your heart." Again, he tipped her chin up so he could see her eyes. "For him to waste that or take it for granted, it makes him the fool, not you. Got it?"

A hint of smile appeared as she gave a half-hearted nod.

It wasn't much, but it was a start. He took her by the hand and tugged her out of the gazebo.

"Where are we going?" she asked.

"Back to the ballroom, of course," he said with a smile. "I was promised a chicken dance—I intend to claim it."

KACIE SLID THE key card into the lock and shoved open the hotel room reserved for the newlyweds. She leaned heavily against the door, holding it open for her sister until Sam's lengthy train made it completely through. As the door fell shut, her sister toppled onto the bed.

"Oh, my God, I'm exhausted," Sam said, kicking off her heels and giving her feet a momentary reprieve.

"Well, you better find your second wind seeing as you've got at least another two or three hours to go."

A groan rose from the pillows as Sam rolled over to her back. "You don't think Bryce will want to have sex tonight, do you?"

Kacie chuckled. "Um . . . I would say that's highly likely."

Her sister sat up and placed a hand to her forehead, the diamonds on her finger shooting sparks around the room. "I don't know that I'll be able to."

"Have you eaten?"

"I had a bite of cake."

"And how much champagne?"

"Not much."

Kacie narrowed her eyes. "What about punch?"

Sam giggled. "Lots."

Kacie shook her head and went straight to the mini-fridge. "I can't believe he was right," she muttered, pulling out two sandwiches and bottled waters. "Ham and swiss or roast beef and cheddar?"

Sam's eyes widened. "Gimme, gimme, gimme. I can't believe you brought food," she said while grabbing indiscriminately for a sandwich. "Where did these come from?"

"Michael bought them. Called them emergency rations. When we arrived, I got your room key from Bryce and stashed them up here."

"Okay. I take it back. You made the right call bringing him to my wedding," Sam said around a mouthful of lunch meat. "I thought he was like those rent-a-dates in the movies, but really, the man is a lifesaver."

Kacie shook her head as she carefully peeled back the cellophane and tossed the tiny packets of mustard and mayonnaise wrapped inside on the dresser. When they stopped at the convenience store en route to the reception and Michael came out with provisions, she'd thought he was nuts. After all, she attended the catering tastings for this shindig and knew just how much food was downstairs. But between the toasts and the first dances and all the relatives wanting to stop and chat and take pictures, she'd somehow missed out on food, just as her sister had. Not even a bite of cake.

As she savored the sandwich, Kacie envisioned the smug look of satisfaction that Michael would give her when he found out he was right. She could always lie and tell him they didn't eat the sandwiches—but she wasn't a very good liar. And he knew it.

"I swear to God, Kacie," Sam said, cracking open her bottled water. "If I weren't married already and he weren't so old, I'd think about marrying that guy myself."

"He's not old," Kacie said before taking another bite of her own sandwich.

Sam snickered. "For you he's not."

And just like that she lost her appetite.

She wrapped the cellophane around her partially eaten sandwich and tossed it back in the minifridge before heading into the bathroom to wash her hands. By the time she returned, Sam had finished the sandwich and was polishing off her bottle of water, so Kacie grabbed her sister's second dress from the closet.

"We need to hurry up. Bryce is going to think he's got a runaway bride on his hands."

Sam rose to her feet, a little wobbly yet, but managed to get herself and her voluminous skirt turned around. One tiny satin-covered button at a time, Kacie freed her sister from her dress, lowering it to the ground so Sam could step out of it.

As she quietly went about stuffing it into its massive garment bag, Sam picked up the cocktail gown she would wear for the remainder of the reception.

"What's the matter?" Sam asked, her tone laced with concern.

"Nothing."

Sam gave a derisive snort. "That's a lie. You're scowling."

Not realizing she was doing so, Kacie made a conscious effort to relax her face.

"I was just teasing you about Michael," Sam said. "If a long-term relationship isn't what you two are about, that's fine. Maybe it's a good thing. I'm glad you've let your hair down a bit. Not every man you have sex with has to be regarded as a potential husband."

Careful to not catch any of the delicate fabric within the teeth, Kacie zipped the bag. "Well, there's definitely no confusion in that regard. Michael and I are only . . ." She wanted to say screwing around. Having a fling. But she couldn't get the words out. "When I leave for Durham, that will be the end of it. If not sooner."

Sam studied her. "It's okay to change your mind, Kacc. The program is only a year long. There's nothing that says you and Michael can't do the long-distance thing for a while. Then, when you're done, you can come back here."

"No," Kacie said emphatically. "I'm not going to make any more career decisions to accommodate a man. Especially not one who plans on being career military. Do you want me to zip you up or not?"

Sam turned her back and Kacie took hold of the small tab and yanked upward. Considering the fabric and the dress, she should've taken more care, but at this point she just really wanted out of the room.

"When I suggested a fling, I'd hoped it'd teach you to

not be so damn rigid." Sam grabbed a small kit off the dresser to touch up her makeup and eyed Kacie with suspicion via her reflection in the mirror. "You don't have to be so stubborn all the time. He could decide to leave the military. You never know."

That, in her opinion, was a pipe dream.

Men of Michael's rank didn't just choose to leave the military. They might be medically retired. They might be forced to resign due to conduct unbecoming. But they didn't just wake up one morning and say, "You know what? I'm tired of being in the military. I think I'll quit."

Sam slicked on a fresh layer of lipstick and pressed her lips together. "I meant to ask you, did you happen to see a guy in uniform?" she asked while reaching for a tissue to blot the excess. "Bryce wondered if it was someone from our side of the family since the guy talked to you, but I was in the bathroom and never saw who it was."

Kacie took a seat on the end of the bed. "It was Mike. Davis."

"Oh, shit." Sam's eyes went wide with surprise. "I assumed it was someone who accidentally wandered into the wrong reception." Sam sat down on the bed next to her. "How on earth did he know where to show up? I swear I didn't send him an invitation. The first thing I did after you told me you'd broken up was delete him from the invitation list."

"Google calendar. I put it in his phone as soon as you

guys set the date, time, and place. That was before we broke up."

"Oh, crap. Kace, I'm so, so sorry." Sam took Kacie's hand in both of hers. "But that doesn't explain why he'd just show up here. Was he wanting you to take him back?"

Kacie could only shake her head in response as the anger, frustration, and exhaustion from the day caught up with her. Unshed tears burned her eyes and clogged her throat. "More than that. He had a ring. Even suggested a long engagement so I'd have time to move and find a job. I passed on his offer."

After hearing herself recount the encounter, the dam broke and Kacie covered her face and began to cry in earnest. Seven years she'd wasted on a man who had never even loved her.

Sam slipped an arm over her shoulders, holding her as best she could. "If you turned him down, why are you so upset?"

"I don't honestly know."

Except deep down inside she did know. She still wanted everything she had once dreamed of having; she wanted to know love and be loved. She wanted to be a wife and a mother and have a career.

The only problem was that now she wanted that future with a man she already knew she had no future with.

Chapter Eighteen

MICHAEL SIPPED HIS drink as he stood at the bar along with the groom and his friends. They were all nice guys, especially Bryce, but listening to them talk about their jobs, their wives, or girlfriends made him feel uneasy. These were men who were five to ten years younger than himself and yet many of them already had a family and a future in the works.

And what did he have?

Yeah, they thought his job was cool, but what they didn't realize was how much he'd sacrificed to have it. Fifteen years ago he'd assumed he'd be married, maybe even have a kid or two by now. But somewhere along the way, things changed without him ever really noticing.

Or maybe time had just gotten away from him.

It was then he noticed Kacie's father approaching the bar. From their brief conversation at the church it was easy to tell he was quite protective of his daughters. And while her mother was easily charmed, her father, not so much. Mr. Morgan wasn't big in stature, but he was still one of the most intimidating people Michael had ever met. And considering some of the men he worked with over the years, that was saying something.

"Looks like someone's about to have his intake interview," Bryce said with a slap to the back. "Best of luck, man."

As Mr. Morgan stepped up to the bar and ordered a scotch and water from the bartender, Bryce and his buddies quickly scattered. Michael, however, was not going to tuck tail and run. If Kacie's dad wanted to chat, they'd chat.

"Michael, is it?" Mr. Morgan gave him the side-eye as he waited. "I apologize. I'm not the best with names."

"Yes, sir. Michael MacGregor."

"I'm sorry we didn't get much of a chance to talk earlier, but I thought now might be a good time." Her father rested his hands on the counter and carefully watched the bartender mix his drink, even instructing him to dump the ice and go easy on the water. "So my daughter tells me you're in the military. She also told me you two met at Samantha's bachelorette party?"

"Kacie told you that?"

"No. Samantha did." Her father took a cautious sip of his drink, all the while glaring at him over the rim of the glass. "Kathryn, on the other hand, hasn't said a single word about you. Aside from when she introduced you at the church."

It took a moment for Michael's brain to catch up with what the man was saying. His sunshine, Kacie, was a Kathryn? At that point he could've been knocked over with a feather.

This time her father took more than a sip of his scotch.

"What is it you do in the military, Mr. MacGregor? You're not a pilot like the last one, are you?" The tone of her father's voice was a low, slow rumble that reminded him of an old cowboy.

"No, sir. I'm the battalion surgeon for the 75th."

"You're a doctor, then?" His tone lightened.

"Yes, sir."

From that moment forward her father appeared far more relaxed and eased off the intimidation factor. Instead, they spent the next fifteen minutes or so chatting about a variety things—golf, fishing, you name it. Then their conversation turned to Kacie, how her name was actually Kathryn Claire. They spoke of her career plans, her upcoming fellowship and relocation to Durham. It wasn't long before Michael learned just how much Mr. Morgan disliked Kacie's ex, how he thought the guy lied to and manipulated Kacie for years in the hopes that Mr. Morgan would hook him up with a posh job as a test pilot where he worked.

From across the ballroom Bryce let out a loud whistle and Michael, along with everyone else, turned to see what the commotion was all about. Sam had returned to the ballroom wearing a dress far shorter and far more revealing than her wedding gown. While she was beautiful in her own right, in his mind she would never compare to her sister. Then, right on cue, Kacie appeared from the hallway. She scanned the room, presumably looking for him, and her eyes widened the moment she spotted him standing with her father.

She made a beeline for them. "Are you being nice, Daddy?"

"Of course, Kacie-cakes," he said before placing a kiss to her cheek.

Michael could hardly believe what he was seeing. In an instant, the cold, hard intimidator had been replaced by an old softy.

"It's about time you girls made it back. I was about to send out a search party." Mr. Morgan turned to Michael and extended his hand. "It was very nice talking with you. I have to go report back to my wife now." He smacked Michael's shoulder. "Take my girl for a spin on the dance floor and enjoy the rest of your evening."

"Thank you, sir. Same to you."

Michael placed his half-full beer on the bar top and offered her his hand. "You heard your dad, Kacie-cakes. I'm supposed to show you a good time."

"Do not call me that." She crossed her arms, refusing his hand.

"Okay, then. How about Kathryn Claire?"

Kacie shook her head in disbelief. "Oh, my God. How long were you two talking before I showed up?"

Still holding out his hand, he wiggled his fingers.

"Come on, sunshine. It sounds like they're playing our song."

Her laughter was light and sweet as he took her hand and towed her out onto the parquet dance floor.

"We don't have a song," she said as he twirled her to face him.

"Then this can be our song."

Kacie tilted her head, listening closely to the wedding band. As she focused intently on the lyrics being sung, he found himself enchanted by the loose strand of hair curling along the side of her neck. "*This* can't be our song."

With the hand at her waist, he pulled her closer so there was no space between them, and stared down into her face. "And why not?"

Her head fell back as she smiled up at him. "Because it's Taylor Swift."

"You have a problem with T-Swizzle?"

She laughed out loud then. "I don't even want to know how you know she's called that. But yeah, seeing as I'm closer to thirty-two than twenty-two it feels a little young for me."

"Fair enough." He sent her into a quick spin, only narrowly avoiding a couple of her fellow dwarfs who were . . . well, to be honest he wasn't sure what they were doing. It didn't look like dancing. It was more along the lines of them all struggling to hold each other up.

As the band segued into a slow song, Kacie wrapped her arms around his neck, her fingertips stroking his nape. She looked up at him with an inquisitive grin on her face.

"What is running through that head of yours?" he asked.

"I'm just curious."

"Are you now?" He waggled his brows suggestively at her. "I like it when you're curious."

Kacie punched his shoulder.

"And rough," he added. "I like that, too."

She pretended to be offended, but couldn't keep a straight face as she tried to get away. He tugged her back into his arms. "What is it you want to know?"

"I want to know what you and my dad were talking about."

"The standard stuff. What I do for a living. Where I'm from. What my intentions are." He took hold of her hand and held it against his chest. "One thing is for certain, he does not like your ex. Had more than a few choice words about him. And then he asked why I didn't wear my uniform to the wedding."

Her eyes widened. "What did you say?"

"I told him: one, because I was off duty, and two, it's not a military event. But if he wanted I could rush home and change, especially if there was some kind of parade following the reception."

"What did he do?"

"He laughed and smacked me in the arm!"

She smiled while shaking her head in disbelief.

"Now I know where you get it."

"It's a bad habit. I admit it." Kacie tossed her arms around his neck. "But that definitely means he likes you."

And for that, he was very glad.

ALTHOUGH SHE DIDN'T really want to be there, Kacie stood with the other single ladies as they awaited the tossing of the bouquet. While she didn't make any move for the small bundle of roses as it sailed over her head, she did have to raise her hands in order to protect herself; the drunken bridesmaids went crazy, turning the bouquet toss into a death match, scrambling to get it. By the time the small nosegay was held high in the air by one of her sister's friends, it was a shadow of its former self with a carnage of white petals scattered all around the floor.

Kacie quickly edged away to where Michael was standing.

"That looked scary," he said.

"You have no idea."

As the single men reluctantly gathered for the garter slingshot, Michael made no move to join them. Unfortunately for him, the garter still dropped right at his feet. And unlike the women, no man made a play for it.

Kacie laughed as Michael stared down at the lacy blue elastic draped across the toe of his shoe, waiting a significant amount of time before he finally picked it up. "You looked like you could hardly contain your excitement. I didn't realize you were in such a rush to get married?"

Michael twirled it around his index finger. "Me neither. But now that I have it . . ."

He waggled his brows at her and a silly thrill of excitement rushed through her.

But the thrill dissipated the moment the aforementioned drunken bridesmaids forced him to the middle of the dance floor where the one that wrestled the bouquet into her grasp sat on a banquet chair, eagerly awaiting him.

The brunette crooked her finger, then lifted the hem of her dress high upon her thigh.

The crowd gathered in a large circle around them and of course the groomsmen were all clustered together, laughing to the point of tears. Michael looked back at her with an expression that undoubtedly meant he did not want to do this.

Sam sidled up next to her. "You were supposed to catch the bouquet, idiot."

"Was this all a setup?"

"Mmm-hmm. And I didn't get a chance to tell Bryce to abort mission before he sent it flying." Sam shook her head. "There is no good that will come of this. Did you know Tara hit on him that night on the bar? And she doesn't have an ounce of subtlety. There's no telling what she'll do."

"Why is someone like that your bridesmaid?"

"Because she's my friend?" Sam said as if it were no big deal.

Kacie's stomach turned a bit as Michael knelt at the woman's feet and the bridesmaid immediately lifted her foot and placed it on his shoulder.

Sam laughed. "See what I mean?"

Howls of laughter went up all around her as Michael took hold of her foot and carefully lowered it to the ground. Then he made quick work of slipping the garter on, placing it just below her knee. As he rose to his feet, about to make his getaway, the girl reached out and grabbed his tie.

"It's supposed to be higher up," the bridesmaid said, loud enough for everyone to hear. "You need to fix it."

Michael smiled politely. "Well, you should probably just put it wherever it feels comfortable."

"I was kinda hoping you'd do that." She tugged again on his tie, trying to bring him closer.

"Sorry about that, but you'll have to handle it yourself."

After prying his tie from the bridesmaid's grip, he made a hasty escape, taking hold of Kacie and towing her out of the ballroom. With her free hand, she grabbed as much of her skirt as she could so she wouldn't trip in the layers of fabric as they ran across the back lawn. The farther they went, the more they laughed, and the lower the bodice of her strapless dress got. By the time they found a secluded outdoor sofa a safe distance away, she was on the verge of indecent exposure.

Michael collapsed into the cushions, still laughing as

Kacie stood in front of him, blatantly tugging the top of her dress back up where it belonged.

"Pervert." Kacie grinned.

"Yes," he said, and followed the pronouncement with a wink and a charming smile.

He stretched out nearly the length of the sofa, so she settled between his legs, reclining against his chest, her head resting on his shoulder. Once their laughter subsided, they both stared up at the starry night sky and released a contented sigh.

"So . . ." she began. "As dangerous as the bouquet toss was, it appeared you had it far worse in the end."

"I was worried I'd have to put my SERE training to use to get away from her," he said with a chuckle.

"I'm sorry. I had no idea they'd act that way." She turned so she could see his face. "But I really appreciate you coming, especially since you didn't know anyone besides me."

He pulled her back against him and wrapped her up in his arms. "Don't worry about that. I had fun. And the food was amazing."

"Was it?"

He craned his neck so he could to see her face. "You didn't eat?"

"Didn't get the chance."

Michael settled back against the corner of the sofa. "Well, I hate to tell you, but you really missed out."

"I did have a few bites of the ham and Swiss you bought. Sam ate a whole sandwich." His laugh was a low rumble in her ear. "As much as I hate to admit you were right, it was a damn good thing you made me take them up to her room. She'd likely be passed out cold by now if it weren't for that convenience store roast beef and cheddar."

"I'm glad to be of assistance."

She turned to look at him again. "If anyone owes you, it's Bryce."

They both snickered a bit before the silence returned.

As far as she was concerned, their time together had passed way too quickly. And even though she wasn't ready for the night to be over, for this thing, this arrangement between them, to be over, the fact remained she would still be leaving in a month.

Her practical side said to go ahead and put an end to it tonight, just as planned. Treat it like the proverbial Band-Aid and rip it right off. But her other, less practical, side told her to soak up every possible minute she could and just enjoy the time they had. Because in a month, she would be far away from family, from friends, from the only job she'd ever known, and she'd need these memories to keep her warm at night.

A cool breeze kicked up off the water sending a shiver right through her. Immediately, Michael tightened his arms around her and lowered his mouth to her ear. "So I guess this is it, huh?"

She shifted in his embrace, turning just enough so she could see his face. "What do you mean?"

"The dress fit, the wedding's done," he said matter-of-factly. "We've reached the end of our agreement. This is where we go our separate ways."

Even though she was the one who made the rules in the beginning, set the strict guidelines and established the deadline for this fling, she wasn't ready to say goodbye now that the time had arrived. Not just yet. "I guess once you agreed to be my date, I always assumed we'd at least have tonight."

The corners of his eyes crinkled. "That's really good to hear."

With those words the giant knot in her stomach eased and she breathed a sigh of relief having delayed the inevitable. But she promised herself that tomorrow she would be ready to let him go.

Immediately, she rose to her feet. "Give me a few minutes to say goodbye to everyone and we can get out of here."

"Actually . . . I booked a room." A slow smile spread across his face. "Just in case, you know, we had too much to drink and didn't want to drive home."

"In that case," she said, holding out a hand to him, "what are we waiting for?"

After retrieving her things from Sam's room and saying goodnight to her parents, Kacie headed up to their room on the twelfth floor while Michael grabbed his overnight bag from his car. Kacie placed the key card on the dresser and made her way to the balcony, easing back the curtains and opening the sliding door. From this height, she could easily see the tourists walking along River Street and the hotel pool down below, along with the outdoor sofa where she and Michael had sat just moments before.

She was so caught up in the scenery that she didn't hear him come in until he called her name.

"How's the view?" He asked as she stepped back into the room.

There was something about the way he looked at her while he removed his tie. Something that made the butterflies take flight in her stomach.

"Amazing. You should really take a look."

As he unbuttoned his cuffs, he started toward the balcony, only to be stopped by a knock on the door. He smiled at her. "That must be room service."

"You ordered food?" As if the beautiful room for the night wasn't enough.

"Just a snack, really. You said you hadn't eaten much."

He opened the door and the waiter made his way inside, placing a tray on the table.

"Wine, beer, or water?" Michael asked as Kacie lifted the first cover, revealing a bowl of fresh strawberries. They were nice, but not something she was really craving after weeks of dieting. "Water, please," she answered, investigating the second dish, which turned out to be a delicious hot pile of French fries. "I can't believe you did this." Kacie's stomach growled as she snatched a long crinkle-cut strand from the plate. "I honestly didn't realize I was starving until just this moment."

Michael handed her an opened bottle of water. "If you like that, wait until you see what this is." With dramatic flair, Michael lifted the third cover, revealing a huge slice of chocolate cake with a scoop of vanilla ice cream on the side.

Kacie gasped in surprise. Actually gasped. "I've never seen anything so beautiful."

He laughed, clearly amused by how excited she was.

"Seriously, I think you're underestimating how truly happy I am at this very moment."

He folded his arms across his chest and gave a half smile, downplaying his gesture. "I know how rough the last month and a half has been for you since you gave up chocolate. Figured now was the right time to welcome it back into your life."

She rose up from her chair and leaned across the table so she could press a kiss to his lips. "You, sir . . . are going to get *so* lucky."

Chapter Nineteen

NEVER COULD MICHAEL have imagined just how entertaining it could be to watch a woman eat.

Still wearing her pale blue gown, Kacie sat cross-legged in the chair, head tipped back as she dangled a long French fry above her mouth before devouring it. Then, as she reached for the next fry, she smiled at him in a way that almost challenged him to say something sarcastic about her way of eating. But knowing how long she'd deprived herself of all her favorites, he loved watching the pure enjoyment the food brought to her face even more.

What he wouldn't give to see her tear into a peach fritter.

If he had his way, he'd see it happen. He'd buy her not only one fritter, but an entire store full just to watch her eat them. And it would be only the beginning of him spoiling her.

After the near-miss disaster when her ex showed up at the reception, he'd decided to take his little brother's advice to heart. No more just letting this arrangement he'd agreed to months ago simply play out between them. No more dancing around his feelings. Instead, he would somehow convince her they deserved a shot at something far more long-term. And then he would spend the next month showing her just how perfect they were together.

Once finished with the fries, she moved to his side of the table, taking a seat in his lap, which brought her a bit closer to the dessert plate. "You don't mind if I sit here, do you?" she asked with a sly grin on her face while simultaneously scooping a large bite of cake and a bit of ice cream.

He smiled back at her. "Not bothered in the slightest."

Due to her self-professed love for all things chocolate, he was surprised when she offered him the first spoonful. And not only did she offer one bite, but another, then another, alternating bites between the two of them, stopping occasionally to kiss away a touch of cream on his lips or use her tongue to swipe away a rogue crumb at the corner of his mouth.

Once the cake and ice cream were completely gone, she dropped the spoon into the empty dessert bowl. He watched and waited to see if she would move on to the strawberries. Instead, she reclined against his chest.

Michael wrapped his arms around her. "Long day, huh?" he whispered into her hair.

She burrowed farther into his embrace, tucking her head beneath his chin. "Mmm-hmm."

With her belly full and long denied cravings sated, she completely relaxed against him, her body weighing heavy against his. Several minutes passed and she was so still for that time he was certain she'd fallen asleep. But he made no move to wake her or carry her to the bed. Instead, he rested his head against hers and listened to the soft huffs of her breath as the low hum of the air-conditioning unit played accompaniment.

For most of his life he'd kept people at arm's length unless they were family. Not that he'd figured such a thing out on his own; it was more that the women he'd dated over the years always told him so. And for the past year, ever since he'd nearly lost his brother, he'd walled himself off even more. Because if he dared let someone in, then they were his to care for, his responsibility. And he wasn't sure he could bear the additional weight.

Maybe the tequila he drank that first night exposed a tiny gap in his own fortress. Or maybe he'd grown tired of keeping his defenses up. Either way, Kacie managed to find a way inside and before he knew it, she'd burrowed herself deep beneath his skin and settled somewhere in the vicinity of his heart.

Sometime later she stirred and Michael opened his eyes to see her looking back at him.

"Why don't we call it a night?" Kacie skimmed her hand down his cheek and along the underside of his jaw.

He captured her wrist and pressed a kiss to her palm before holding it to his face. "Sounds like a good idea."

A tired sigh escaped her mouth as she rose to her feet and walked over to the dresser. She stood in front of the mirror, lifting her hands to her hair as she searched for the bobby pins that held it all in place.

Having followed her across the room, he met Kacie's gaze in the mirror. "Let me do that," he whispered.

She lowered her hands and watched as one by one he carefully pulled the pins free, dropping them haphazardly on the dresser. He took his time, enchanted by the way each curl lengthened and brushed her shoulders. Once he found all the pins, he raked his fingers through her long strands, starting at the root and combing to the ends. Her eyes drifted shut and she sighed in pleasure at his touch.

Michael pushed the wild blond curls to one side and placed a kiss on the curve of her shoulder as he wrapped her up in his arms, pressing his front to her back. Her head fell back and rested against his shoulder, allowing him unfettered access. With his mouth he followed the faint trail of freckles across the top of her shoulder. Then he traced the tendons in her neck with the tip of his nose, stopping only when he reached the tender spot beneath her ear. During the past weeks he'd discovered that her scent, blended with the cocoa butter lotion she wore, was always strongest in this one particular spot. And so he lingered there, breathing deep, kissing and tasting her skin as his hands glided over the silky fabric of her dress, teasing her breasts and belly.

"Michael."

His gaze met her reflection. "Yes?"

"Get me out of this dress," she softly ordered. Then added, "Please," with a soft smile.

Never one to ignore that type of order, Michael nodded. "Yes, ma'am."

Mindful of the delicate fabric, he eased the tiny zipper down and held his breath as the dress slowly parted. With the back of his finger he skimmed the length of her spine, following the way of her dress as it slipped from her body. He expected to encounter the edge of her thong, panties, something. Only he never did. Instead, her dress now pooled at her feet and she stood before him wearing absolutely nothing.

"You've been naked beneath this dress the entire day and didn't say a damn thing?" Just when he thought this woman couldn't make him any harder, she went and did something like this. In an instant nearly every ounce of blood pulsing through his veins went rushing straight to his groin.

Her reflection smiled back at him. "It didn't matter if it was a thong or a G-string, everything I tried made lines that showed through the dress. So I went commando." She shrugged.

"It's a damn lucky thing I didn't know this at the church, otherwise . . ." His words were reduced to little more than a growl.

She laughed softly and turned to face him, her hands immediately going to the buttons on his shirt. "Once again, you're completely dressed and I'm naked."

Michael smiled down at her. "I'll never see that as a problem."

He swept his hands from her shoulders to her breasts, taking one in each hand to plump and caress. He loved the feel of her soft skin beneath his palms, liked teasing her nipples to hardened points with his fingers. Meanwhile she continued working on his shirt, releasing each button from its restraint before undoing his belt and unbuttoning his pants. After pushing the shirt from his shoulders and down his arms she did something that took him by surprise. Something she'd never done before in all their times together—Kacie leaned forward and pressed a kiss to his heart. Not his sternum. Not high on his chest near his collarbone, but the exact place where it pounded beneath her lips.

He held his breath as she lingered there, marking him. Because whether she realized it or not, she'd taken complete ownership of his heart, making it hers forever.

Michael took her face between his hands and pressed his lips to hers. He coaxed her mouth open so his tongue could stroke and tease hers. He channeled everything he was feeling in that moment into his kiss, hoping it conveyed the words he desperately wanted to say but knew she wasn't ready to hear.

The next few minutes were a frenzied rush to divest him of those last few bits and pieces of clothing before he led her to the bed, holding back the covers as she climbed in. He followed, sliding across the cool sheets until they lay face-to-face with only inches separating them.

The moonlight streaming through the sliding glass door backlit her wild hair and he was reminded of that first night they spent together. How beautiful and funny and smart he thought she was even then, when he hadn't really known her.

And now that he did know her?

He was convinced he'd found his perfect match, his other half. To hell with the idea of opposites attract. He and Kacie were so alike it was downright scary sometimes. But that meant she understood him at his core, and vice versa. She was everything that had been missing from his life, the final piece of the puzzle.

Kacie stroked the crease between his brows with her fingertip. "Penny for your thoughts," she whispered.

Michael didn't dare tell her. Instead, he tried his best to show her.

He took his time, touching, tasting, worshipping her body. Every sigh he incited, every whisper of his name that escaped her lips, was music to his ears. And then he made love to her while staring down into those gorgeous green eyes as she welcomed him into her embrace. Once inside her, he was in no rush to move, luxuriating in the warmth and softness that surrounded him. As she ran her fingers through his hair, she gifted him with a smile before pressing her lips tenderly to his.

It was then he knew, without a doubt, he would never want to let her go.

KACIE WOKE UP to bright sunlight streaming through the windows and an empty bed.

She bolted upright, clutching the bedsheet to her chest while her eyes scanned the room, looking for some sign that he hadn't just up and left her with no intention of coming back. That's when she spotted the piece of paper folded over on itself and sitting on his pillow, her name scribbled across the front.

Her heart dropped into the pit of her stomach, fearful of what it might say. Never in a million years would she have imagined this would all come to an end with a Dear John letter.

Before her imagination could get the best of her, she snatched up the piece of paper to read it.

Ran out to pick up a few things. Checkout isn't until 1400 so don't run off.—M

Below his initial, he scrawled a postscript.

P.S. Don't bother getting dressed.

Kacie flopped back on the pillow and covered her face with the piece of paper as she giggled. The note was so typical Michael. Direct, bossy, arrogant and sweet all at the same time. Of course he'd automatically assume they'd have sex one more time before they left. Not that she was complaining about one final sendoff.

But how would it be between them this time?

Would it be fast and hard like so many times before? Maybe up against the balcony wall or in the shower? Would he trap her wrists in his hands and whisper filthy nothings in her ear? Would he have her climb on top and ride him until her thighs shook and muscles burned, all while he lay back, hands tucked behind his head, enjoying the view *and* reaping the reward?

Or would it be more like last night?

She wasn't exactly certain how or why it happened, but something had definitely changed. Last night certainly didn't feel like a fling and what they shared wasn't just sex. It was far more intimate. And if it weren't for the fact she was afraid to even *think* the L-word . . . .

Kacie unfolded his note and was reading it a second time when she heard the key in the lock. The door opened and the scent of coffee and warm pastries preceded him into the room and had her stomach growling by the time the door closed behind him.

The moment he appeared around the corner and saw her, a smile overtook his face. "You're awake."

"I am." She, of course, smiled back. She couldn't stop herself if she tried because he simply made her that happy. "What do you have there?"

In one hand, Michael held a familiar pink pastry box. "Two peach fritters, two bear claws—a cherry-filled, a lemon-filled—and a chocolate chip muffin. And one coffee, of course," he said, showing her the cup in his hand.

"You sure do know how to spoil a girl."

"What? This stuff?" He set the items on the dresser, well out of her reach. "I got all of this for me. But if you'd like I could run downstairs, see if they have anything left at the complimentary breakfast. There's probably a bagel. Maybe a banana. Or would you prefer one of those little bowls of dry Froot Loops?"

He held his straight face just long enough that she started to believe he might be serious. Then, once he realized he had her, the corners of his mouth lifted.

Asshole.

Kacie grabbed the closest pillow and sent it sailing across the room, hitting him square in the chest.

Without any warning, he dove onto the bed, landing on top of her. She squealed as he trapped her beneath the sheets, pinning her with his body as he nuzzled her neck and huffed hot breath into her ear. He kept it up as she wiggled and squirmed with laughter, until tears streamed down her face, until she was breathless. Finally, Michael rolled off and stretched out alongside her.

One side of his mouth hitched up as he pushed her hair back from her face and swiped the wetness from her cheeks with his thumb.

"Don't tell me you've been up hours, gone for a run, showered, changed, and made a breakfast run already this morning."

"I have not." Capturing her hand in his, Michael pressed a kiss to the underside of her wrist. "You're such a bad influence, sunshine."

Giving in to the sudden urge to touch him, she stroked along his jaw and underside of his chin. "I can't believe you skipped your run," she said, enjoying the unfamiliar scrape of whiskers on his face.

"I'll make up for it by going for a run when I get home, no matter how hot it is outside."

Kacie groaned and rolled herself into his embrace. "Can't we just live in this hotel forever? I'm not ready to go home just yet. Especially since Sam and Bryce are on their way to Italy by now."

"Well, I can't take you to Italy, but how about a little weekend getaway?" He tightened his arms around her, pulling her even closer so he could tuck her head beneath his chin. "The next couple of weeks will be busy with the change of command, but after that we could go somewhere. Just you and me."

Kacie held her breath, her mind racing as she attempted to decipher the underlying meaning of his invitation.

"But I have so much packing to do."

"I'll help you. It's not like you have a ton of stuff to begin with. I know of a place not far from here. We can leave after work on Friday, return Sunday. What do you think?"

She wanted to say yes. But she knew herself well enough to know if she signed up for a weekend away . . .

if they spent more nights like last night together . . . there would be little doubt she'd be leaving Savannah heartbroken at the end of the month.

"I'm not sure how I feel."

Needing to put distance between them, Kacie rolled out of his arms and off the bed.

"Kacie."

She wrapped the sheet around her body once, twice, then glanced in his direction and found him moving to the edge of the bed.

"In case you haven't noticed, or I haven't been perfectly clear, I like you. A lot."

She dropped into the desk chair and Michael followed, positioning the other chair so he was directly in front of her, his knees straddling hers. He took hold of her hand and held it between his own, silently willing her to look at him.

"I know you're leaving in a month and I know you'll hardly have time to catch your breath much less do the long-distance thing, but it's only a year." He lifted his shoulders and smiled, making it all sound so easy. "And I'm not ready to say goodbye to you."

She opened her mouth, prepared to argue, despite not knowing what on earth she would say. But Michael raised his hand, effectively cutting her off. "Before you say anything, let me explain. Please."

Kacie nodded.

He took a deep breath, then gave her hand a gentle squeeze. "In a few months, I'll have fulfilled my commitment to the army. Which means for the first time in fifteen years I have options. *Real* options. Anything from moving to a different unit to resigning my commission."

She could hardly believe what she was hearing. "You're leaving the army?"

"I haven't decided anything yet."

"What about that whole twenty-year thing?"

"I don't have to do twenty years. It might make sense financially. I'd be leaving a lot of money on the table if I just resigned. But . . ." He shook his head as if trying to get himself back on topic. "Don't worry about all of that right now. All I'm asking is that we not end this when you move to Durham. Let's give whatever this thing between us is a chance to see where it can go."

It was difficult to swallow around the lump in her throat. Especially since her insides were a jumbled-up mess of panic and excitement.

If there was one thing ex-Mike had taught her, it was to never get her hopes up.

And now, this Michael was asking her to do that very thing.

She looked at their joined hands, how he cradled both of hers in his, his thumbs gently stroking her skin.

"Kace?" He'd ducked his head lower, bringing his eyes level to hers. "Tell me what you're thinking."

At the moment she felt like she was caught on an amusement park ride, one that tilted and turned and tossed her about, making her so dizzy she could hardly walk a straight line when it was over. But it was also the kind of ride that made her feel alive. The kind that had her running to get back in line so she could have another turn.

She, like him, wanted to see just where this relationship might lead. But there was one thing she needed to make clear: her fellowship, her career, came first. At least for now.

"You do realize I probably won't have time to come visit? And you can't be farther than two hours away from Savannah. How will that work?"

He shrugged it off. "You'll be so busy it's likely we wouldn't see much of each other even if we lived in the same city."

"But that's basically saying we might not see each other for the entire year. Are you sure you're okay with that?"

Another shrug. "Absolutely."

It would be so easy to say yes. Almost too easy. "You'd really be willing to go without sex for an entire year?" she asked skeptically.

"For you, yes. Besides, a year isn't that long in the grand scheme of things." An arrogant smile spread across his face. "After all, that's what phone sex is for."

Chapter Twenty

KACIE SMILED TO herself as Michael sang along to the twenty-year-old Black Crowes song that blared from the car speakers. Any nerves she might have felt about having dinner with his brother and sister-in-law eased the moment he arrived on her doorstep. And now, as she watched him bang out the drumbeat on the steering wheel as he navigated his way through Savannah traffic, she found herself completely relaxed.

In the three weeks since her sister's wedding, despite the fact they'd been sleeping together for months, she felt she'd finally come to know the *real* Michael MacGregor. And what she'd learned was that he was the closest thing she'd ever known to a grown-up Boy Scout. Although he'd be quick to deny the suggestion, his actions told the story. He was a man who routinely checked on the elderly woman who lived on the first floor below him and often carried out her trash and fetched her mail. He had a photo of his mother in his wallet and spoke to his father every weekend. He loved southern rock almost as much as he loved sweets and often preferred to drink lemonade over almost anything else.

Michael was also a man of his word. Despite being busy with work, he found time to haul the things she no longer needed to donation centers and helped her pack the remainder. Then, just as promised, he whisked her away to Sapelo Island, where he rented a house on the marsh for the weekend. That was really when she caught a glimpse of what a future with Michael might be like as they spent the weekend talking, laughing, and making love.

And then there was the other, decidedly non–Boy Scout side. The side that liked to say the dirtiest things she'd ever heard in her life. The side that liked to tie her hands, so he could tease and torment her just a little bit. The side that didn't protest when she suggested doing the same to him.

"What are you thinking about?"

Kacie turned to find him watching her. "Nothing, really. Why do you ask?"

He flashed that cocky smile, the one that showed off his dimples. "Your cheeks are rosy pink."

She brushed her hair back from her face and felt the heat rising off her skin. "I was just thinking about last weekend."

"Hmm . . ."

That was his only response; he kept his eyes on the road, finally turning onto his brother's street where he parked along the curb in front of a small bungalow. Then he shut off the engine and stared intently at her with those deep blue eyes. "Making plans for dessert already?"

His words were a low rumble, scraping across her nerves and setting them afire.

She swallowed hard, then laughed because that's what she always did when he made her just the slightest bit uncomfortable. He, of course, chuckled because he took great satisfaction in teasing her.

Then he climbed out of the car and rushed around to help her out. Even held her hand as they made their way up the front walk. But before they reached the porch steps, the front door swung open. And there stood his brother—a slightly shorter, bulkier version of Michael, with dark brown hair and a dimple in his chin.

"It's about damn time he's brought you for dinner," Danny bellowed as he shoved open the screen door. "How are you doing, Kacie?"

She was somewhat surprised he remembered her name seeing as they had only met the one time, months ago. Either he had a really great memory or someone had been talking about her.

"I'm well, thank you," she replied.

Within moments of stepping inside, they were joined by his wife, Bree. "Welcome to our happy little construction zone," she said with a smile. She then gave them a short tour through the two-bedroom, one-bath house they had hopes of transforming into three bedrooms and two baths by knocking down a wall and expanding into the backyard.

As they made their way into the kitchen, Danny appeared through the back door with a metal tank in his hand. "I gotta run to the store. Just realized I'm outta propane." Danny grabbed a set of car keys off the counter. "Anything else I need to pick up while I'm out?"

"Not that I can think of," Bree replied.

As the two of them talked, movement on the other side of the kitchen caught her eye. Kacie turned just in time to see Michael swiping cookies from a jar on the far counter. He had no shame though, smiling proudly at her as he replaced the lid. As he made his way back to her, he shoved one into his mouth.

"I can't believe you," Kacie whispered as she brushed away a stray crumb from his chin. "Stealing cookies?"

"I didn't steal anything," he said around a mouthful of cookie. "Those cookies are for me. I bought Bree the cookie jar for Christmas, therefore what gets put inside belongs to me. Do you want one?" he asked, offering her the other.

"No!" she whispered harshly.

"Suit yourself." Michael smiled wide, then shamelessly shoved the second cookie in his mouth as well.

"In case you didn't know it already, Michael is a dessert whore."

Kacie looked back at Bree, who was not at all upset. If anything, she was quite amused.

"I've seen what he can do to a box of pastries," Kacie replied.

Bree laughed as she unloaded a variety of fruit onto the counter. "He'll do just about anything for sweets. As a matter of fact, I'm surprised he hasn't been kicked out of regiment for his habit since it's bad enough it could compromise operational security."

Michael shook his head. "You all exaggerate."

Bree arched one brow. "If you say so."

The three of them spent the next few minutes chatting about their work and her upcoming fellowship. They talked about sports and avoided politics. As far as first dinners with the family went, things were going relatively well until they began discussing the planned renovations for the house.

"When are you going to start on the master suite?" Michael asked. "I'll need to make sure my calendar is full so I don't get wrangled into any home improvement projects."

"Please." Bree arched one brow and flashed him a look before going back to chopping up salad ingredients. "Like you've helped with anything so far."

Kacie sat on the bar stool, completely entertained by the conversation that ping-ponged back and forth between Bree and Michael. Especially since Michael had told her they were far closer than in-laws, more like true siblings. Actually, more than once he'd referred to her as the bratty little sister he never had.

"I wanted to start on the master suite after the first of the year," Bree admitted. "But Danny wants to wait until next summer, since he doesn't want me dealing with construction and renovations while he's deployed. But with that logic, we might never get all the remodeling done."

"Not if he doesn't re-up."

Suddenly, the mood shifted and the once happy and light room grew cold. Bree deliberately placed the large kitchen knife on the cutting board and looked Michael directly in the eyes. "We're not going to have that discussion again."

"We have to. He should be getting his reenlistment papers any day."

Bree broke eye contact and snatched up a kitchen towel to dry her hands. "He already has them."

"And what? That's it?" Michael swore under his breath and pounded his fist on the island. "I can't believe you're going to let him re-up."

"And I still can't believe you tried to get your own brother thrown out of the army when you know how much he loves it," Bree countered.

Michael looked as if he'd been slapped. "Who told you that?"

"Please, Michael. Do not play dumb."

Kacie held her breath, uncertain of whether or not she should intervene or remain silent. After all, this was a family affair and she wasn't family.

Michael took a deep breath, trying to regain his

composure. From where she sat, Kacie could see his pulse thrumming in his neck, the heavy rise and fall of his chest. When he finally spoke, his words were low and cold.

"I gave the same recommendation for Danny that I would've given anyone else."

"Are you sure about that?" Bree challenged. She looked at him for a long moment, before tossing the dish towel over her shoulder and resuming her dinner preparations. "What I say doesn't matter anyway. Danny's not going to leave the army, at least not in the next ten years if he can help it. You know this. I know this. Anyone who has ever met him knows this."

"You can talk him out of it, Bree. He'll listen to you. If you tell him not to, he won't do it, because he'll do anything for you."

Bree shook her head. "I would never ask him to leave the army."

"Why the hell not?" Michael yelled.

Unable to stand by and watch any longer, Kacie rose from her seat and placed her hand on his arm. "Michael, you need to calm down."

He jerked his arm from her touch and closed the space between himself and Bree, to the point he was practically hovering over her. "Do you remember how you felt when that chaplain knocked on your door? Do you remember waiting hours on end to get an update on his condition? He might not be so lucky next time. Tell him you want him to quit."

"I won't do it, Michael."

"Why not?" he bellowed again.

Bree refused to look up at him, choosing instead to halve and quarter the cherry tomatoes on the cutting board in front of her. Michael finally backed away and began pacing across the small kitchen, running both hands through his hair in frustration.

Kacie could see the tears welling in Bree's eyes. "Because it was the one thing he asked me to not do before we married."

"Before your arranged marriage, or whatever you two called it?" Michael folded his arms across his chest and laughed without humor. "That's a bullshit excuse."

"It's called a marriage of convenience," Bree answered calmly. "Besides, you know damn well that's not what we have now."

"Exactly!" Michael smacked his open palm against the island counter. "So why are you still adhering to stipulations he made back then? Put your damn foot down."

Bree dropped the knife and walked right up to Michael, took hold of his arms and looked him straight in the eyes. "You know he found himself in the army. I will not ask him to give that up. I will not ask him to leave his friends and what he believes in, for me. And I sure as hell won't make him choose."

Michael scoffed and attempted to pull away, but Bree held strong.

"Don't think I'm not scared to death every time he's

deployed. Every time he's out training. I know how easily things can go wrong." Her voice was shaking. "How do you think I felt when I received the call about so many of the guys getting killed and injured last year?"

This time he did pull back, yanking himself from her grasp so violently Bree nearly fell down in the process. "How do you think I felt?" he shot back. "I was there, Bree. You don't need to fucking remind me how many men we lost on our last deployment. Who do you think signs their death certificates?"

Bree's expression crumpled and the tears finally streamed down her face. She closed the distance between them once again, placing her hand on his cheek. "Michael."

He pulled away from her touch without ever looking at her. "Maybe we should do this another time."

Kacie was still trying to process all that she'd seen and heard when Michael stormed past her, headed for the front door. "I'll be in the car."

Kacie turned to face Bree, her heart racing. "I'm so sorry. I don't know what's gotten into him."

Bree waved off her apology. "Don't worry about it."

"I've never seen him so upset. I'm kind of surprised."

Bree took a settling breath and tried her best to smile. "Michael's under a lot of pressure and has been for a very long time. Most of it is self-imposed. But he's one of the best men I've ever known. So don't let what happened here tonight change your opinion of him." Bree leaned in to give her a quick hug. "We'll do this another time."

By the time Kacie made it outside, Michael already had the car running, clearly impatient to get the hell out of there.

"If you don't mind, I'll just drop you off at your place," he said after she closed the passenger door.

It definitely wasn't a side of him she'd ever seen before. Rigid. Uncompromising. She'd be lying if she said it didn't trouble her more than a bit.

"Are you sure you don't want to talk about whatever it was that happened in there?"

"I'm sure."

And with those two words, he effectively ended the conversation.

As he wove his way through Savannah traffic, she watched him closely. How he held the steering wheel in a death grip. How the muscles in his jaw flexed. There was little denying his anger, and if she had to give him credit for anything, it was keeping it in check for the most part. When they reached her street, he didn't even pull into the driveway. Instead, he just stopped along the sidewalk.

"Why don't you come in for a while?" she asked, reaching for the door handle. "I can make us something to eat."

Silently she hoped he would say yes. Then she'd try her damnedest to make things better for him, because clearly he was hurting.

"I don't think I'd be very fun company tonight," he said. "I'll talk to you later."

She had been, in a word, dismissed.

He made no movement to kiss her goodbye. As a matter of fact, he never even shifted the car into Park. Just kept his foot on the break long enough for her to climb out and shut the door behind her before he roared off down the street.

MICHAEL SLAMMED HIS apartment door closed behind him and threw his keys on the coffee table. When he looked up, his mother's face stared back at him from the framed picture on his bookshelf. For most of his life she'd been a two-dimensional image rather than a flesh and blood person. His recollections of her were few and far between and were becoming less and less vivid as each year passed. But one thing that remained, her voice as crystal clear as the day she said it: *Take care of your brother, Michael.*

The memory of it was like a record skipping in his brain.

Take care of your brother.
Take care of your brother.
Take care of your brother.

Sometimes he could bump the needle and the song would continue on to another verse instead of hanging up on the chorus that had played in his head since he was ten. It was during those times he was able to go on living normally—well, as normal a life as someone could while bearing that kind of responsibility.

But ever since that afternoon in Mali, from the moment he heard Danny's teammates over the command radio alerting the rest of the squad he'd been injured, when he heard them calling for a medic, followed by the eerily calm request for a medevac, he'd been in a heightened state of panic. It didn't matter that his brother was back home now, not only completely recovered from his injuries but living life with the woman he loved. What mattered was that Michael couldn't let it happen again. Because in his gut, he knew Danny wouldn't be so lucky the second time.

Take care of your brother.
Take care of your brother.
Take care of your brother.

Michael scrubbed his hands over his face, wanting it to stop. He spun on his heel, his fist meeting the wall, then disappearing into the hollow space behind the shattered Sheetrock. Sparks of pain shot up his wrist to his elbow and his hand throbbed in time with his heart as he pulled his fist from the hole.

Clutching his hand, he turned and slid down the wall until his butt met the floor. As he wiggled each digit and tested the flex of his tendons, he realized just how lucky he was to not have hit a wall stud. Aside from a few minor cuts and bruising, it didn't appear he'd done any major damage. Otherwise he'd be on the way to an emergency room for at the very least a cast, if not surgery.

He was an idiot.

He propped his forearms on his knees and leaned his head back against the wall, trying to calm his mind and racing heart.

At least the skipping had stopped for the moment.

It was hard to believe only a few weeks earlier he had thought he was about to have some control over his life, have real options for the first time in years. But all he'd succeeded in doing was kidding himself.

Chapter Twenty-One

KACIE SPENT THE next hour running so many loops around Daffin Park that she actually lost count. When she returned to her packed-up house, she was still in disbelief, trying to figure out how their evening ended so abruptly. There was even a moment where she wondered if she ought to count her blessings and call the whole long-distance thing off. The last thing she needed was to be committed to a man who would completely shut down and push her away when he was upset.

But then she'd recalled the look on his face when he talked about signing death certificates, his pain so evident. She hadn't known he was hiding so much hurt.

After a quick shower, Kacie dressed and slipped on her flip-flops, convinced that he needed someone to talk to. And that person might as well be her.

Within a matter of minutes she was on his doorstep,

but unlike the last time she had shown up unannounced, there was no music blaring from inside his apartment. No sounds of any kind from within. The only indication he might be home was his car in the parking lot. She stood there for several minutes, knocking on his door at regular intervals. Finally, she had no choice but to give up and head back to her car. But as she followed the walkway to the parking lot, something drew her attention to the swimming pool in the middle of the complex. There, in the fading light of day, was a man sitting all alone on the deck and staring out over the water.

Kacie cut across the lawn to the pool gate.

Michael had his back to the gate and headphones in his ears, so she was able to walk right up without him noticing. Although he wore swim trunks and no shirt, it was evident he hadn't gotten in the water. Instead, he sat on the stairs leading into the shallow end of the pool, the water reaching only midcalf. And sitting beside him was a half-empty bottle of Gentleman Jack.

She placed her hand on his bare shoulder and he jerked around in surprise. "I didn't mean to scare you," she said once he pulled the earbuds free.

"Go home, Kacie," he said flatly.

"Sorry about that, Major MacGregor," she said while picking up the half-empty liquor bottle. "I'm not required to follow your orders."

She'd intended to move the whiskey out of her way, but after a moment, she picked it up and walked over to the fence where she poured out the remaining liquid into the bushes before tossing the bottle into a can for recyclables.

He didn't react. He just sat there. Like a bump on a log. Numb.

And her heart broke for him.

Despite his unwillingness to fight, she noticed the tension in his body, how his neck and shoulders were hard as stone. Instead of trying to squeeze in between him and the pool railings, she slipped off her flip-flops and settled on the deck behind him, her legs astride his body. Then she smoothed her palms over his back and began massaging his muscles, hoping it would help him relax. Much to her surprise, it wasn't long before his held fell forward, almost in surrender.

She continued working as the light dwindled around them. She began with the trapezius muscle, its fibers lean and powerful, but not so overdeveloped that his neck disappeared into his shoulders. Next came the anterior, medial, and posterior deltoids forming his strong shoulders, each muscle clearly defined. Then there was the shadowed valley of the infraspinatus and teres major and the strong vee of the latissimus dorsi.

For a long time they sat in silence as she worked the tense muscles until her hands ached and fingers cramped.

"I need to take a break," she said, shaking out her hands.

Again, there was no protest.

She could only hope she'd helped somehow. Moving from back to front, her palms smoothed the exterior abdominal obliques before sliding upward to the pectoral majors. She flexed her arms and scooted closer, her feet now resting in the water alongside his, her pelvis flush with his backside, her breasts pressing into the newly worked muscles.

"I know I talk a lot," Kacie said, pausing just long enough to press a kiss to his spine, "but I think I'm a pretty decent listener, too."

She held her breath, waiting for a response. Finally, she turned her head, resting her cheek against his skin as she hugged him close.

He covered her hands with his. The left he moved to cover his sternum where she felt the powerful beat of his heart beneath her palm. The right was lifted higher, her palm turned upward to receive a tender kiss in the center.

"Thank you," he whispered across her skin before kissing it again.

"Are you ready to talk?"

"Not just yet."

She nodded against his back just so he knew she'd heard and then held him a little tighter.

IT WAS FULL dark by the time Michael stood up, took Kacie's hand, and led her back to his apartment. He knew she was still waiting for him to say something, anything. And he wanted to tell her everything—but he didn't even know where to start. He wanted to tell her how much he appreciated her being there for him. He wanted to tell her that he was falling in love with her. He wanted to ask her to stay here with him forever because the idea of her leaving made it difficult to breathe.

Because she would leave. And he had to stay.

He unlocked the door to his darkened apartment and reached past the doorjamb to flip on the light. Kacie followed him inside, and before he even closed the door and turned the bolt, she noticed the massive hole in the wall.

She turned to look at him with concern in her eyes. "What the hell did you do?"

He lifted one shoulder, then let it drop. He was all out of excuses. "I was stupid."

But she didn't turn tail and run like he thought she might. Instead, she took his left hand, his good hand, and led him into the kitchen. After grabbing a bar stool and positioning it beneath the bright overhead light, she pointed to it. "Sit," she ordered.

"There's no need," he protested. "I've already checked it. It looks worse than it really is."

But one thing was for certain—while the whiskey had temporarily dulled the pain, his hand was going to hurt like a son of a bitch come morning. His head, too.

With a look of disgust, or maybe disappointment—to be honest he was having a hard time reading her at the moment—she pointed at the empty bar stool once again. "Sit."

This time he sat.

"If there is one saying that is completely true, it's that doctors make the worst patients."

Obviously, she was not going to take his word that his

hand was fine. For a split second the smart-ass taking up space in the back of his brain suggested asking just where the hell she got her medical degree. But while he was drunk, he wasn't that drunk. Saying something that stupid in this moment was essentially a death wish.

She stepped closer, bringing herself to stand between his knees, and instantly he was enthralled by that wild hair of hers. She must have showered, because bits and pieces were still damp; and even though he smelled like a distillery, there was an overpowering scent of cocoa butter in the air.

Kacie tested each joint and bone in his hand, then mumbled under her breath, most of it incomprehensible. But he did manage to catch "doctor," "hand," "idiot." Pretty much summed it up.

Satisfied nothing was broken, Kacie began a full recon of his kitchen instead of just asking where things were. Opening and closing drawers, slamming cabinet doors, all the while looking for . . . whatever it was she was looking for. Finally, she gave up and headed down the hallway only to return within a matter of seconds with one of his ARMY T-shirts. She passed by him, going straight to the refrigerator where she used her hand to scoop ice from the bucket before dropping it into the cotton fabric. Then she gathered the sides and twisted it around a few times before placing it on the top of his hand.

Putting some distance between them, she took several steps backward until her butt met the counter on the opposite side of his small galley kitchen. She folded her arms over her chest and huffed in frustration. "I think you need to start talking."

There had been very few women who had spoken to him that way during his lifetime. Most of them found it was easier to walk away from him rather than tolerate his bullshit. Bree was the exception. And apparently Kacie—at least for now.

"I think it's obvious I lost my temper and punched a hole in the wall."

She shook her head in frustration. "Start talking about what's important. What was that all about at your brother's house? What happened?"

Even through the haze of alcohol, he felt his earlier irritation bubbling up inside him again. "What do you think happened? He was injured last year, spent several weeks recovering in Walter Reed. But instead of counting his blessings and getting the hell out, he's determined to re-up."

Her earlier expression softened a bit. "It's understandable you'd want him to leave."

"Yes."

"What I still don't get is why you got that upset," she said, pointing to his hand.

How the hell was he going to explain this to her?

Despite the sedating effects of alcohol, he could feel his heart rate ratcheting up. "Because if he stays, I stay."

The little crease appeared between her brows. "But you told me you never intended to be career military, or even join the Rangers. That you only did it because you and Danny were so competitive. Surely that's not still the case anymore?"

Damn her and her memory.

Michael rose from the stool and tossed the ice pack into the sink. "I think we're done here."

But as he tried to walk away, she took hold of his arm in both of her hands. "Don't just walk away from me. Talk to me. Why don't you just leave the army if you don't like it, Michael?"

He tore his arm free from her grip and spun around, hovering over her. "Because I can't!"

Immediately, she stepped back. She rapidly blinked her eyes and he knew she was trying to keep the tears at bay, refusing to show any weakness.

God, how he wished he were as strong as her. To take back his life and just start over like she was doing.

"I'm sorry. I didn't mean to scare you, but I just . . ." He squeezed his eyes shut and pressed the heels of his hands to them as he shook his head in frustration. "It's not that simple, Kacie."

It felt like a lifetime passed before he heard her footsteps on the ceramic tile floor. He could only assume she was leaving and he couldn't bear to watch her go. But then he felt the cool touch of her hands on his face. He opened his eyes and saw those calming green eyes, the color of sea glass, staring back at him.

"You just said you only had a few months left." She smoothed one hand over his cheek, along his jaw. "Get a job in a hospital. Get a job in private practice. Go anywhere."

"I wish I could." He wanted it. He dreamed of it. But he couldn't have it. "You make it sound so very easy."

"It is that easy—"

"You. Know. Nothing."

Stunned into silence, Kacie pulled her hands from his face.

"You don't have any idea what it's like to hold your brother's life in your hands. To be covered in his blood. To know that if you fail, if you make one wrong move or make one tiny mistake, you'll have to live with his death on your hands for the rest of your life. That you'll have to face your father and admit your absolute best wasn't good enough."

Kacie stepped back again, folding her arms over her body as if protecting herself. Michael watched as tears welled in her eyes and eventually spilled over to race down her cheeks. She so badly wanted to know what happened? Well, he'd tell her now.

"He was shot three times. Twice in the lower torso. One bullet tore through his kidney and spleen, another perforated his small intestine. He damn near bled out before the medevac even got him to me, and I was only five minutes away. He was sweaty and breathing hard when he arrived. And he was suffering. He was fighting, but he was suffering. Abdominal wounds are the worst. Take a shot to the head, you at least lose consciousness. And you'll die in minutes from a shot to the heart. But abdominal wounds . . . it takes people *hours* to die. And then there's the fact he was shot with an AK-47. Do you know what that's like? What it does to a person? It's like an explosion going off inside someone's body. There's microscopic pieces of bone fragments everywhere. Everything is torn to shreds. And in order to save a person, you basically have to fillet them. Cut them wide open. Because you need to see everything in order to find out where the damage is. And the amount of bleeding . . ." Michael shook his head. "By the time the surgery was over I was covered in as much of his blood as he had left in his body."

Kacie swiped a tear from her cheek. "You performed surgery on your own brother? No wonder you're so screwed up about this."

"He crashed twice on the medical transport to Landstuhl. Once he got there he spent several more hours in surgery. And then the infection damn near finished him off. It is truly a fucking miracle he is alive."

Needing an outlet for his pent-up energy, Michael began pacing across the small kitchen.

"He shouldn't even be in regiment. Having only one kidney should have disqualified him from service. I personally recommended his medical discharge, said he wasn't fit to remain in the military. But my brother, I'll be damned if he didn't convince the higher-ups to let him stay."

"Is that what you're mad about? That he had you overridden?"

He slammed his already bruised and swollen fist against the counter. "I'm mad that he damn near died!

And instead of appreciating the second chance he has at life and staying safe and having a future with Bree, he's just signing his death warrant."

A short silence followed until Kacie made her way to his side, her hand skimming across his spine as she tried to calm him. Soothe him. "But the important thing is Danny didn't die. You saved him. And he's happy and healthy, building a life and a house with his wife. He's making the most of every minute and that's because of you. But you? You're just sitting here waiting for the other shoe to drop."

"And when it does, I'll be here to pick it up. That's *my* job. I promised."

This time he did turn his back and walk away.

He was so tired. So fucking tired.

He made his way to the bedroom where he collapsed on the end of the bed and held his head in his hands.

And of course she followed right along behind him. "Promised who, Michael?" She dropped to her knees in front of him and took hold of his wrists, pulling them away from his face. "Michael, look at me. Who did you promise? Your father? Bree? Who did you—"

He was staring into those beautiful green eyes of hers the moment they widened with surprise.

"Oh, my God," she whispered.

And he knew she had figured it all out.

Chapter Twenty-Two

MICHAEL SAT IN his desk chair and stared out the window, watching what seemed like the entire population of Hunter Army Airfield pass by. Although he was up to his eyeballs in new medical training policies and procedures, supply requisitions, and other assorted paperwork, he couldn't bring himself to go through any of it.

A quick knock on the door interrupted his thoughts and had him spinning his chair around. Speak of the devil. There was his brother standing in the doorway, a huge grin on his face.

"You mean to tell me the US government pays you the big bucks to stare out the damn window all day?"

Michael smiled back. "Today they do."

After his argument with Bree on Saturday, Michael had anticipated a visit from his younger brother sometime the day before. Especially since Danny was quite protective of Bree and wouldn't tolerate anyone raising their voice to her—much less his own brother. He'd fully expected Danny at his door, fists a-flying, but the visit never happened.

"What brings you here?"

Danny's boots thumped across the floor as he made his way to the empty chair on the opposite side of the desk. "I was just dropping off some paperwork, saw your door was open and thought I'd stop by and see how Kacie was feeling."

Now he was confused. "What's that?"

"Is she feeling better?" Danny repeated. "Bree said that Kacie had a migraine or something that came on pretty strong. That's why you guys left before I got back with the propane, right?"

Not only had Bree not told Danny about their argument, but she'd covered for him as well. And if that didn't make him feel like shit.

"Right, yes. Kacie's fine. Thanks for asking."

Danny smiled. "Well, maybe we can do it next weekend if she's up to it."

Suddenly, talk of a reschedule made it impossible for him to smile back. "Afraid that won't happen. She's moving to Durham this weekend. She starts her fellowship on Monday."

His brother folded his arms over his chest and reclined in the chair with a smug smile on his face. "Now the staring longingly out the window makes sense. You're moping."

Michael shook his head. "I'm not moping."

"The hell you aren't."

Irritated that his brother had indeed caught him moping, he rose from his chair and began organizing the massive piles of manila folders on his desktop. "Don't you have somewhere to be? Someone else to harass?"

"Nope," Danny answered without dropping his smile. "Bree and Marie are going to some women in construction thing so I'm on my own for dinner. Ben invited me over to their place but I passed on that one."

Michael chuckled. Dinner with four kids wasn't his idea of relaxing either.

"So I thought I'd see if you want to get something to eat. But that was before I realized your girl is leaving this week." Danny waggled his brows. "I'm sure you have better things to do than hang out with your little brother."

"Fuck off," he muttered. "So about that paperwork . . ."

"Signed, sealed, and delivered for another four years at least," Danny said matter-of-factly.

Although Michael had expected it, the news still came like a dagger to the gut.

"I thought you were getting out?" He dropped into his chair. "The last time we talked you sounded like you were considering it."

Like the soldier he was, Danny sat up straighter in his chair. "That's true. I was. But several guys with ten years recently decided to get the hell out for various reasons. If I left now, 1st Batt could be in one hell of a lurch."

"You don't owe them your life, Danny."

"That's true. But I like it here," he said with a smile. "I'm happiest here. And Bree wants me to do what makes me happy."

His stomach churned. If only he'd been able to convince Bree . . .

"What about you?"

Michael looked at his brother. "What do you mean?"

"Your time is about done. Are you ready to get the hell out of here? It's not like the army was ever your style to begin with."

He was trying to decide how best to answer when they were interrupted by a cell phone chime. Danny pulled his from his pocket and, after reading the message on the screen, typed out a quick reply. "Change of plans, big brother," he said with a grin. "Marie had to cancel on the meeting and Bree didn't want to go alone. So I get to spend the evening with my wife."

Immediately, Danny rose from his chair and was halfway through the door when Michael called out to him. Danny stopped to look back. "Yeah?"

For a split second he considered asking Danny to go and get his paperwork and tear it to shreds. But really, what was the point?

"Have a good night," he said instead. "Tell Bree I said hello."

"Will do. And you," Danny said, pointing a figure at

him, "go spend time with Kacie before she leaves. If you don't you'll regret it." Then he gave two quick taps to the doorjamb with his knuckles before disappearing down the hallway.

Michael leaned heavily on his elbows. If Danny was in for another four years, then that meant he was in for another four. He never should have told Kacie about the possibility of him getting out in a matter of months. She was willing to put up with the military thing for maybe another year, but no way would she ever agree to four years—not after the game her ex played. So in one fell swoop, he'd lost his freedom to choose and he'd lost his girl, too.

Unless . . .

Once again, his little brother was right. He could sit here and mope about Kacie leaving or he could do something to make her stay.

KACIE STOOD IN front of her pantry, pulling items from each shelf and deciding whether or not the contents were worth keeping. She gave a box of cereal a shake, and when she didn't hear anything, she opened the top and peered inside. Empty. Which was surprising because she was pretty sure she hadn't eaten this variety of cereal in the past few months. Her guess? Sam. Her little sister had a bad habit of putting empty things back in the refrigerator, or pantry, or wherever, because she was too lazy to throw them away.

This chore, along with clearing out the refrigerator, was the last big job she had to do before she moved. Everything she didn't need over the next few days was already packed in labeled boxes that now overtook her living room. Anything not packed had to fit into one large suitcase, so when the movers arrived all she had to do was toss those last few items in her car.

Although she was nervous about moving to a new city where she knew no one, and starting a demanding residency and fellowship, she was excited, too. Especially since the door had been left open for Michael to possibly join her in the coming months. At the very least, he would be able to visit her during the next year.

She was just about to text him when she heard heavy boot steps coming up her front porch. Immediately, she ran to the door and yanked it open, before he even had a chance to ring the bell. "Speak of the devil."

Michael smiled and immediately reached for her, wrapping his arms about her waist and lifting her until her feet were well off the ground. To make things easier, she wrapped her legs around him and burrowed her face beneath the collar of his jacket so she could press a kiss to his neck. He'd come straight from work and smelled of starch since he was still wearing his ACUs.

Without saying a word he walked the two of them inside and nudged the door shut behind them, then continued on to her bedroom where he stripped her bare and made love to her before ever saying hello.

But as she lay there next to him, looking into those

deep dark eyes and raking her fingertips through his hair, she knew just by looking at him what he was feeling. Because she was feeling it, too.

He took hold of her wrist, brought it to his mouth, and pressed a kiss to her pulse. "How was your day?" he asked.

"Fine. Dull. Spent most of the day scheduling utility shutoffs and setting up connections for my place in Durham. How was yours?"

She was taken by surprise when he dropped her hand and pushed himself up to sitting, his back leaning against the headboard. "To be honest, pretty shitty. Didn't get much of anything accomplished. It's hard for me to concentrate knowing you're leaving at the end of the week."

Her heart fluttered. It was the closest thing to a declaration he'd offered.

She sat up as well and dragged her finger along the edge of his jaw. "The long-distance thing won't be forever." And then she smiled, so wide it made her face hurt. "Besides, we'll have phone sex to keep us warm at night."

But the smile on his face was hardly a smile at all. Only one corner of his mouth lifted and even then it only rose up halfway at best. She skimmed her palm up his arm to his shoulder and back down again, trying her best to soothe him. "Tell me what's wrong."

Michael sighed, slightly shaking his head like even he couldn't believe what he was about to say. "Danny stopped by my office tonight. Right after he turned in his reenlistment papers."

He didn't say another word. Didn't need to.

The way he looked at her she already knew what was coming next. Her stomach twisted and knotted and suddenly it was difficult to breathe.

She slid off the bed, gathered her clothing from the floor, and made a beeline for the bathroom so she could have a moment to herself. As she closed the door behind her, she let herself cry. Her heart was too involved now; a few months with Michael, and she'd grown closer to him than any other man she'd previously been with.

She knew they weren't done yet. That Michael could still change his mind.

All she could do was pray for the best.

She steadied herself, putting on her clothes, ready to face him and their uncertain future. She stepped out into the hall and noticed him sitting in the living room. Like her, he'd also dressed and was in the process of lacing up his combat boots.

If ever there was a bad sign.

She made her way down the hall and took a seat on the end of the sofa, sitting on the rolled arm and tucking her toes beneath the cushion. "So your brother signed up for four more years. Did you sign up for four more as well?"

Michael rested his elbows on his knees, his fingers laced together. "I haven't done anything yet, but that's the plan. I wanted to talk to you first."

Inside she felt a tiny flicker of hope. The fact he was asking her opinion, that he was including her in such a life altering decision, meant something. Didn't it?

"Well, then." She pushed a loose strand of hair behind her ear. "If you want my advice, I suggest you do what's right for you. I know you promised your mother you'd watch over your brother, but that was twenty-five years ago. You're not little boys anymore. You need to live your own life. And you can't do that if you're baby-sitting your little brother for the rest of your life."

His expression hardened. "I would hardly call it baby-sitting."

She took a deep breath, trying to calm the jumble of nerves inside her. "You're right. I apologize. But the fact remains, you need to do what's best for you. Right now you're living a life of obligations. You do your job because you have to, not because you want to."

"True. But having the right person by my side would make everything better." He stared at her with those intense blue eyes. "And that person is you."

Kacie shook her head. "If there's one thing I've learned in the past year, it's that no one person can make you happy. At least not long term. You have to find that happiness for yourself. In yourself."

"But I'm happy enough where I'm at right now. This past month is proof of it. And a job doesn't have to be everything. If I have my family, my brother, and if I have you, then it will be just fine."

Needing to put distance between them, she climbed

off the sofa and moved to the other side of the room. Feeling a sudden chill, she wrapped her arms around her middle. "I told you from the beginning I wouldn't get involved with another military guy. I can't do it again."

"News flash, Kacie, you already are," he said, his tone sarcastic and borderline cruel. "All I'm asking you to do is stay here with me. Don't go to Durham. All your things are packed—just move them in with me. Or if you want, we can find a new place to call our own."

Kacie gasped. Tears welled in her eyes, blurring her vision. "You're just like him," she whispered.

"You're comparing what we have to how that asshole used you? Led you on? I wouldn't do any of that!"

"What you're asking me to do, put my dreams on hold, my career on hold, all so everything in your life remains neatly in place? *That* is something he would've asked. Did ask actually."

He threw his hands in the air, incredulous. "A job can't be your whole life, Kacie. Believe me."

"I realize that!" She pounded her fist against her chest. "But I can't be with someone who wants me to give up everything I've worked for just to be with them. I can't put my life on hold until that person decides I may or may not be what they want."

He rose from the sofa. "Okay, then. Let me make it perfectly clear. I want you with me. I want you to—"

"No!" she shouted, cutting him off with a wave of her hand. "Do not say another word. Don't even think about proposing something else in order to get me to stay." The tears she'd fought to control spilled over onto her cheeks and she roughly swiped them away with the palm of her hand. "That's nothing but straight-up manipulation, Michael, and I wouldn't have thought you were capable of it. But I guess when you're desperate to have everything your way, you'll do or say just about anything."

He crossed over to her, invading her personal space. "Kacie . . ."

She sidestepped him and marched to the front door, pulling it open. "You need to leave."

"Kace . . ."

"Just go, Michael."

She couldn't force herself to look at him. For what felt like an eternity, they waged this standoff. Him likely watching her, while she stared at the floor. Finally, his combat boots pounded across the wood floors as he made his way toward the door, but paused momentarily in front of her. Still she didn't look up. Couldn't look up. Instead, she watched as his neatly tied boots walked past her, through the door, and out of her life.

Chapter Twenty-Three

MICHAEL PLACED THE ball on the tee and stepped back to enjoy the view. Long expanses of manicured grass. Towering trees. Additional bursts of color in the form of blooming shrubs lining either side of the fairway.

He hadn't stepped on a golf course since that Saturday afternoon Kacie called him out of the blue, asking him for a ride home from the bridal shop. But while out for his morning run he decided today would be a good day to break out his clubs, take out his frustrations on a little white ball, and maybe, just maybe, get her out of his head for a few hours.

After a couple practice swings, Michael addressed his ball, adjusted his grip one final time, drew back his club, and gave it his all. But the moment his club struck the ball, he knew it was going to be an ugly shot. Sure enough, it sailed right, slicing far off the fairway and into the trees.

He gritted his teeth and swore under his breath.

"I heard wood on that one but didn't see it come down," came a voice from just off the tee box.

He wasn't sure which of the three men he was playing with said it since the moment he turned around they all stopped talking. With shoulders slumped and head hanging, he fought the urge to wrap his fucking driver around the closest tree, grab his shit, and leave.

But his father didn't raise a quitter, so he'd tough it out.

"Sorry about that." He leaned over, picked up his broken tee, and tamped down the divot. "I haven't touched my clubs in a few months. Guess I'm rustier than I thought."

"Take a mulligan, kid," said the round white-haired gentleman holding a cigar between his gloved fingers. "We can turn our backs and pretend we didn't see you take one if it makes you feel better."

The other two men with him laughed and Michael decided to laugh along, because really, what choice did he have at that point?

Six months ago, everything in his life was fine. Just fine. And now, everything was total shit. His golf game. His career. His love life. It was all pure shit, and he had no one to blame but himself.

When his phone vibrated in his pocket, he'd never been so thankful for a distraction from his golf game. Even better when the group text message from Lucky, announcing the early-morning birth of Baby James and an invite to visit, came through. While he wasn't one to rush right on over to ooh and aah over a newborn, this one came at a time he needed an excuse to grab his clubs and head out.

"Fellas," he called. "I'm afraid duty calls. You'll have to finish this one without me."

As he loaded his bag on his back and prepared to walk back to the clubhouse, the drink cart rolled up the concrete path. To apologize for his behavior and hopefully redeem himself, he told the men drinks were on him, then handed the cart girl two twenty-dollar bills before grabbing a Gatorade for himself. As he cut across the first fairway, his phone buzzed again.

"How is my favorite sister-in-law?" he asked.

Her contagious laugh came through the phone. It was nice to know Bree wasn't the kind of woman to hold a grudge. "I'm your only sister-in-law."

"Yes, yes. I know. Do I need to stop and get some flowers or a gift or something?"

"I'm taking care of it for you as we speak. They have quiet time on the maternity ward until four, so no visitors until then. We'll meet you downstairs in the lobby and you can sign the card before we go up to the room."

"You're the absolute best," he said while winding his way down the cart path to the first tee. "If you weren't married to my brother, I'd marry you myself."

She scoffed in disbelief. "I'd never marry you."

Now it was his turn to laugh. "And why is that? I'm a catch, you know."

"I wouldn't marry you for the simple fact you're in love with someone else."

Shit. Well, he couldn't really argue that point.

"By the way." Having reached the clubhouse, he looked both ways before crossing the drive and heading for the parking lot. "I owe you an apology. For yelling at you. For storming out. For being an ass."

He could practically hear her smile through the phone. "You've always been an ass, Michael. It's one of your endearing qualities."

Of course it was impossible for him to not smile back, even though she couldn't see him. "Obviously, you never said anything to Danny either."

"You were talking from a place of hurt and fear. I understand that. Now you just need to understand that Danny can't quit being a soldier any more than you can quit being a doctor."

She was a smart woman, his sister-in-law.

They spoke a few more minutes as Michael tossed his clubs into the trunk of his car, then, after they disconnected the call, he took a moment to drink down the last of his Gatorade. With three hours to kill before he met Danny and Bree at the hospital, he decided now was as good a time as any to go see Kacie, to apologize face-to-face before she left for Durham.

It had taken the better part of a week for him to realize his monumental fuckup, asking her to give up everything she'd worked so hard for, all so she could stay right here and make him happy. He owed her an apology. Knowing her like he did, a phone call, email, or a text message wasn't going to cut it. And rightfully so.

He drove across town to Baldwin Park and her little carriage house, rehearsing all the things he needed to say in his head. He only hoped she'd give him a chance. Like so many times before, he parked along the curb in front of the main house and made his way down the driveway to the back. But as soon as he reached the corner he saw it, the black and red FOR RENT sign posted in the front window. He climbed the front steps anyway and knocked on the front door, hoping the owners had jumped the gun with the sign since the moving trucks weren't supposed to be coming until tomorrow.

"Are you looking for a place to rent?"

Michael turned to see an older man carrying a shovel and garden hose.

"I'm looking for Kacie."

The man pulled off his hat and scratched the top of his head. "She moved out two days ago. Said her place in Durham was ready early so they loaded up her things and headed out."

Michael's heart sank, but he thanked the man and headed back to his car, telling himself along the way it was probably for the best.

To KEEP OUT of the way, Kacie stood in one corner of her kitchen and watched her apartment slowly fill up as the movers brought in stacks of boxes and furniture.

She wasn't quite sure how she had accumulated so much stuff.

"Thanks again for the movers, Daddy. You didn't need to do this."

His low chuckle came through clear on the phone. "Of course I did, because I wasn't going to move all of your things. I'm too old for that."

Kacie shook her head. "You aren't that old."

Again, he laughed. "Aren't you the one always asking which is less: the price to pay someone or my insurance deductible? I can promise you, the movers were cheaper."

They talked a few more minutes, but had to say goodbye when a call he'd been waiting on all day finally came through. She hadn't been in Durham two days and already she was homesick. Which was silly, of course, seeing as she usually only saw her parents once, maybe twice a month when they lived in the same town.

But it felt different now. The security in knowing she could drive across town and see them anytime she wanted was gone.

By lunch the movers were done and the cable guy took their place, wandering back and forth from the living room to her closet as he hooked up her router and cable boxes. Once he finished, Kacie walked him to the door and was shocked to find her sister standing in the hallway.

"Surprise!" Sam yelled, and rushed in through the

doorway at the same time the cable man squeezed his way out.

"What are you doing here?" Kacie asked as her sister threw her arms around her neck.

"Bryce had some work stuff here and I decided to come with!" Her sister stepped back to look her in the eyes. "Are you surprised? Are you happy to see me?"

Kacie felt the burn of unshed tears in her eyes. "You have no idea."

An hour later they were both sitting crisscross on top of her kitchen island because she had no bar stools, eating Chinese food from the containers because her dishes were packed away, as Kacie told her how badly things ended between her and Michael.

"Have you heard from him at all?" Sam asked. "A text message? Voicemail at least?"

"Not a word."

"Maybe he's trying to give you some space," Sam said while swapping the vegetable lo mein for Szechuan chicken. "Maybe let things cool off a bit before he calls you."

Kacie rolled her eyes at the suggestion. "There's more than three hundred miles between us now. How much damn space do you think he needs to give me?"

"I was just trying to give him the benefit of the doubt." Sam pointed at her briefly with the chopsticks, then went back to picking chicken from the container.

Kacie slid off the counter and stashed her leftovers in the refrigerator. "And you're right. I should give him the benefit of the doubt. He was pretty upset about his brother reenlisting."

"The only reason I'm even suggesting it is because of what happened with his brother. And you yourself said how great a guy he was. That he treated you well and made you laugh." Sam jumped off the counter and threw the remaining containers in the trash. "I saw how happy you were at the wedding. Bryce noticed, too."

"You're so full of it," Kacie muttered under her breath.

"I'm not." Sam took hold of her shoulders and looked her in the eyes. "You deserve to be happy, Kacie. And you will be. Don't give up on him just yet. It's only been a week. Maybe, just maybe, he'll change his mind."

God, she wanted to believe everything her sister was saying. That somehow, magically, things would just work out and she and Michael would end up together. But she'd gotten her hopes up once before, and it had all come crashing down.

"I don't know Sam. I just don't see him leaving the army." Kacie lifted one shoulder and let it drop, feeling the familiar sting of tears in her eyes. "And I can't do the long-distance thing with a military guy again. I just can't. I won't make that mistake twice."

"Oh, shit. Don't cry, Kacie. You know I'm a sympathetic crier." Sam pulled her into a hug and squeezed her tight. "I'm so sorry, Kacie. So, so sorry."

And within seconds they were both crying. But then the tears gave way to laughter once they both got a glimpse of each other and the raccoon eyes their mascara had created. And as they dried their eyes with the scratchy take-out napkins because they couldn't find anything else, they laughed a bit more.

"I'm so glad you came to see me," Kacie said.

And then, as if her kind words were a jinx, Sam's phone buzzed with a text message.

"Bryce is on his way to pick me up," she said with a disappointed look on her face while shoving her phone in her pocket. "We're going to dinner with his boss and a few other people. But you can definitely come along, if you want."

Kacie squeezed her sister's arm. "Thank you, but I'm not much in the mood for going out."

Sam's face brightened. "I could ditch the dinner and stay here with you."

Just her sister offering to stay was enough to lift her spirits. "Go to dinner with your husband. I'll be fine."

Sam gathered her things, and as Kacie opened the door, her little sister turned to hug her goodbye. "I miss you."

"Same here."

Her sister stepped back, putting space between them, but still reluctant to let her go. "Now I'm going to try not to bother you too much. I know this next year is really important and you're going to be super busy. But don't think that means I don't miss you. Or that I don't want to talk to you. You can call me anytime. Okay? Anytime day or night."

After one last hug, Sam headed down the corridor and Kacie closed the apartment door behind her. She and Sam hadn't had an exchange like that—one that wasn't loaded or challenging—for so long she had almost forgotten what it felt like.

For the first time that day, she was alone in her new apartment. She surveyed the room, at the towering stacks of boxes and the furniture still wrapped in cellophane. Finally, she picked up the box blade on the counter and began cutting away the plastic covering the sofa cushions, all the while reminding herself this was what she wanted.

Chapter Twenty-Four

AFTER YET ANOTHER bad round of golf, Michael stopped off for a twelve-pack of beer and headed home to his lonely apartment. Only once he opened the door, he saw he wouldn't be too lonely. His father, Mac, sat in his reclining chair, feet propped up, a beer in one hand and Michael's remote in the other.

"It's about damn time you got home," his father said.

Michael turned and closed the door behind him, then made his way into the kitchen where he shoved his beer in the refrigerator alongside the ones his father had brought. But before he closed the door, he pulled two longnecks out, both of which were for him. He had a feeling he was going to need them.

"Dad, I love ya. And I realize you usually like to chat on Saturday nights." Michael twisted the top off his beer as he dropped into the sofa. "But what in hell are you doing here?"

His father took a leisurely sip of his beer, flipped through the cable channels a bit more, until he landed on a game. "I was told my son was having a hard time of it, so I decided to come see for myself. Especially since he hadn't bothered to tell his old man about any of it over the past few weeks."

Michael intended only to take a short pull from his beer, but ended up drinking down damn near half in the first go.

"Let me guess, Bree called you."

"Yeah, yeah, smarty pants," his father said with a wave. "She called me a few weeks ago, said she was worried about you. And I chalked it up to Bree just being Bree. She's very empathetic."

"Doesn't explain why you're here now." He was on the verge of taking another drink when his father turned and locked eyes with him. The familiar blue eyes bored into his soul.

"I'm here because your brother called me this morning."

Fuck.

Suddenly, he wasn't so thirsty.

Michael placed his half-full beer on the coffee table and tried to change the subject before things got out of hand. "Have you eaten? Are you hungry? I was going to order pizza if that sounds good to you?" He began scrolling through his contacts, looking for the pizza delivery place just down the street.

"Put your phone away, Michael. We're going to talk."

Jesus Christ. If there was a way for a man to go from thirty-five to fifteen in ten seconds flat, being chastised by his father was one.

He did as his father asked and placed his phone on the coffee table. In turn, Mac lowered the footrest and spun the chair around to face him. There was little doubt the man meant business.

"Your brother tells me you haven't decided on whether or not you're going to resign your commission."

Fucking Danny.

"I have not."

"Your brother seems to think you're considering staying in regiment since he reenlisted. He thinks you feel obligated to stay here."

Michael laughed without humor. "Because I am. There's a whole battalion of men counting on me."

His father shook his head, clearly not buying it. "There were battalion surgeons before you and there will be battalion surgeons after you go. That's not a reason. Are you staying here in order to keep an eye on your brother?"

"Don't be ridiculous. Why—why would I do that?"

Mac shrugged. "You tell me. Your brother has thought so for years. But I didn't buy into the idea until right now."

"Why now?"

His father leaned as close as he could get without leaving the chair. "Because you're doing everything you can to not look me in the eyes. So tell me, are you stay-ing in the 75th so you can watch out for your brother?"

He had no choice but to answer truthfully. His father was like a dog with a bone when it came to matters like this. "Yes."

Michael picked up his beer from the table and drank the remainder in a matter of gulps. He placed the empty on the table, then grabbed the second, twisting off the cap and tossing it next to the bottle.

"Tell me why," his father said, crossing his arms over his chest. "Why are you staying here when everyone can see you aren't happy?"

Michael stared down into the narrow opening of his bottle, wondering if his lack of enthusiasm for the job was really that obvious.

"Michael. I'm waiting."

He took a deep breath and resigned himself to the fact he had to tell the truth. "Because Mom told me to. It was the last thing she asked me to do." Suddenly, it was like the floodgates opened up; the truth came rushing out of him. "It was just before she slipped into the coma. I'd come home from school and Mom was in her room. She was practically skin and bones by then. All she kept saying was that I was the oldest and he was the youngest and he was so little and he could get hurt so easily. She'd told me the same thing weeks before, but this time she kept saying it over and over, 'Take care of your brother. Take care of your brother.' So you see? It's *always* been my job to watch out for him. And then he almost died."

It was only then Michael realized he'd started crying, his face now damp with his tears. Maybe he should have talked to someone about all of this baggage long before now.

"I can promise you your mother never meant for you to watch over Daniel to this extent," his father said softly. "She would never want you to sacrifice your own happiness as a result."

"But what if I leave and something happens to him, like last time?"

"If, God forbid, your brother were to be killed while serving his country, it would not be your fault any more than if he were killed in a car accident down the street." His father sat quietly for several minutes, studying him. "Tell me about the girl."

Michael swore at Bree under his breath.

His father smiled. "No. Not Bree."

He spent the next twenty minutes pouring out his soul as he talked about Kacie, what an amazing a woman she was. Smart. Funny. Beautiful. He told his father how they spent most of their time laughing and now how he missed her so much it hurt. He told him how he saw future with her. One that had kids and grandkids in it.

"Do you realize I was your age when we lost your mother? Thirty-five is too damn young to lose the love of your life, Michael. The difference is your mother and I had fifteen years together and she gave me you two boys. So while I've missed her every day since her death, she's never been too far away either. But that's not the case with you and Kacie." Michael nodded and one corner of his father's mouth hitched up. "You two had only, what . . . a few months together? And you have nothing to show for it. That's not enough to sustain a man for a lifetime, Michael.

Michael couldn't stand it anymore. He held his head in his hands, wondering how in the hell he fucked everything up so badly.

"If you want to spend the rest of your life in the army, then do that," his father told him. "But do it because it's what you want to do, not because it's what you think you have to do. It's time to go out on your own. And if you think this girl is worth the trouble and uncertainty of starting a whole new life, then do it."

Mac stood up, walked over to Michael, and waited with open arms. His father had never been one to skimp on affection, especially not after their mother died. Tonight his father held him for a long time. Michael imagined it was longer than most fathers and sons would embrace, but he didn't care.

As he stood in front of his father, he realized his dad had become a little shorter, a little rounder, and his hair a lot grayer over the past couple of years. But he was still the great man he'd always been.

"There's one other thing your mother used to always say: 'Go where your happiness lies.' Whether it be a job you like, or place you feel at home in, or in the arms of someone you love. Don't be afraid to chase after it." Mac patted Michael's cheek. "Life is far too short to not be happy, Michael."

KACIE STEPPED OFF the elevator with grocery bags in hand and breathed a sigh of relief when she saw the corridor between her and her one-bedroom apartment was empty. Months ago, when she leased the unit in Durham's tobacco district, the idea of being surrounded by people, many of whom were single and close to her age, held a great deal of appeal.

But now, the idea of going out, being social, held zero appeal. Instead, she just wanted to climb into bed and curl into a ball and stay there until she had to get up the following morning.

She shifted her bags to one hand and pulled her keys from her pocket. As she went to unlock her door, a voice called out to her from down the corridor.

"Hey there." A dark-haired man wearing a Cubs T-shirt, madras plaid shorts, and flip-flops was making his way toward her.

For a split second she considered darting inside and slamming the door closed behind her, but he seemed friendly enough and didn't appear to be the serial killer type. So she'd suck it up and be nice, but only because she had forty-nine weeks until her lease expired and the last thing she wanted was to be labeled "that" neighbor within the first month of living here.

She offered a polite smile but nothing more.

"You just moved in, right? I'm Paul." He extended his hand to her, only to drop it when he noticed both of her hands were occupied.

"Kacie."

She spent the next few minutes listening to him chatter away, about how he had moved from Chicago to The Triangle to do research in immunogenicity. He talked about the outdoor concerts, the street festivals, the rooftop parties, all the things that had made her want to live here in the first place, but now was doing her best to avoid. He asked where she was from, what she did for a living. His eyes drifted to her left hand and she knew it was only a matter of time before he asked her relationship status.

"One of your bags is dripping," Paul said, pointing to the floor.

"Well, then, I guess that's my cue to get this stuff put away." She smiled politely and shoved open her door. "It was nice meeting you."

"Some friends of mine and I'll be barbecuing in the courtyard around six if you want to join us."

"Another time, perhaps."

He nodded in understanding, then finally turned to leave. Kacie let the door close behind her and breathed a sigh of relief as she leaned against it.

For all intents and purposes, she should have been interested in a man like Paul. He was obviously smart and polite and nice looking, even if his clothing choices were questionable. And, from what he told her, didn't tick any of the boxes on her no-fly list. But it didn't matter, because he wasn't a tall, arrogant man with dark blond hair and deep blue eyes and a smile that could charm the panties off a nun.

Pushing herself off the door, Kacie made her way into the small kitchen and placed her bags on the counter. As much as she hated to admit it, she missed him. Despite telling her body and her heart for months it was just a temporary fling with Michael, he'd somehow found a way to burrow beneath her skin and take hold of the very places she had previously vowed to keep closed off.

She'd read and kept each text, each email. Listened to the dirty voice mails he'd left months earlier thousands of times just to hear the sound of his voice.

Her phone vibrated across the kitchen counter and her heart leapt at the thought of him calling her at the very moment she was thinking of him. Only when she looked at the caller ID it wasn't Michael. It was Sam.

For days she'd been avoiding her sister's calls, too, despite the great time they'd had together when Sam had visited. Not because she'd done anything wrong— aside from having a perfect life and being blissfully happy. Despite the new job, the new apartment, the new city, it was as if Kacie's life had regressed to that same sad, lonely point it was months ago. Once again she was the woman standing all alone at the bar, watching her sister and her friends enjoying everything life had to offer, while she was left feeling like a total buzzkill.

It was as if the summer never even happened.

The call went to voice mail, but almost immediately it began vibrating again. Kacie sighed. At some point in time she'd have to talk to her sister. Might as well do it now.

"Hey, Sammie!" Kacie hoped she at least sounded convincingly happy. "How are you?"

"I know I promised not to bother you too much but I've been calling you for three days."

"I know. I've just been swamped." It wasn't a total lie. Between her fellowship and seeing patients and unpacking the last of her things, she'd been busy.

"I was worried."

She held the phone with one hand and unpacked her grocery bags with the other. "I'm fine, I promise," she said, pulling a container of Phish Food out of the bag.

"Have you heard from him?"

"Nope."

"You're not moping, are you? Your freezer isn't stockpiled with Ben & Jerry's, is it?"

Kacie stared at the small carton of ice cream in her hand. Sometimes her sister had scary intuition. "Nope. No moping. And no ice cream." She shoved the container in her freezer, to hide the evidence of her lie.

"Oh. That's really good."

"As a matter of fact, I just met a nice guy who lives in the building. He invited me to dinner."

"Oh! That's really great news. When are you going out?"

"We haven't set a night just yet." Kacie desperately needed to change the subject. "So what's up? Why have you been trying to call me?"

"I have fantastic news. Are you ready for it?"

Kacie moved on to the next bag and unloaded a container of apple fritters she'd found in the bakery. While they weren't peach, they were close enough. "Absolutely. Hit me with it."

"You are going to be an auntie."

The silence stretched too long as she tried to process the words.

"Kacie?"

She pressed the heel of her hand to her eyes. Surely she heard wrong. "I'm sorry, Sam. I'm going to need you to repeat that."

"I'm pregnant! Bryce and I are going to have a baby."

Suddenly, Kacie was struggling to swallow around the lump in her throat. "Congratulations."

She slid down the kitchen cabinets and sat on the cold, polished concrete floor, holding her head in her hand while Sam spent the next forty-five minutes recounting every symptom, every second of the first doctor visit. She even forwarded the ultrasound images, pictures that looked like nothing more than a white bubble floating on a sea of black.

An hour later, she was finally able to get off the phone. By that point she had no desire to eat, to read, to watch TV, to unpack. She had no desire to do anything. So she climbed into bed, closed her eyes, and cried. Like she had done every other night since she arrived. Because if she'd learned one thing over the course of the last year, it was that happy endings weren't meant for her—they were meant for everyone else.

THE FOLLOWING DAY, Michael found Danny in his backyard, coated in sawdust and drenched in sweat as he sawed through a large sheet of plywood. As the wood began to slip and fall from the sawhorses, Michael ran over and grabbed the opposite end, stabilizing it. Only then did Danny even realize he was there.

His brother gave a nod of thanks, finished the cut, then lowered the circular saw to the ground. "That was good timing," he said while shoving his safety glasses onto the top of his head.

"No problem." Michael stacked the two pieces on the grass. "What's this for?"

"The subfloor in the mudroom has rotted. I moved the washer and dryer out first thing this morning and started tearing out the existing floor. I need to get this nailed down, install some linoleum, and move everything back in before the weekend is up."

Michael chuckled. "Bree's got you on the clock, huh?"

"You know it." His brother smiled at him, then took a moment to brush the sawdust from his clothes. "Okay, then. Let's hear it."

"Hear what?"

Danny folded his arms over his chest. "How you're

pissed off that I called Dad and made him worry to the point he drove down here to check on you."

Michael shook his head. "I'm not pissed."

His brother stared at him in surprise. "Huh," he finally said, then gestured to the back porch where a large cooler sat between two deck chairs. "Want something to drink?"

Michael was indifferent about the drink, but followed anyway, because this conversation was a long time coming. He'd just sat down when his brother tossed him a bottle of Gatorade. But instead of cracking it open, he stared at the orange top a few seconds, trying to decide how best to start the conversation. Ended up, he didn't have to.

"Were you able to talk to Dad about what's got you all twisted up inside?" Danny drank down half of his bottle and swiped an orange droplet from his chin. "That's why I called him, you know. Since you wouldn't talk to me or Bree, I'd hoped you'd at least talk to him."

"I didn't realize you were wanting me to talk to you."

Danny scoffed. "You haven't noticed how often I've been stopping by your office? Especially when I haven't seen you in a couple of days? What about the number of dinner invites Bree has made in the last six months? I thought you'd talk when you were ready. And just for the record, Bree got tired of waiting before I did."

"Jesus." Michael shook his head. "You act like I should have had all sharp objects and my shoelaces taken away from me."

"Hey." Danny said it with such force, it got Michael's attention. "We've just been worried about you. And when I found out you were dating someone I thought, 'Maybe this is what he needs. This will help.' And I think it did for a while. But since Kacie left for North Carolina, you've had the look of a man on the edge."

"Don't be so fucking dramatic."

Danny grabbed his arm. "Really? You're calling me dramatic? Dad phoned me the minute he got to your apartment yesterday. Said there was a fresh patch and paint job on your living room wall. I may not be a fucking doctor, but I seriously doubt punching holes in apartment walls is some newfangled form of therapy."

He was silent for a long time as he thought about all Danny had said.

"Tell me what's running through that head of yours?"

Michael set his drink on the ground and looked his brother in the eyes. "I'm thinking about leaving the 75th."

A smile spread across his brother's face. "I've been waiting a long time to hear you say that."

"You're serious?"

"Hell, yes, I'm serious. As a matter of fact, this calls for a celebration!" Danny rose to his feet and slapped him on the shoulder before he headed inside. A few minutes later he returned, handing one of the opened longnecks to Michael. "The scotch will have to wait for another time. Preferably when I'm not required to use power tools and on a tight deadline. But for now, here's to new adventures!"

Danny held out his longneck, waiting for Michael to join in on the toast. "I didn't realize you wanted me out of your hair this bad," he said, finally tapping the neck of his bottle to Danny's.

"Don't get me wrong, I like having you around. But you need to do your own thing." Danny dropped into the empty deck chair beside him. "What finally changed your mind?"

"Dad."

And then he told Danny everything. About the conversation he'd had with their dad the night before, about the nightmares, the constant worry. He told him why he changed specialties in medical school, all he had done to make sure he'd become battalion surgeon for the 1st/75th. Even told him about that late-summer afternoon when their mother asked him to take care of Danny.

When he was finally done telling the secret he'd carried around for twenty-five years, he looked up to see his brother smiling at him, almost on the verge of laughing.

He frowned. "What's so damn funny?"

Danny shook his head in disbelief. "Mom told me the same thing."

Michael stared at his brother. He couldn't have heard right. "She *what*?"

"Before she died she asked me to watch out for you. She told me that it was my job as your little brother to make sure you remembered to have fun. Because even at ten years old you were so damn serious."

"You're lying." But even as he said the words, Michael knew Danny was telling the truth. And as the fact sunk in, it felt as though a weight was finally lifting off his shoulders.

"You can ask Bree. I told her years ago," Danny said with a chuckle. "So, big brother, the question now is what do you *want* to do?"

Michael stared down into his longneck, nearly overwhelmed by all the possibilities. "I don't even know where to start."

"Okay, then. Let's do this." Danny leaned forward in his chair and looked him straight in the eyes. "You can go anywhere in the world. You can see or do almost anything. Scuba diving in Hawaii. Golfing in Scotland. Skiing in the Alps." He poked Michael in the chest. "Who do you want to do it with?"

"Kacie."

He said her name without hesitation. She was the first answer, the right answer, the *only* answer that would ever come to mind.

"There you go," Danny said with a smile. "I think you know exactly where to start."

Chapter Twenty-Five

THREE MONTHS INTO her fellowship and Kacie had to remind herself every day this was everything she had ever wanted. Her clinical work kept her unbelievably busy, and the research for her fellowship took up the rest of her time. She loved working with kids who needed her assistance to have as normal a life as possible—it was far more rewarding than working with grown men who strained a muscle or hurt their back in a pickup basketball game. And when her residency was over, she shouldn't have any trouble finding a job since she was participating in one of the most prestigious programs in the country.

So why was she so damn miserable?

Well for one, her imagination had been running away with itself, coming up with scenarios where Michael had met someone new. Someone prettier. Someone who wasn't so rigid. Someone who knew how to dance.

Meanwhile, she sat in her closet-sized office facing the prospect of eating another lunch at her desk, all alone. What a pathetic sort she'd become when it came to her social life.

A knock on her open door interrupted her thoughts. She spun around in her chair to see a fellow therapist leaning against the doorjamb. "My lunch meeting was canceled," Valerie said. "Want to go down to the cafeteria with me?"

"I'm not very hungry."

"You don't have to be hungry, but you do need to get out of this office even for a little bit. Just a thirty-minute break. You're allowed that. And it just so happens it's unseasonably warm today. So let's sit outside and soak up some vitamin D."

It was all the prodding she needed. Kacie grabbed her wallet and headed downstairs with her coworker. She couldn't very well expect to move on with her life if she spent every spare minute of her day hiding in her closet, could she?

The moment they stepped off the elevator, Valerie's phone beeped; she pulled her cell from her pocket to check the message.

"Ooh . . ." Her face lit up as she read the message on her screen. "Seems like this break is even better timed than I imagined."

"Oh, yeah? Why is that?"

Valerie's thumbs flew across the touch screen keyboard as she typed out a reply. "Georgia from radiology said she just saw one fine hunk of man down in the solarium. Word on the street is he's a new hire in the ER."

If there was one thing Kacie had learned in her short time here, a new doc in town always caused a stir.

The message chimes came faster and faster and the typing continued as they made their way to the cafeteria.

"What is going on?" Kacie finally asked.

Valerie looked up at her with a smile that stretched from ear to ear. "Group text. We're tracking his movement."

"Oh, my God. Y'all are stalking this poor guy now?"

Valerie laughed. "Hey now. We're just having a little fun." Her phone chimed again and she looked to the screen. "I wonder if anyone has been able to snap a picture of him."

Kacie chuckled as she selected a large chef salad and placed it on her tray, then followed it with a small dish of banana pudding with vanilla wafers. She looked over at her friend only to realize she didn't have one. "Are you getting a tray or what?"

Valerie thunked her forehead, then raced off to grab one. She'd barely returned to her spot in line when she let out a whoop. "Yes! Someone got a pic. And my goodness. He is pretty."

Valerie held out the screen for her to see, but Kacie wasn't really interested. "Later maybe," she replied, fishing through her wallet for change.

With her curiosity now satisfied, Valerie was able to focus on lunch once again, and the two of them headed outside to an empty table in the small courtyard and took a seat in the sunshine.

Valerie's phone continued to chime as they ate, but she didn't bother to reach for it. "Do you need to check those?" Kacie asked, pointing to the phone.

"Nah." Valerie stabbed a bite of pasta with her fork. "They'll be going on all day. Lord help the man if he truly is single."

They shared a laugh, at least until something caught Valerie's attention. "Oh, my God, Kacie. He just came outside," she said without really moving her mouth.

"Really?" Kacie made a motion to turn around and check this guy out for herself, but Valerie stopped her.

"Hang on a second," she whispered. "If you turn around right now it'll be obvious."

Kacie laughed. "As opposed to all the women already staring at him with their mouths hanging open? Including you?"

But Valerie wasn't listening. Instead, her jaw dropped and her eyes widened. "He's coming this way," she said while sitting up a little straighter in her chair.

Although she really wanted to turn around, Kacie didn't want to make a scene. She watched Valerie's eyes grow wider and wider, her line of sight now somewhere directly above Kacie's head.

"Kacie?"

She knew that voice. Knew who it belonged to without any need to see his face. She took a deep breath and scooted her chair back so she could stand and face him.

It was no wonder he'd caused such a stir. His hair was a little longer now, and the way the sunlight hit the golden strands, he looked like an actor from a movie, an image only enhanced by the fact that he was dressed in a tailored navy suit, starched white shirt, and patterned tie.

She swallowed hard and tried to find her voice. "What—what are you doing here?"

"Getting the full tour." He flashed that charming smile, the one that showcased his dimples, and Kacie was almost certain she heard a half dozen women behind her swoon. "My new boss thought it was important I knew my way around the hospital before I officially start next week."

At some point her heart migrated northward and was now pounding out a rhythm in her throat. "You took a job here?"

"I did."

"You left the regiment?"

"I did," he said, staring at her with those intense blue eyes. "For the moment I'm on inactive ready reserve. I haven't made a final decision yet as to whether I'll stay my full twenty. I was hoping to talk to you about it. Get your thoughts."

Kacie couldn't believe what she was hearing. "But what about Danny?"

Michael took her hand in both of his and stroked the

back of her knuckles with his thumbs. "He's a big boy. He'll take care of himself."

She couldn't believe this was happening. Kacie grabbed hold of his suit jacket and buried her face against his chest, unable to hold back the tears of joy and relief any longer. She'd thought she had lost him forever—and that she would regret losing him every day of her life.

He wrapped his arms around her, pressed kisses to the top of her head. It wasn't until this very minute, having been without his touch for so long, that she understood just how much she really missed him.

Once she caught her breath, she put just enough space between them so she could look up at him.

Using his thumbs, he swiped the tears from her face as he smiled down at her. "I hope these are tears of joy. Otherwise I'm kind of fucked."

Kacie laughed in a way she hadn't laughed in months, not since the last time she was with him. "God, I've missed you. You'll never know how much I missed you. I kept telling myself that this new job, new fellowship, new life, would somehow be enough, but it just wasn't."

He grasped her face in both hands and kissed her. He was not gentle. He was not polite. He kissed her like she was the air he needed in order to survive. He pressed harder, deeper, with his mouth, bruising her lips, marking her in such a way everyone in this place would know she belonged to him. And then his kiss softened into the merest brush of his lips against hers, once, twice, and one more for good measure.

Their private moment was interrupted by the shutter sound from a camera phone. Kacie turned to see Valerie typing out a quick message. "What are you doing?" she asked, bewildered.

Valerie smiled. "Just letting them all know that this man is taken."

Michael cupped her chin and tipped her face upward to his. "Am I?" he whispered so only she could hear. "Taken, that is?"

She smiled at him through her tears.

"Absolutely."

MICHAEL HATED LETTING Kacie go, even for a matter of hours. But she had patients to see and work to do and that was priority. He wouldn't ever make such a stupid mistake again, implying her work was somehow less important than his. So he kissed her goodbye and headed off to the human resources department to complete his new-hire paperwork.

They planned to meet in the solarium at the end of the day, since it was one of the few places he was able to find on the sprawling hospital campus. And for the third time in less than ten minutes, he checked his watch. She was only five minutes later than she'd said she would be. But the time seemed to crawl.

He took a seat on an empty bench and waited. He'd wait a lifetime for her if he had to, without complaint.

From the night he returned to his apartment to find

his dad kicked back in his reclining chair, he knew what needed to be done. Although he didn't resign his commission, he did give notice to the new battalion commander that he no longer wished to serve as 1st Batt's surgeon. He had stayed long enough to assist with the transition once a replacement was found, but that was all.

As fate would have it, once he decided to go inactive ready reserve, an opening came available in the emergency department at Duke. He was told by his new boss that his top notch education and years of trauma experience made him an easy selection. The job was his if he wanted it.

In that time, he hadn't heard from Kacie. He didn't know how she'd react. Part of him feared being kicked to the curb, in much the same way she'd rejected her ex at the wedding.

But he knew it would have to be all or nothing. He wouldn't have been able to approach Kacie and say he may or may not take a job with Duke. Or that he may or may not leave the army. He needed to make these decisions on his own. Like she had told him, he had to be responsible for his own happiness. So he had done that. And he was all the better for it.

"Hey there, handsome." His heart jumped as she approached his bench and gave him a shy smile, followed by an unexpected wink. "Care to give me a ride home?"

After how things ended between them in Savannah, he never expected to see her smile like that at him again. God, how he'd missed the sight of it. Missed *her*.

He rose to his feet and handed her the small bouquet he had bought at the gift shop. Then, he pressed a chaste kiss to her mouth, right before he leaned close to whisper in her ear. "Sunshine, I'll give you any kind of ride you want, anytime, anywhere."

Then he stood back and watched in amusement as that slow blush burned across her cheeks.

They chatted about unimportant things as they made their way to her place: football, the weather, his drive up from Savannah. But once her apartment door closed with a thud behind them and they were inside the privacy of her home, everything they were carrying was dropped. Including the bouquet, which met the concrete floor in an explosion of petals.

Wasting no time in picking up where he left off in the courtyard, Michael cradled her neck with one hand, his lips skimming the delicate skin of her throat. But for Kacie it wasn't enough. Immediately, her hands went inside his suit jacket, sliding up to his shoulders until she pushed it free from his arms. And then she took hold of his tie, practically leading him to the bedroom. Their hands worked in frenzied motions as they removed each other's clothes. And then finally they tumbled onto the bed where they made up for three months' worth of being apart.

As day turned into night, he propped his head on one hand, content to watch her sleep. He brushed the tiny strands of hair back from her face; he listened to the soft huffs of her breath. All the while counting the moments until he could stare into those green eyes of hers. He didn't have to wait long as Kacie roused herself from her catnap and rolled over to face him.

"So . . ." She skimmed her hand along his face, under his jaw to his chin. "I never asked, but when do you start your new job?"

"Two weeks."

"Why so long before you start?"

He raised one shoulder and let it drop. "Because I needed time to find a place to live. And to pack up all my stuff and bring it up here."

Kacie shot straight up in the bed, covering herself with the bedsheet. "No."

"No?"

"That's right." Her tone softened and a smile appeared. "You don't need to find a place to live. Because you're going to live here. With me."

Part of him had hoped that's exactly what she'd say. But he'd been afraid to hope too much.

"You're sure?"

"Absolutely." She climbed out of the bed and picked up his white dress shirt off the floor, slipping it on. "As a matter of fact, I think we should start right now."

She disappeared into the living room and then returned with his suit jacket and his bag. He couldn't help but think how sexy she was when she walked past the bed, towing his suitcase along behind her. He liked how her wavy blond hair fell wild over her shoulders, liked how she rolled the sleeves of his shirt up her arms, and especially liked how the hem of it only reached midthigh. And since he knew she wasn't wearing anything beneath it, it made for one helluva sexy version of peekaboo.

One by one she unpacked his things. She hung his suit in the closet along with the golf shirts and pants he'd packed. She made room in a dresser for his socks and underwear and then gave him two drawers in the bathroom for his toiletries.

With his suitcase empty, she brushed the imaginary dirt from her hands and smiled. "Done and done."

They ordered pizza for dinner because neither wanted to go out. And since they had nothing else to do during the forty-minute delivery wait, they made love yet again. Once it arrived they sat side by side in bed and ate straight from the box as they watched the Thunder and Warriors play. He climbed out of bed to refill their water glasses, but was struck by the view upon his return. Wearing nothing more than a white bedsheet, Kacie sat cross-legged in the middle of the bed. Her hair was pulled haphazardly into a knot on the top of her head, while a few tendrils dangled against her shoulders. Hovering over the open pizza box, she took another bite of pepperoni while watching the game.

When he told all the guys he was leaving 1st Batt, they couldn't understand why. What could possibly be better than life at HAAF?

If he could, he would tell them all about this moment, about this woman who captured his interest from the start, who he fell in love with by accident. The one who was only supposed to be a summer fling, but ended up stealing his heart.

Handing her one of the water glasses, Michael settled on the bed next to her, reclining against a stack of pillows.

At the commercial, she turned to look at him and smiled. "There's a few slices left if you're still hungry."

"You go ahead."

"No, I think I'm done," she wiped her fingers on a paper napkin. "As a matter of fact, I know it." She tossed the napkin in the box before closing the lid. She climbed off the bed to take the box to the kitchen and he found himself amused as she struggled with the bedsheet and fought to not drop the box every step of the way.

He was still smiling when she returned sans pizza box, an excess of white fabric trailing on the floor behind her. She circled around to the opposite side of the bed and climbed in.

"Why does this always happen? I end up naked while you're fully clothed."

"Haven't the faintest idea. I still don't see the problem with it."

Kacie arched a brow. "Says the man wearing clothes."

"Well, one of us had to answer the door when the pizza man showed up. Of course, if you'd answered the door wearing *that*, we might have gotten the pizza for free."

She took hold of a pillow and swung it, scoring a direct hit to the head. Unwilling to let such an attack stand, he countered by tossing the offending pillow from the bed. And then he reveled in the sounds of her shrieks of laughter as he wrestled her to the mattress, finally pinning her down with his lower body.

With his breath rushing in and out of his lungs and heart racing, he caged her between his hands and hovered above her, staring down into her calming sea-glass eyes. "You know I love you, right?"

Her smile was soft and warm and sweet and tender all in one. "I suspected as much."

"If I'm going to live here with you and spend every night in your bed, you're going to have to get used to me saying it," he said with all seriousness. "Life is too short to not be happy. And I don't ever want you to think you don't make me so very happy."

Kacie slid her hand free from his grasp and smoothed her fingers across his forehead, his brows. She traced the line of his nose and the edge of his jaw. And after pressing a kiss to his lips, cheek, and jaw, she whispered in his ear. "I love you, too."

Chapter Twenty-Six

February 2014

As they crossed the intercoastal waterway, Michael reached across the center console and took Kacie's hand in his. "Are you ready to do this?"

"As I'll ever be?"

The tone of her voice raised concern, and when he glanced over at her, she wore a smile on her face that said she was trying to convince herself as much as him.

He chuckled and gave a quick kiss to the back of her hand, along with a squeeze for encouragement. "You'll be fine, I promise. My dad is going to love you."

Since he had started working in the emergency room four months ago, this was the first full weekend both of them had off at the same time. Kacie was busy with her fellowship and required clinical hours, and with his ever-changing work schedules, there were some weeks they were like two ships passing in the night. But they were making the best of it. And as far as he was concerned, it was far better than the alternative.

He'd adjusted well to civilian medicine and found himself far happier working in the hectic environment of a level-one trauma center than spending the bulk of his time pushing paper. After all, treating people and saving lives was the whole reason he became a doctor in the first place.

Talking to a therapist also helped. Once every couple of weeks he'd take the time for a tune-up, so to speak, to keep him from falling back into old habits and destructive ways of thinking.

And his relationship with Kacie was all the better for it.

But he didn't leave the military completely behind, choosing to serve in the army reserve medical command with a support team out of Fort Bragg. There would be deployments in his future, but not as long or as often as the 75th, and not always to a war zone.

With 1st Batt returning to Afghanistan within a matter of weeks, Danny and Bree decided to take a break from home renovations and spend the block leave with their families instead. And when Danny suggested making it a family reunion of sorts, Michael quickly jumped on board. While it required weeks of planning, some careful negotiating, and swapping shifts here and there, he and Kacie were able to get the job done. So early that Saturday morning, they loaded a small suitcase into the trunk of his car and hit the road for a short getaway.

As they neared the Grand Strand, traffic slowed as usual, despite the fact it wasn't tourist season. He pointed out a few of his old hangouts along the way and noted how much the city had changed since he'd last visited. Finally, they reached the mid-'60s single-story ranch where he grew up, one of many on the street with an American flag waving proudly from the front porch.

"I'm not sure what I was expecting. A frat house, maybe," Kacie teased as they pulled into the long, single car driveway. "But it's cute. I like it."

Admittedly, Michael never thought much of the generic redbrick house with black shutters when he was growing up. It was on the small side and felt more than a little run-down when compared to some of the newer, larger houses his friends lived in. Now that he was older, he had greater appreciation for this place. In a way, it was exactly what he wanted in his future: a nice house on a quiet street with a yard big enough for kids to play in and large trees for them to climb. He wanted a wife who loved chocolate, kept him on his toes, and made him laugh all the time. He wanted two, maybe three kids with eyes the color of sea glass and wild, wavy hair. And finally, a dog. Maybe a cat or some fish if the kids asked nicely, but otherwise he'd be perfectly content with just a dog.

As they climbed out of the car, the screen door flew open and Danny came bounding down the front steps. "It's about damn time you got here!"

He made a beeline for Michael, grabbing hold of him

in a bear hug, lifting him from the ground and shaking him a bit. Then after dropping him back on his feet, Danny dramatically grabbed at his lower back.

"Damn! Civilian life is making you soft. How much weight have you put on? Twenty? Thirty pounds?"

Michael gave his brother a healthy shove. "You're so full of shit. If anything I've lost weight I've been so busy."

Danny laughed at him as he walked away, circling around the car to Kacie. "It's really wonderful to see you again." He flashed her what Kacie had teased him was the trademark MacGregor grin and extended a hand.

Kacie's cheeks pinked. "Same here."

Always the flirt, his little brother.

"Okay, that's enough." Michael jokingly stepped between them. "Do me a favor and grab our bag from the trunk, would ya? I'm going to introduce Kacie to Dad."

Danny snapped to attention and saluted his brother. "Yes, sir."

"Come on, Kacie." He placed his hand at her lower back and walked her to the front door.

"Wow," she whispered. "I'm kinda surprised you let that go so easily."

"What can I say, sunshine," he said with a wink. "I've grown in the past few months."

No need for her to know that he was using his free hand to flip Danny the bird. And when his brother laughed, there was no question as to whether or not he'd seen the gesture.

They climbed the front steps, but just before he pulled open the door, he stopped and turned to her. "I forgot to warn you that it's kind of a time warp in there."

A little crease appeared between her brows. "What do you mean?"

"The house looks just the same as it did when my mom died."

Kacie's eyes widened a bit. "Oh."

"Yep." Michael took a deep breath and opened the door for her. "Here we go."

But the joke was on him the moment he stepped into the living room.

The wood floors had been sanded and stained and the walls and trim had received a fresh coat of paint. His father's recliner had been replaced with a far more stylish and modern leather version and no longer was there an '80s floral sofa occupying the middle of the room. In its place, a comfortable-looking tan sectional and ottoman that offered far more seating than ever before. And there was actually room for a wall-mounted flat-screen TV.

His jaw was still on the floor when Danny walked in, the screen door slamming shut behind him. "What's the matter with you?" he asked.

"I want to know what the hell happened in here," Michael said as his brother dropped the small suitcase at his feet. "And why does it seem brighter?"

"The new windows are bigger than the originals. And the recessed lighting makes a huge difference as well."

Michael turned to see his dad standing in the doorway leading into the kitchen.

"Well, do you like it?" his dad asked.

As he struggled to find the right words, Kacie quickly spoke up. "I think it looks fantastic."

"And I like you already." Mac chuckled and walked toward her with open arms. "You must be Kacie."

Michael watched as his father embraced her as if he'd known her his entire life. And vice versa.

"It all started with a leaky shower pan in the bathroom. The fixtures looked worn out with all the brand-new tile, so I replaced everything in there." He tucked Kacie's hand in the crook of his elbow and led her down the hall for a tour. "But soon I realized I was the only person who ever saw the best-looking room in the house. And that's a very bad thing."

Their laughter echoed as they disappeared down the hall and out of sight.

Michael smiled, then looked to his brother. "Why didn't you tell me?"

"Dad wanted it to be a surprise." Danny gave a slight shrug as he folded his arms over his chest. "Marie did most of the design. For free, I might add. Bree came home a few weekends to help him pick out furniture."

"But that doesn't explain why he decided to change everything now."

His brother gave him a knowing smile. "He did it for you, for me. He wanted this house to be a place where we'd want to bring our families." He nodded at the suitcase at Michael's feet. "You should go check out your bedroom by the way."

His curiosity piqued, Michael picked up his bag and headed down the hallway, passing the closed door to Danny's old room along the way. "Surprised" didn't even begin to describe how he felt the moment he stepped in his old room. Gone were the old, dusty books and small, worn-out bed. The windows were noticeably larger now and the room had been painted the color of a peacock. The color could've made the room feel small, but the new queen-sized bed covered in white bedding made it feel big. Only his large wooden dresser remained, although it had received a face-lift of its own: on top sat several framed photos. The first was of him and his mom. Another was of him, his dad, and Danny while on a fishing trip they'd taken years earlier. But the largest was a family photo taken at Danny and Bree's wedding. And Michael knew in his gut that one day a similar photo from his and Kacie's wedding would take its rightful place next to it.

"Now that door we're not going to open," he heard his father say. "That's the last room to do. And as my wife used to say, 'It looks like a bomb went off in there.'"

Their combined laughter led them down the hallway to his room.

"Ooh." Kacie's eyes brightened the moment she walked stepped through the doorway. "I love the color. Did you pick it yourself?"

Michael chuckled. "Yeah, Dad. Did you pick everything yourself?"

"You know damn well I didn't pick any of this out." Mac then turned to Kacie and smiled. "But I'm glad you like it just the same."

When the house phone rang, Mac excused himself to go answer it, giving Michael a few minutes alone with Kacie. He took hold of her hand and tugged her close, wrapping his arms around her waist. "See? I told you he'd love you."

Her palms skimmed up and over his chest, finally wrapping around his neck. "I gotta say I think he's pretty terrific, too. You're one lucky man."

Michael pressed a gentle kiss to her lips, then whispered against her mouth. "Don't I know it."

IT WASN'T LONG before Mac returned to finish his guided tour, once again taking her hand and tucking it in the bend of his elbow. Kacie liked how he took time to tell her the stories behind each photograph that hung on the wall or sat atop a dresser, and his pride for his sons was undeniable. It was also plain to see he was a man who remained deeply in love with his wife despite her death so many years before. Photos of her could be found in nearly every room, making certain her presence was there in spirit if not in body.

Since the weather was unseasonably warm considering the time of year, they all settled on the back porch where the three MacGregor men attempted to one-up each other with their stories. They teased. They bickered. They harassed each other. Most of all they laughed a lot, their affection for one another obvious and genuine. However, the fun was interrupted momentarily when a familiar default ring tone caused all three men to reach for their pockets, which of course ended up being just another reason for them to laugh.

Danny held his ringing phone in the air. "Winner winner chicken dinner," he said before swiping his thumb across the screen. "Hey, sweetheart." Within a matter of seconds he was rising to his feet. "Bree just turned in the neighborhood and she's got a carload of groceries."

And that was enough for the three of them to hop up out of their chairs and rush out the front door. Uncertain what to do, Kacie wandered through the kitchen and into the living room. Just then, Bree pulled open the front door and held it as the men paraded inside, each with several bags in their hands. Without further prompting, they dropped everything on the small dining room table and pulled items out left and right.

"No, no, no." Bree rushed to stop them. "You all just stay out of it."

"But don't you need help?" Danny asked eagerly.

"Not that kind of help." Bree snatched a large bag of chips from her husband's hands. "Kacie can help me in here while you all argue about who'll be manning the grill—out there, of course," she said, pointing to the back porch. "So grab your beers and shoo."

There was minimal grumbling as Michael grabbed three longnecks from the fridge, pausing only long enough to drop a kiss on Kacie's cheek before he followed his dad and brother outside.

Having successfully ushered them out, Bree went about unloading the items onto the table. "If given the chance, those three would eat almost everything in these bags before we even got around to having lunch. The way they act, you'd think they hadn't eaten in days."

"I've seen firsthand the damage Michael can do," Kacie said with a laugh. "If Mac and Danny eat anything like him, I can only imagine."

"No one eats like Michael," Bree said with a roll of her eyes. "That man, I swear to God. With the amount of junk he consumes, he should weigh a solid six hundred pounds." She grabbed a few frozen items, then crossed the small galley kitchen to put them away. "So . . . how's life in Durham? And things with you and Michael?" she asked from behind the open refrigerator door.

Kacie ducked her head over the bag she was unloading, trying to hide her smile. Damn if he hadn't predicted Bree would ask about their relationship within five minutes of getting her alone. A quick glimpse of her watch had her stifling a laugh. Three minutes. She glanced out the dining room window and caught him staring at her. A slow grin spread across his face as if he could read her mind.

Damn that man.

He'd won the bet with two minutes to spare and there was little doubt in her mind he'd make her pay up. Not that she'd really care. Especially since it was the kind of bet where they both won in the end.

Instantly her imagination went wild, thinking about all the delicious things he'd promised to do—

"Kacie?"

She shook herself from her daydream and found Bree's head cocked to one side, an eyebrow raised in silent question.

"Oh, sorry. I thought . . ." Without a way to explain herself, she pointed to the window and the man who derailed her train of thought in the first place. Of course he wasn't looking now; instead, he appeared to be completely engrossed in conversation.

Kacie cleared her throat. "Things are good."

"Just good?" Bree's brows drew together, her concern obvious.

"I should say *very* good." Upon her admission she felt the heat rise up from her chest, consume her throat, and set her face aflame. "Michael being there is the best part actually."

"I'm glad to hear it," Bree's face relaxed into a smile. "And you like the work?"

"I love it. It's exciting and exhausting all at the same time, but I'm learning a lot. It's almost hard to believe my fellowship is halfway over."

There was no telling where their careers would lead

them six months from now, but she knew in her heart they'd go wherever the road led together.

Her gaze drifted to the window, to him, once again.

"I've loved him like a brother my entire life," Bree said quietly. "And I've never seen him so happy. I have a feeling it won't be long before we'll be sisters-in-law."

Kacie's heart began to race despite trying to keep her feelings in check. Although she'd mentally prepared herself for this kind of polite inquisition, she still held a deep-seated fear that she'd somehow jinx things if she spent too much time talking about their relationship. "We're trying not to get ahead of ourselves."

"Well, I'm not afraid to jump the gun, especially since you are the first woman he's ever brought home."

That little tidbit took her by surprise. She looked at Bree and tried to determine if she was exaggerating. "Since college?"

Bree's smile widened. "More like since high school. And even then I don't remember any girls coming around."

The back door swung open and Mac breezed inside. "Are you ready for me to fire up the grill?"

"Not just yet," Bree answered. "Give it about ten minutes. I have to run across the street and grab a few things first."

"And how about you, Kacie dear?" Mac tossed an arm over her shoulders and hugged her to his side. "Anything you need?"

Kacie smiled. "I'm just fine, Mr. MacGregor."

"Oh, no! Don't you call me that." Mac made a dramatic showing of shaking his head. "It's Mac. Got it?"

Bree excused herself, but not before she gave her a knowing wink and smile. Her polite way of silently saying, "I told you so."

While Bree was gone, Kacie went about preparing the hamburgers, chatting with Mac about Durham, the loft she and Michael shared, and the baseball stadium just within walking distance.

"Sounds like a fun place to live," Mac said while rummaging through a kitchen drawer in search of a grill lighter.

"You should come visit and we all can go to a game."

Mac pointed at her with the stick lighter. "I'll do that."

It was only as Kacie made the last few patties and placed them on the tray did she wonder if she had overstepped a boundary.

The back door opened behind her. Without even turning around she knew it was him, and sure enough, he appeared at her side as she dried her hands. "Did you invite my dad to visit us in Durham?"

From his tone, it was nearly impossible for her to determine what he was thinking.

"I did. I thought it'd be nice for him to come visit while your brother was deployed, that maybe it'd be good for the both of you. Not that you'd worry any less about him . . ." Finally, she looked up into his deep blue eyes. "I'm sorry. I shouldn't have invited your dad to come visit without checking—"

Michael reached for her, taking her face in both of his hands and silencing her with his lips. She clung to his forearms as he poured every ounce of feeling and emotion into his kiss, until they were both breathless.

Afterward, he pressed his forehead to hers. "I love you. You know that, right?"

She smiled at his question. Of course she knew it, because he told her every day. Not just with words, but through his actions.

"I do know that." Kacie placed her palm on his chest, felt the strong, steady beat of his heart. "And I love you."

And she couldn't imagine a day would ever come where those words wouldn't be true.

LATER THAT NIGHT, after having spent the entire day with family, Michael was anxious to have Kacie all to himself if only for an hour or so. And since she'd never been to Myrtle Beach, it was the perfect excuse to take her down to Ocean Boulevard and the Grand Strand.

Although the tourist season wasn't in full swing, many of the bars and restaurants were still busy. The beach, however, was nearly deserted. They walked along the shore, hand in hand, beneath an inky black sky, where the only light came from the businesses along the promenade and the Sky Wheel.

They'd just reached Ninth Avenue when a bright red door was flung open and a parade of women streamed out of the iconic Myrtle Beach country bar wearing hot-pink T-shirts with TEAM BRIDE across the front. Among them was a woman dressed in white with a BRIDE-emblazoned white satin sash draped across her body—as if the veil on her head wasn't enough of a clue.

Michael chuckled. "That brings back some memories."

"Don't remind me." Kacie feigned a full-body shiver. "It still gives me nightmares."

"Now, now. If it hadn't been for your sister's bachelorette party, we might not have met." He wrapped his arm around Kacie's shoulders and pulled her to his side. "Someday, I'd like to see you wearing one of those."

"What? A satin sash?" Kacie snorted. "I've never been a fan of the pageant look."

He leaned down to whisper in her ear. "I was thinking more along the lines of the veil."

She stiffened slightly beneath his touch so he quickly added, "No rush though," and pressed a kiss to her temple.

Despite his moving to Durham and moving in with her, he knew she was still scared about the subject of marriage. After all, ex-Mike had toyed with her feelings for years and then made their breakup out to be her fault.

If he had his way, he would've proposed to her that afternoon in the hospital courtyard. He could've proposed at Christmas. Hell, he had half a mind to drop to one knee and propose this very second. It wasn't the fear she'd say no that kept him from popping the question. He knew in his heart and his gut she'd absolutely say yes.

But he wanted her to focus on her fellowship, wanted her to achieve her dreams because she'd waited too long and worked too hard to get to this point. And he didn't want anything, not a proposal or an engagement or a wedding, to overshadow her accomplishment.

So he'd patiently wait until the time was right. He'd waited his whole life for her. What was another six months?

The doors into the club opened and the sounds from the live band playing inside filled the air.

"I think they're playing our song."

She stared up at him with those light green eyes and a smile on her face. "We don't have a song."

"Well, then, we need to keep searching until we find one that sticks."

As he reached for the door, he leaned down and gave her a quick kiss, then ushered her inside for a dance.

Acknowledgments

IT IS MY belief that sometimes when everything is going your way, the universe kicks you right in the teeth just to keep you humble. Fortunately, I have great friends who picked me up, dusted me off, and faced me in the right direction so I could keep on going. Kendall, Liz, Mary Ann, and Michelle: I'll never be able to thank you all enough for your loving support and encouragement over the past year.

And so many thanks to my editor, Priyanka Krishnan, for working her magic with this story and giving me the opportunity to bring Lily MacGregor to life.

Don't miss the first fantastic romance
in Cheryl Etchison's American Valor series,

ONCE AND FOR ALL

Rule #1: Military and matrimony don't mix.

But if there's one person Staff Sergeant Danny
MacGregor would break all his rules for, it's Bree—his
first friend, first love, first everything. Maybe he likes
playing the hero. Maybe he's trying to ease ten years of
guilt. Either way, he'll do whatever he can to help her.

Wish #1: A little bit of normal.

Bree Dunbar has battled cancer, twice. What she
wants most is a fresh start in a place where she can find
a new job, and where people aren't constantly treating
her like she's sick. By some miracle her wish is granted,
but it comes with one major string attached—the man
who broke her heart ten years before.

The rules for this marriage of convenience are
simple: when she's ready to stand on her own two feet,
she'll walk away and he'll let her go. Only, as they both
know all too well, things don't always go according to
plan . . .

Available Now!

About the Author

CHERYL ETCHISON graduated from the University of Oklahoma's School of Journalism and began her career as an oil and gas reporter. Bored to tears and broke as hell, it wasn't long before she headed for the promised land of public relations. But that was nearly a lifetime ago and she's since traded in reporting the facts for making it all up. Currently, she lives in Austin, Texas, with her husband and three daughters.

www.cheryletchison.com

Discover great authors, exclusive offers, and more at hc.com.